A NOT SO PEACEFUL JOURNEY

JOURNEY

SECOND CHANCES ~ BOOK 3

SANDRA MERVILLE HART

WILD HEART
BOOKS

Cover design by: Carpe Librum Book Design

Author is represented by Hartline Literary Agency

ISBN-13: 978-1-942265-67-2

"Sandra Merville Hart's *A Not So Peaceful Journey* will take the reader on the adventure of a lifetime. This story mixes in wonderful details of train travel in the 1880s alongside the emotional and physical challenges facing the main characters during their journey. From Ohio to Chicago and all the way to California, Rennie, John, Veronica, and a child companion, will experience beauty and trials faced in the western states and territories as they deal with resolving their personal differences. Intriguing historical research, found in the back of the book, supports this wholesome romance. Ms. Hart has created another historically reliable and entertaining account that will keep you turning pages and wanting more."

— BETTIE BOSWELL, AUTHOR OF *ON CUE*
AND *FREE TO LOVE*

"In a story chock full of colorful descriptions and sweet interactions, creative John and his pragmatic fiancé Rennie take their struggle to understand each other to the rails from Ohio to California. Sandra Hart vividly describes 1884 train travel as if she'd taken that trek herself. A wonderfully immersive experience."

— LINDA YEZAK, AWARD-WINNING AUTHOR
AND FREELANCE EDITOR

"When Rennie and John journey by train from Ohio to California to escort a young girl, we get to go too. The sights, smells, sounds, fears and joys collide in an epic ride of fun, angst, a bit of bickering and misunderstanding—and danger. You'll fall in love with little Livie, and you won't be able to put it down."

— SUSAN G. MATHIS, AUTHOR OF TEN GILDED AGE NOVELS

Dedicated with love to Charlotte, Veldon, Wendy, and Shirley,
Belonging to these four strong, loving, courageous, funny, and fun
sisters
Blessed me in countless ways over the years.
Remembering my contentment when listening to you
Sing together in perfect harmony—these memories
And so MUCH more
Gave you all a permanent place in my heart.

"Who shut up the sea behind doors when it burst forth from the womb, when I made the clouds its garment and wrapped it in thick darkness, when I fixed limits for it and set its doors and bars in place, when I said, 'This far you may come and no farther; here is where your proud waves halt'?"

— JOB 38:8-11 (NIV)

CHAPTER 1

Friday, July 4, 1884,
Hamilton, Ohio

*R*ennie Hill picked her way across tufts of grass in the churchyard toward the Great Miami River at John Welch's side, one hand firmly tucked in her beau's arm and the other holding a colorful quilt. For an hour, she'd waited outside the church in the hot sun with her family for him to arrive from Cincinnati. She'd worn her favorite peach gingham dress with a bustle and small puffs at the shoulders leading to tight, elbow-length sleeves. He'd often complimented her on it. As he had when he'd arrived today.

"I know it doesn't seem like it, but my job was done today in record time." John carried the basket as he maneuvered them around families and couples who'd already picked their spots for the Fourth of July picnic. His new brown suit enhanced his dark good looks.

Children dangled their legs over the riverbank or climbed trees while indulgent mothers emptied food onto blankets beside plates, utensils, and bottles of tea or lemonade. Men, some wearing suits and others in trousers and collared shirts, talked in small groups near the river while keeping an eye on their family's ever-growing array of dishes.

"I took the first train out." John held up stained fingers. "I left without scrubbing all the ink off."

His job in the composing room at the *Times-Star* newspaper was a messy one. "No matter. Thank you for coming as soon as you could." No one ever claimed that patience was her virtue, but Rennie refused to complain about anything today, especially since his work had kept him from coming home for nearly a month. She'd convinced her family to eat together and allow her and John to enjoy their picnic alone. "All you missed was the reading of the Declaration of Independence. Games will come later." Aromas from platters of fried chicken and fragrant peach pies caused her mouth to water. It had been difficult to wait for him for more than one reason.

He grinned. "I know what the document says."

The riverbank was a dozen feet away. Rennie stopped under the shade of a tall hickory tree. "Let's eat here." They were close enough to the church to hear when the races started and far enough away to speak privately. "I'm surprised no one claimed this spot."

"Me too." He helped her spread the quilt on the grass.

Rennie and her mother had cut out a steepled church shape from a bolt of fabric and sewn it in the middle of a green background. A white house with a picket fence like the one in front of John's home ought to give him the hint that it was time to propose. At least, that was what Mama had said.

"Is that a new quilt?"

Rennie nodded. Mama said it never did hurt to put the idea of marrying into a man's head, especially if you could do it without words.

"You sewed this?" He quirked an eyebrow.

"Mama helped me."

"I'll bet she did." John looked like he wanted to laugh. He bent down.

On both knees.

To empty the basket.

Sighing, she joined him. It might take a while for the message to sink in.

Now that she and John had settled their differences and John had forgiven her foolish mistake, Rennie didn't want to wait too long. Why, she'd turned nineteen two months ago. She knew her mind and figured she knew his too. After all, their courtship had started nearly three years before.

They settled into munching roasted beef sandwiches, Saratoga potatoes, rice pudding, and blackberry turnovers, occasionally sipping lemonade as the placid river rolled by. John's handsome face was constantly turned to her, and his brown eyes seemed parched for the sight of her. That dark-brown hair had a tendency to curl when he let it grow too long, as it was on the verge of doing now. She loved his wavy hair when it curled all about his head.

They ate a leisurely lunch as John peppered her with questions about her job at the telegraph office, and then, leaving their repacked basket with the quilt, walked arm in arm along the riverbank. John was quieter now, but there would be plenty of time to talk before he returned to Cincinnai on Sunday evening. And they had plans that would fill the weekend.

Children all around dashed toward the church building.

"The games started." Rennie spotted her youngest sister, Bettina, in a sack race, her red pigtails leaping with every jump. "Want to watch?"

"In a few minutes." His shoulders tensed. "There's something I need to tell you first."

That sounded ominous. He couldn't intend to go on that trip... "What's wrong, John?"

"Let's sit on that bench." He nodded toward one facing the river. After she settled onto the seat, he sat with his knees grazing her dress. "I'm quitting my job. I'll turn in my resignation next week."

Relief flooded her. Now that Cora, his twin, had moved from Cincinnati, there was nothing to keep him there. "That's the best news." She brought his hand to her face and kissed it. "Now you can obtain a position at a Hamilton newspaper, and we can see each other every day again—"

"Rennie, no." He put his fingertips over her lips. "I'm going west."

"Wh-what? You're leaving?" He wasn't moving to Hamilton as she had dreamed. No, he'd be hundreds of miles away.

"Not forever. Just for a few months." His brown eyes pleaded for understanding.

Months? She was ready to marry him *now*. Her heart plummeted. "I thought you changed your mind about that." He had first mentioned the possibility around Christmas. They'd argued about it. She'd figured he'd decided to use the brain the Good Lord gave him and forget the whole thing.

"Once we...settle down..."

Hope sprang with her blushes at his hints about their future together.

"There won't be time or money for such a trip. Seeing some of the world will spur my imagination, enable me to write authentically about different locations. Can't you see? It's an investment in my career. Those adventures will end up in my stories. Other authors have done the same." His hand moved to cup her cheek. "Now that I've sold two stories, my dreams of becoming an author are closer than ever."

There he went again, always with his head in the clouds. It was a good thing he had her to snatch his feet back to the ground. "John, publishing two stories in that magazine doesn't make you an author." *The Atlantic Monthly* had published his stories in May and June.

His hand slid from her face. "Of course. I know that. It's a humble beginning, yet it *is* a beginning. Won't you be happy with me?"

"I *am* happy for you. Five copies of each of those magazines are stored in my hope chest." There. That ought to remind him that he needed to be thinking of their future together.

"Ah, Rennie. Thank you for that." He tapped a loose fist against his chest, rustling his black string tie against the collar of his blue-and-brown plaid shirt.

"I'm glad. I truly am." The intensity of his gratitude surprised her. Did her support mean that much to him? Then she was the right person to help him see reason. "But it might be years before your book is published. Why, you haven't even begun to write a novel."

Scarlet surged up his throat. "That's why I'll travel. Experience new adventures for my stories."

"You don't need to travel to experience adventure." A chill crept into her heart. What if he discovered that he liked living in the West? What if he decided to stay? Would he leave her an old maid after all their years together? It was as if she could hear the distant whistle of a train, see all of her hopes fading with puffs of charcoal smoke in the blue sky.

His jaw set. "It's my best opportunity. Now's the time."

It seemed her opposition to his plan actually strengthened his determination. "Where will you go?"

"To California. Colorado. Maybe Wyoming Territory. I've a hankering to hike a trail in the Rockies, the Sierra Nevadas." He turned toward the river with unseeing eyes, as if his imagination fueled visions of places only he could see. "Can you understand?"

"No. I don't understand." Would he return by Christmas? "How long will you be gone?"

"I don't know. Three months, maybe more. I've been saving for a while."

She gasped. And here she'd imagined his savings were for *their* future as husband and wife.

"Rennie, I'm building for the future." Earnest brown eyes met hers. "I'll see something of our country. Meet new folks. Experience an adventure to inspire some of those books you seem to doubt I can write."

"Throwing good money away on such a journey is the height of foolishness." Sounded like the prodigal son to her. She must convince him to abandon this crazy plan. "Why, what you'd spend could go a long way toward the purchase of a house."

His hand dropped to the bench. "I've counted the cost. I bought a tour guide to give me an idea what's required. That's why I've been saving so long."

"Then don't throw it away." Rennie's shrill tone was attracting attention. She'd best calm herself.

Her humble childhood home had always had sufficient food but rarely an abundance. She'd grown up listening to her parents voice their worries over how to provide more than the necessities for her and her siblings. Those concerns lived on and reminded her to watch every penny. A portion of her earnings went to her father every week and had eased the financial strain on her parents. The rest was in the bank, waiting for John's proposal.

"I don't believe I am wasting it." His voice softened. "Please support my decision. This is important to me."

"Well, it's not important to me." Rennie was used to speaking her mind, but she regretted the remark when his body stiffened. When would she learn to temper her words with grace? "I'm sorry. I didn't mean that exactly."

"What *did* you mean, exactly?" His gaze held hers.

"I don't understand. There's plenty of adventure right here in Ohio. Did you forget the flood? Or the riots in the spring when Ben's father was shot?" Just the memory of it had her shuddering. John had been with his twin sister's future husband and Mr. Findlay when it happened.

"I remember." His shoulders sagged. "You're right."

Phew. She hadn't believed she could talk him out of his crazy plan so easily. But then he continued.

"You don't understand."

The pain in his eyes pierced her heart. She loved him, wanted his happiness, but his thinking about this was all wrong. Becoming a husband and father would surely spark more stories than a Wild West trip. But he'd made his decision despite her wishes. Her feelings didn't matter. He truly intended to leave her. Would he return a changed man? How could such a trip *not* change him?

The youngest of her five siblings ran up and plopped on the bench beside her. "Rennie, come with me."

Blinking away her sadness, she looked down at her sister's freckled face. "What is it, Bettina?"

"I'm in the three-legged race with Flo."

Rennie could barely think coherently. All her focus was on the silent man sitting beside her.

"You promised to watch." Bettina tugged on her arm. "John, you come too. Cheer for us."

"Wouldn't miss it." John stood and extended his hand to Rennie.

She put her hand into his clammy one.

As soon as she was on her feet, he released her. "I think we've said what needed to be said."

The finality of his comment slammed her senses. How could she make amends for her blunt honesty while convincing him to find a job here?

7

Walking between them, Bettina chattered, but Rennie paid her no mind.

She didn't get an opportunity to speak with John alone the rest of the day. They walked home with her family. At least he seemed at ease with them.

He didn't linger for a kiss.

She tossed and turned so much during the night that Veronica, her fifteen-year-old sister, snapped at her to be still or sleep in the living room. Rennie, afraid of waking her other two sisters, bit her tongue. She and Veronica hadn't been getting along since Rennie had started working. It didn't help that the four of them shared one large bed in the small room.

Rennie spent the remainder of the night on the sofa. An aching neck the next morning was her thanks.

She avoided conversations as she donned her prettiest green dress. John was taking her to lunch in the city followed by an afternoon stroll to the Lane Free Library.

She wove her waist-length brown locks into one long braid and pinned it around her hairline. She stared into the mirror as she patted it into place, sighing over the liberal streaks of auburn, which she'd inherited from her red-haired mother—though John had often complimented its sheen in the sunshine.

What was she to say to him? Best start with an apology and then convince him to stay in Ohio. If he was bent on quitting his job in Cincinnati, all the better. He'd find one easily enough right here.

Mama often warned Rennie to curb her outspokenness...to sprinkle her words with grace. Mama was a fine one to talk, for she rarely had a thought that didn't tumble from her mouth in some way. And all her children were just as blunt.

Papa was the quiet, reserved one. Maybe she'd do better to emulate him.

Her nerves stretched as tight as a guitar string at the sound of a knock. She gripped her reticule and headed down the hall.

But it wasn't John who stepped inside when Mama answered. "Cora, how nice to see you. Are you going to lunch with John and Rennie?"

"No, Mrs. Hill." John's twin shook her head. "Rennie, come outside into the yard with me."

"Where's John?" Mama's bright eyes darted to Rennie.

"He's not coming," Cora said.

Rennie's heart plummeted. "Is he sick?"

"Not coming?" Mama sputtered.

"That's right. Please, Rennie," Cora said. "Let's sit on that old log in the woods between our houses."

Rennie stepped outside, dread settling in her midsection, and silently followed Cora.

They sat in the same place Rennie had often visited with John of an evening. Cora stared out at the forest before turning to face her. "He wrote his regrets to you." She extracted a letter from her skirt pocket and handed it over.

Rennie tore open the letter and read John's apology that he had to return to Cincinnati unexpectedly with growing dread.

"John went back to the city this morning. He said to tell you he's sorry." Cora's brown eyes, so like her brother's, filled with compassion.

"We had plans..." He didn't even stay for the weekend. She must have wounded his pride. They had so little time together, and now he'd robbed her of precious hours.

"I know." A brown tendril escaped the bun at the nape of Cora's neck. "Look, I'm not certain what happened, but he came home in a dejected mood. I've never seen him so forlorn."

"I tried to make him see reason. To talk him out of going on this foolish trip."

Cora's eyes widened. "You didn't actually tell him his idea was foolish, did you?"

"Someone has to tell him the truth."

"Oh, Rennie." Cora gave her head a slow shake. "This is his dream. Can you imagine how tough it is for him to pursue a career in writing when the woman he..." Her voice trailed off.

"He what?" The woman he loved? The woman he wanted to marry? The woman he wanted to ask to wait for him? She tapped her foot. What had he said?

John had told her he loved her several times, most recently on her birthday. The kiss that accompanied his words had left her breathless and full of dreams of her own.

"Those words are for him to say." Cora's glance slid to the Hills's small white one-story home visible through the trees.

"You can tell me." Rennie had to know.

She shook her head.

Drat. A little coaxing had worked when they were children. "Do you think he'll come back for me?"

"His plans are to be gone three months, maybe twice that. No longer."

Plans changed all the time. Mark Twain, his author hero, had gone out West and ended up living there for years. That mustn't happen to John.

She must find a way to make him stay.

~

*J*ohn held the resignation letter he'd just typed on Ben Findlay's typewriter. This was it. His next step toward his dream of becoming a writer.

"Are you certain?" Ben, John's future brother-in-law, was an up-and-coming reporter at the newspaper where they both worked. Except John worked in the composing room, a far cry from the fellows who actually got to write stories.

They were the only ones still in the reporters' office because the day's edition had already been printed. Newsboys were selling it now.

"I've no doubt you're in line for the next reporter position that becomes available," Ben said.

Not you, too, Ben. John's excitement ebbed. He didn't need his closest friend to second-guess his decision, not after what Rennie had said. He'd almost abandoned the entire idea after talking with her. Her comment that he hadn't yet begun his first novel had stung, and he'd returned to his Cincinnati boardinghouse to pour his heart out on the page. Unfortunately, those two days of writing bore little fruit. Nothing worth submitting, anyway. But hearing his girl all but ridicule his dream? He couldn't stay around for more of the same from his friend.

"You know I'll put in a good word for you with our editor if you like. Assist you to get started in a way no one helped me." Ben didn't quite meet his eyes.

"Did Cora put you up to asking me to stay?" John's twin didn't want him to leave almost as much as Rennie. Both of them were making this whole situation harder than they realized.

A flush stained Ben's clean-shaven face, causing his brown hair to appear even darker. "Well, she might have mentioned that you'd be content to remain with the *Times-Star* if you had a writing job."

"It's not the same." John ran his fingers over the typewriter's keys. "I'll not deny typing anything that sells brings a certain satisfaction. But my choice is to write novels that might be loosely based on actual occurrences."

Getting two stories published in the popular *Atlantic Monthly* magazine after four rejections for other pieces had filled him with joy that couldn't be contained. He'd bought a ticket on the afternoon train to Hamilton. Rennie had just been leaving her job at the telegraph office for the day. Her happiness at his news was all he could have wished. For about ten seconds. Her joy had quickly dissipated into blunt warnings that fifty dollars was a nice start but hardly enough to make a living.

She was right. Doggone it, she was right. But he had needed her to celebrate the milestone with him. She was the first person he'd told. He didn't need her sensible observations to ignite doubts about his abilities. He needed her support. Her negative reaction had deepened a wedge between them that had been growing for months.

"That story about your first week on your family's farm was both funny and insightful," Ben said. "It brought the plight of orphans to the public's mind without bashing them over the head." Ben met his gaze squarely. "You have talent. Your hard work is bearing fruit."

John and Cora had been adopted when they were fourteen, and he had plenty of experiences relating to that difficult time. Trouble was, that pain still struck a chord too deep for him to reach. He found the courage to look at his friend's face. Read the honesty in his expression. "I wish Rennie saw it that way."

"Cora said that Rennie wasn't as happy about your success as you expected."

John grunted. "That's putting it mildly." He crossed the room to stare out the window at the city street bustling with pedestrians, wagons, stagecoaches, carriages, and horsecars filled with passengers. They all had a destination. What was his? "Her idea of the perfect job for me is to continue working at a composing room—in Hamilton, mind you. She says I can write in my free time."

"That won't satisfy you."

"No." John gripped the window sill. "Not until I give it my best effort." Maybe Rennie was right. Maybe those two stories were the only ones a publisher would ever buy from him.

No. There must be more in him.

"Writing advertisements and the like never satisfied me, so I understand your dilemma." Ben moved to sit on the edge of a reporter's table nearest the window. "It's writing the articles about special events—and everyday occurrences—that bring me satisfaction in my job."

"I've studied your articles for months."

"That means more than you know. And I understand. If you don't work at a job that fulfills you, every day can be drudgery."

"Exactly." John stared at a lamppost outside the office. In his imagination, he pictured Rennie standing there, looking beautiful in her peach dress. She'd throw her arms around him in shared joy over his first published pieces.

But reality had painted a very different picture. "It wasn't merely the fact of publishing two pieces but also writing them that brought a sense of rightness."

"Folks can't read them unless they're published."

Didn't he know it. "Rennie won't be happy unless I get a job in Hamilton."

"Sounds as though she wants to settle down and get married." Ben quirked an eyebrow.

"I've got some things to figure out first."

"Agreed." Ben crossed his arms. "For what it's worth, I understand why you quit."

"That's worth a lot." John turned to face him. "So, you don't think it's foolishness?" Rennie's description.

Ben shook his head.

"Will you help Cora understand?"

Ben shifted against the table. "Few people know you better than your twin. She knows this writing dream consumes you. She loves you. Don't fret about her."

John and Cora enjoyed a rapport that went beyond words.

"So...two more weeks?" Ben said the words flippantly, but there was something troubling in his expression.

"Something eating at you?"

Ben opened his mouth as if to say more. Then shut it. "I'll be praying that you find what you're searching for."

John had been praying for guidance for months. He appreciated someone else bending God's ear on his behalf.

CHAPTER 2

*R*ennie trudged to work using the back roads leading to the city on Friday, a week after John had announced his plans to go all the way across the country.

California, no less.

Rennie had no hankering to see the wildness of the West. The violence of the gold rushes. Train robberies. Towns where vigilantes took the law into their own hands. Her sensitive, head-in-the-clouds, loyal-to-a-fault beau would be crushed in such surroundings. And he intended to go alone, for goodness' sakes.

But how was she to make him see reason when he hadn't stayed to talk with her? She'd sent a letter of apology that included her arguments against his travels.

His response had come yesterday. He'd given his resignation and would work until July nineteenth. He'd prayed about all her objections and still felt he was on the right path. Their future was simply a little farther down the road. He asked for her patience.

That request frustrated her to no end. She'd waited while John lived in Cincinnati to watch over his sister for two years.

And now this? At least he hadn't closed the door on their relationship. Perhaps she should take the train to Cincinnati to speak with him directly.

A horse's clopping hooves nearby shook her from her gloomy thoughts. She looked up to find a wagon filled with crates stopping in front of a dry-goods store. A harassed mother led a passel of grumbling children down the sidewalk ahead of Rennie. Horseback riders and buggies shared the road with a dusty stagecoach on a sunny morning that promised to be a scorcher.

A glance at the corner clock quickened her step. Almost time to begin work. She pushed the door open at the telegraph office and greeted Mr. McMahan, her boss and the grandfatherly man who had trained her to send and receive telegraphed messages.

"Morning, Miss Rennie." He glanced at the mantle clock.

She was precisely on time. He preferred she arrive early.

"Glad you're here to wait on customers. Busy morning already." He began tapping in a rhythm while staring at the page in front of him.

Someone must always be available to decipher incoming messages and send outgoing ones. Brian and Todd must be out delivering telegrams, for the two tables behind the counter were empty.

Fine with her. She wasn't in the mood for idle conversation. After her reticule was stored in the back room that was little more than a large closet, Rennie sat on the stool behind the counter in time for her first customer of the day.

She carefully wrote the stranger's message to be sent to Columbus, Ohio, and then collected the money. Rennie waited for Mr. McMahan to complete his telegram so that the line was clear for her to send her message. By the time she was finished, another customer had arrived.

The clatter of dots and dashes came across the sounder

while she stowed the money in the box kept on the counter shelf.

"Rennie, I need your help." Mr. McMahan rubbed the gray stubble on his chin while studying the page. They got all kinds of messages, from personal to business, and the telegrapher had to read them as part of the job.

"What is it?" Because she'd been occupied with a customer, she hadn't bothered to decipher the incoming message. Rennie wanted to peer over his shoulder at the telegram that anyone on their wire might have heard, but she restrained her curiosity as she pushed the newest telegram in front of him.

"Well, this message appears important, but Brian and Todd aren't back from their deliveries." He peered at her over the top of his round spectacles. "You know Miss Eleanora Bennett."

"Yes." The talkative brunette came in occasionally to send messages to California, often accompanied by a quiet girl she called Livie. "She's the governess for little Olivia Sherman."

"This message concerns the health of Mrs. Sherman. Brian should be back within minutes, but you're probably the best choice to deliver this one."

"I'll be happy for the exercise." Hopefully, it wasn't a serious illness. This was one customer who had become a friend. The poor daughter didn't need bad news. "Shall I go now?"

Tapping noises had the gentleman rushing to open the call, pad and pencil ever ready.

While he took the message, Rennie fetched her reticule.

When he finished, he handed her the folded telegram and a slip of paper with the address. "I can manage until Brian returns."

"Then I'll go and return as quickly as possible." She stowed the page in her reticule while scurrying toward the door.

"*I* hoped that Mrs. Sherman had improved." Eleanora Bennett rubbed her forehead. The pretty governess who appeared to be in her late twenties had sent Olivia upstairs to work on her studies as soon as Rennie arrived with the telegram—almost as if she expected the news. "She's a young woman. About my age."

"What does the telegram say?" Rennie sat in the comfortable front parlor of the Sherman's two-story brick home located near the river on the fringe of the area's more elegant homes.

"That she's still ailing. And to prepare to travel." Eleanora paced in front of the empty fireplace.

Rennie's heart skipped a beat. No wonder Mr. McMahan had sent her out with the message immediately. Clearly, he understood that the governess might need to talk with a friend. "What's her ailment?"

"She suffers bouts of fever and ague." The ruffled hem of Eleanora's blue dress brushed the brocade curtains at the front window as she turned to pace toward the pianoforte at the opposite wall.

"I'm sorry to learn that." Malaria. Such bouts could be severe. Folks often lived with the illness for months or years without having a spell. When the fever struck, sufferers were made more comfortable with quinine.

"She had a bout last year, soon after I came. It lasted a month." Her cheeks were flushed as if she were the one with the fever.

"Perhaps this one will be milder." Rennie spoke gently. "Has there been a letter sent that gives more information?"

"The last one arrived from Mr. Sherman yesterday. He wants us to join them in California. He's unflappable given the most serious of business matters but tends to panic whenever his wife falls ill." Eleanora sank into her chair. "They lost a baby three years ago during one of her spells with the ague."

No wonder the man wanted his daughter with him. "If she's suffered for two or three weeks, do you believe she'll be recovered by the time you arrive?"

"I'm not going." Eleanora's cheeks were as ashen as they had been crimson moments ago.

Rennie gave her head a little shake. Surely, she'd misunderstood. Eleanora couldn't ignore such a summons from her employer. "What do you mean?"

"I avoid travel by train. I suffer from a queasy stomach on an hour's journey to Cincinnati. It takes over a week to get to San Francisco...longer, depending on overnight stays along the way. The Shermans made their trip a leisurely journey of three weeks." She raised tormented eyes. "I hate to lose my position here, but I'd be of no worth taking care of a child in such circumstances."

Sympathy for Eleanora's dilemma surged through Rennie. She'd seen her often enough to build a rapport with her. And yet..."A seven-year-old child cannot travel across the country unaccompanied."

"Of course not, though I fear a companion as sick as I'd be on such a trip would be more of a detriment." She wrung her hands. "That leads to my major concern. Who can I ask to accompany her?"

"Miss Eleanora, is Mama sicker?"

Rennie twisted in the low-backed, cushioned sofa to see the girl standing in the doorway, her green eyes wide with fear.

"I'm afraid she's not better yet." Eleanora stood and held out her arms.

Livie rushed into them and buried her face against her governess's waist, sobs racking her body.

"Shh. I have every reason to believe she'll be just fine." Eleanora crouched to look at her directly. "Remember when she was sick last summer? And we had to play quietly for a while?"

Chin quivering, Livie rubbed her eyes.

"Your mama got all better and started playing with you again, right?"

She nodded, her sobs quieting as she hung on every word.

"That will happen again. Only this time, you'll be in California with her."

"You'll take me, won't you?" She raised pleading eyes to her governess.

Just how much of the conversation had the child overheard?

A spasm crossed Eleanora's face. "I'll find someone who will take excellent care of you. Someone you know. Someone who's comfortable around children."

Livie turned a forlorn face to Rennie. "Will you come with me, Miss Rennie?"

She blinked at the sudden turn of events. Every maternal emotion had been touched by Livie's misery. But how could she agree when she'd given John such grief about—

It was as if lightning struck her. What if she could arrange to travel on the same train as John? Would he agree to escort her and Livie?

Clutching the locket at her throat, Eleanora said, "That would be the perfect solution. I'll have to ask Mr. Sherman's permission. Will you consider it?"

"Please, Miss Rennie?" Livie laid a shaky hand on her arm.

"I-I don't know what to say." Would her parents agree? How would she get home if John wouldn't bring her? And if he did, the expense would eat up his savings, and he'd still want to go West again. "Can I think about it?"

"Please give it every consideration." Eleanora's gaze darted to Livie's crestfallen face. "It will require a few days to make preparations. I expect they'll send a letter with instructions. The route to take, money required for meals, possible overnight stays and the like, so you won't leave immediately. Pray about it. Talk to your family and John. He might even agree to escort you, though I imagine your parents will not like the idea of him traveling alone with you back to Hamilton."

True. Her protective father would balk at that. As would John, no doubt.

"Mr. Sherman will bear all expenses for you and anyone your parents deem necessary for your safe return. Just please make your decision quickly."

Rennie's head swirled. She'd never been farther from home than Cincinnati, less than forty miles away. Never wanted to go anywhere else.

And here she was actually considering escorting a frightened little girl to California.

~

"John didn't even stay last weekend for your plans. That's what comes of speaking before you think. Never call a man's dreams foolish, or you'll die an old maid." Mama folded her arms across her faded green bib apron. "He's angry, so I doubt he'll adjust his plans for you."

"He will. He loves me." Rennie, sitting across from her parents at the supper table, prayed that her mother was wrong. John loved her as much as she loved him, she was certain of it.

The meal had finished a half hour before, and she was still trying to convince her parents of the soundness of her idea. Her sisters were cleaning the dishes, but as the main room served as parlor, dining room, and kitchen, the conversation wasn't private. The unaccustomed silence in which they worked convinced Rennie they hung on every word.

"You wounded his pride, pumpkin." Her father's gray eyes turned smoky, as they did when something troubled him. "When a man's got a big dream, one he don't know if he can succeed in, he needs encouraging, not belittling."

Heat flooded Rennie's face. Her father was a man of few

words—possibly because her mama spoke her mind from sunrise to sunset—so when he gave Rennie guidance, she listened. If Papa thought she'd said too much, she believed him. She should have tempered her words. "What if I believe he's doing wrong, Papa? I can't hold my tongue."

"No, I don't reckon you can...no more than your mama or your sisters can." He sighed. "Did you try to look at the situation through his eyes?"

Rennie thought back to the first time John had mentioned wanting to travel. Her immediate thought had been that the journey would increase the distance between them. "Can't say I did."

"That's not our biggest concern, Trent." Mama's glance slid back to her oldest daughter. "What we've got to decide is whether Rennie should take that poor angel to her ailing mama. Then we can discuss who's going with her."

"Someone must. For safety's sake." Papa didn't back down from his original demand that someone accompany her. "And to protect your reputation."

She'd been right. He wasn't keen on the idea of her and John traveling to California with only a child as chaperone, which she understood.

"Why do you want to do this?" Mama's bright blue eyes pierced through her. Probed the truth at the core, as she always did.

"Livie's scared for her mother. Since Eleanora can't take her, she wants me to."

"That ain't the only reason." Mama tilted her head to the side.

"No." Rennie became aware that even her brothers playing checkers on the porch had stopped their game to listen. "If John goes with us to San Francisco, maybe it will be enough adventure for him."

"Unlikely." Papa shook his head. "You're the one dreaming this time, pumpkin."

Her spirits deflated. "Then at least I will have tried to see his way of thinking. Make amends."

"Can't argue with the wisdom in that." Mama exchanged a long look with her husband. "You did say that Mr. Sherman would pay everyone's way."

Rennie nodded.

"Then Veronica is going with you, no matter what John decides."

"Veronica?" Rennie's worst nightmare. She'd smarted too often from her sister's sharp tongue. Given as good as she got, if she was honest. She shot a glance at her sister, who was unashamedly listening as she scoured the stove. "But we haven't been getting along—"

"Don't matter." Mama gave a satisfied nod. "Any man who tries any funny business with either of my feisty daughters won't get far with the other one around."

"I'll go along with that." Papa's glance bounced between his two oldest daughters.

Candlelight turned Mama's red curls almost copper. "It'll take too long for you to write to John and get a reply, bein's Eleanora wants an answer soon."

Mama was right. Rennie needed to talk to him face to face. "I don't work tomorrow. I'll go to Cincinnati on the train and be there when John gets off."

CHAPTER 3

"*Y*ou're doing what?" John's fork clanked against his plate.

He'd stumbled to a halt upon finding Rennie waiting for him on a bench outside the *Times-Star* at the end of his work day. Her sweet apologies had softened a bit of the hurt lodged in his heart. They'd strolled to his favorite eatery, Molly's Home Cooking on Vine Street, talking of his preparations for his trip without a peep from her concerning her upcoming one.

He shook his head to clear it. No one could ever accuse Rennie of being boring. It was one of the reasons she'd captivated his heart back in school, though her impetuous behavior often frustrated him. Like now.

"I haven't accepted the job yet." She took a bite of her pork chop, the day's special they'd both ordered. "I wanted to talk with you first."

"Let me ask you something." He pressed his fingertips together, his own delicious meal forgotten. "You wouldn't accept this task if I weren't already going, right?"

She chewed her lip. "That's a good question."

He tried not to smile. One of the things he loved about her was her honesty, though he had to admit it often wounded his pride.

"Maybe not." She twirled her fork through her mashed potatoes. "Your trip might be part of the reason."

Just as he suspected. And this after she'd berated *his* travel plans. "What's the rest?"

"Livie asked me." She raised troubled blue eyes to his. "She trusts me because of my friendship with Eleanora. Even if not for your upcoming trip...if you saw the child, you'd understand. I can't bear to disappoint her."

That changed things. A little. "You can't go alone with a child."

"Papa's making Veronica come with me."

Those two had been butting heads for the better part of a year. Why did Mr. Hill believe that was a good idea? "She's barely out of pigtails herself." He rubbed his jaw. Should he alter his plans to meander through the western half of the country, making multiple stops and taking on temporary jobs if he settled in one location more than a few days? "Veronica won't be helpful. You'll have two charges to watch over. Can't someone else from the Sherman household take her?"

She shook her head. "There's nobody else willing to do it."

"And Miss Eleanora?" He'd met the woman once when he was there to escort Rennie to supper at the end of her day. Pleasant type. He was glad to see Rennie become more sociable with her customers. For all her outspoken ways, she'd been a bit of a recluse when he met her.

"Trains make her sick. She can't watch over a little girl in such a state. The worst part is she fears this will cost her job— and her home, since she lives with the family—so the nausea must be pretty bad."

"My mama suffers in the same way. It took her two days to recover when we traveled from Bradford Junction." And that had only been sixty miles. John couldn't imagine his mother on a train all the way to California. He chewed his last bite of pork while he considered. Though he didn't want Rennie to take on this responsibility, his heart went out to the child. He remembered how worried he'd been for his ma before she died. He could barely stand to leave her long enough to attend school. Of course, Pa had died the year before his ma, adding desperation to his fears all those years ago. "This won't be a cheap trip. Trains stop for breakfast, lunch, and supper. Count on every meal stop to cost one dollar each."

"So much as that?" Tilting her head, she studied him.

Knowing her so well, he figured she was trying to calculate how much *he'd* spend on his meals westward—the trip she'd called foolishness. Tension tightened his gut.

"Eleanora assured me all the expenses of the trip will be covered." Rennie heaved a heavy sigh. "My parents weren't pleased about all this, especially coming out of the blue as it did. They want us to leave when you do."

"And follow the same route?" Now they were getting to the crux of the matter.

"Right." She leaned closer. "Change trains when you do and all. You'd escort us all the way to San Francisco. If you do, Eleanora will pay for your trip out there."

Saving a portion of his money slated for, as Rennie would say, foolishness. His gut wrenched. If only she believed in him. "What if I can't alter my plans?" He needed some time to mull over the changed itinerary before committing to it. He'd wanted freedom from the responsibilities that had ensnared him since his pa died, yet the possibility of traveling with Rennie to begin his journey was growing on him. It could work. No tickets had been purchased. His plans were to move his things from his boardinghouse back to the farm next Saturday, spend a week with Rennie and his family, and then be on his way.

She shifted in her high-backed wooden chair. "Papa said something about sending Zach along if we can't go with you."

Zach? That adventurous boy had barely outgrown chasing the neighbor girls with snakes.

"Papa will sure feel better if you escort us." She crumpled her cotton napkin in her fist.

"Your father is a wise man." Zach would protect his sisters, no doubt about that, but he'd also give Rennie someone else to fret over.

"The best ever." Rennie's face softened into a sweet smile.

Rennie had always been close to her father. "When do you plan to leave?" He was training his replacement and felt good about how quickly the former newsboy was learning the job. The seventeen-year-old soaked up every detail like a sponge.

"Eleanora's waiting for a letter of instructions. Unless Mrs. Sherman's condition worsens. Then it will likely be a telegram telling us to leave immediately." Rennie touched his hand resting on the table. "You're going, anyway. Why not rearrange your departure date?"

"You'd prefer me to Zach?" He teased as he considered his decision. Once they married, she'd balk at the expense of such a trip. Perhaps this was his only opportunity to show her the beauty of the western half of their country.

"I'm already saddled with Veronica." She rolled her eyes heavenward. "Don't make me take Zach along."

He suspected she had another reason for this mission of mercy. A deeper one she wasn't talking about. His heart hadn't recovered from her harsh words. He needed her support to sustain him in the months he was away from her.

He turned his hand so that it clasped hers. How right it always felt tucked inside his. "How about if I take the train back to Hamilton with you? I'll wager Miss Eleanora will want to talk with me."

Rennie squealed. "You'll escort me? I mean, us?" Joy mingled with relief in her eyes.

She'd never been fifty miles from her home. She must be nervous, even fearful, of the journey, but she'd overcome those fears to help a little girl.

Pride welled up in him. She was the right woman for him. "I will."

~

John felt more certain about his decision when sitting at the table at Rennie's home later that day with her parents. As usual, Trent Hill had been silent through most of the discussion, allowing his wife to vent her concerns.

"John, I sure am pleased you'll be there to protect my girls on the trip west." Catherine Hill's red curls fairly bounced when she nodded. "Are you sure you won't consider returning to Hamilton with them?"

"Rennie only asked me to accompany them on the journey out because I was already going. The Shermans will hire an escort for the trip back. Since I know the ladies will be safe, I'd best save the train fare and stay in California."

It was nearly as difficult to refuse her as it was her feisty daughter. The house was abnormally quiet with the other children gone or playing outside. Pleasant. Or it would be if not for tension settling in his back. He wanted to do as they asked. He loved them all. They'd be his in-laws if all went according to plan. First, he must convince Rennie of his ability to support them through writing.

He had enough doubts of his own. He didn't need to take on hers, not while his spirit yearned for the expression only the written word gave. He'd spent plenty of time praying for guidance and believed his desire for travel sprang from those prayers.

"He's rearranging his schedule as it is, Mama." Rennie tilted her head toward the stove. "You want me to turn the chicken?"

Changing the subject. A good tactic with her mother. John's mouth watered at the smell of the chicken frying and biscuits baking. Rennie was as good a cook as her mother, and that was saying something.

"It'll be fine another minute." Catherine didn't take her eyes off John. "What if you don't like the person the Shermans hire?"

"If I feel uneasy for her and Veronica's safety, I'll escort them home." He met Mr. Hill's steady gaze. "I give you my word."

Trent offered a nod. "I'll count on that."

"I'd find more comfort if it was you." Catherine's plain brown skirt flounced as she scurried to the stove.

Hopefully, her ire would evaporate with the steam that rose from the pan. The aroma of frying chicken wafted through the room.

"No need for him to alter *all* his arrangements, Mama." Rennie's mild tone belied the disappointment in her eyes.

"You all may as well eat before you go see Miss Bennett." Grease plopped onto the stove as Catherine turned a chicken leg.

John agreed. No need to turn down biscuits, fried chicken, stewed tomatoes, and—he sniffed—candied yams? He'd soon be dreaming of these meals.

"She's not expecting us. Perhaps that's best." Rennie clutched her stomach. "Where's Veronica?"

"Spending the day with George." Trent fingered the condensation on his glass of lemonade.

"That boy acts like his heart's broke in two that his girl's leaving for a month." Catherine rolled her eyes. "He's fifteen, for goodness' sake."

Trent drummed his fingers on the wood table. "Veronica's excited."

"She'll come back with stories of all she's seen."

Mrs. Hill's comment condensed everything John wanted to accomplish into one sentence. He shot a look at Rennie to see if she noticed, but she wouldn't meet his gaze.

~

*T*wo hours later, Rennie sat beside John in the Shermans' front parlor with Eleanora and Livie. She'd explained the plans. "Did you receive more news?"

Eleanora shook her head. "Perhaps we'll receive a letter Monday. So she's either the same or better." She patted Livie's shoulder.

"I'm certain that's right." John gave the little girl a reassuring smile.

"I miss her." The little girl's words were barely audible.

"You'll see her soon." John left his cushioned green chair to squat in front of her. "Her eyes will light up like candles on a Christmas tree when she sees you."

Livie's face brightened.

Rennie marveled at John's ability to understand exactly what Livie needed to hear. She'd witnessed his rapport with his brothers and sisters time and again. He'd make a wonderful father.

She blushed at her thoughts. Best not get the cart before the horse, as her mother often said. John hadn't proposed. Rennie prayed the wall between them would tumble down on the trip.

"I'll wager he's got the right of it, precious one." Eleanora placed an arm around her and drew her close for a comforting hug. "Can you leave Wednesday? That's the sixteenth."

John returned to his chair. "My last day of work is Friday.

Perhaps I can move that up. Will you send a telegram once you hear from Mr. Sherman?"

"Certainly." Eleanora gave a crisp nod. "And I believe you'll want to rest a few days before your return journey. Count on staying in San Francisco for about a week."

Wonderful. One more week with John. "All right." She tilted her head up at him. "How shall I prepare?"

"Be sure to pack clothes for all seasons."

Rennie blinked. "It's July. We'll return in August."

"We'll pass through the Rocky Mountains at high altitudes where you might need wool clothing and an overcoat. We'll travel across the Humboldt Desert." His eyes sparkled in anticipation.

"Is there a women's dressing room?" Trains had conveniences for men and women, but she'd never had to worry about changing clothes while traveling from Hamilton to Cincinnati.

"Overnight passenger trains have dressing rooms. Pack a valise with light summer dressed and warm winter weather." He flushed. "Er...and extra clothing that goes along with wool clothes."

Wearing two sets of underclothes in cold weather for warmth was normal. "Goodness, between Veronica, Livie, and me, we'll be carrying at least two valises."

Eleanora walked to a rolltop desk in the corner. "John, those are the kind of details I need to get Livie ready. What else?" She selected a paper from a desk compartment and jotted down some notes.

"Rennie will keep the valises with her, so tuck items needed daily inside the bag. Pack a trunk, both of you, for what you'll need at the end of the trip." John scooted to the edge of his chair. "Trunks are stored in baggage cars while traveling. You won't get to them until we switch trains in Ogden. Oh, and that's usually an overnight stay in a hotel. There may be other overnight stops in an emergency. We'll buy tickets for the next leg of the journey there. No doubt we'll be happy to sleep in a bed that doesn't jar back and forth."

Eleanora looked a little green at the very mention of the jarring motion.

"This is important." John waited until everyone looked over. "You must eat every meal. Don't skip a meal to save money. Eating at regular intervals can be tricky because trains have particular stops scheduled. Some may be two or three hours apart—say breakfast at eight and lunch at half past ten."

"I can't eat meals so close together." Saving a dollar in such a case seemed the wisest course to Rennie.

"You must. Because the supper stop might be eight hours later." He raised open palms. "Oh, I forgot to mention a lunch basket. Pack food like fruits, canned meats. Bread and milk are easy purchases along the way. Don't pack food that has an odor. No fish or the like."

"How do you know all this?" Her beau never failed to impress her. What was he doing with a backward girl like her?

"Remember that guidebook I told you about?" His expression lightened. "I read it three times last winter."

Three times? He really hadn't been fooling when he'd brought up the idea at Christmas.

"I wish I had one of those books." Eleanora frowned. "What else do I need to know?"

"Is there room in my valise for my doll?" Livie crossed the room where a curly-haired doll rested in a child-sized rocking chair. "I don't want her in a trunk. She can't breathe."

"I'll make certain of it." Rennie knelt beside her. It was a small request for a little girl whose life was being uprooted to cross the continent. "Does your doll remember your mama?"

"Not very well." She rubbed her eye. "She gave her to me the day before she left."

Rennie's heart went out to her. "Then we'll introduce them to each other again."

"All right." Livie rested her head on Rennie's shoulder.

She put her arms around her and rocked her back and forth. A maternal feeling swept over her, akin to her feelings for her siblings.

Focusing on this precious little girl who missed her parents might prevent her from worrying about how her life might change when she waved goodbye to John in San Francisco.

Maybe.

CHAPTER 4

*E*arly the following Thursday morning, John settled back on the hard train seat next to a stranger with graying temples. The man's suit surely cost twice the amount of his own. When his companion buried his nose in a newspaper after a cursory greeting, John let out a breath of relief.

Although he had reconciled himself to losing a week at the farm before leaving, his family had not. His younger siblings, tears streaming down their faces, had clung to him at the depot. Five-year-old Aaron's misery had tugged at John's heart as he'd promised to write often.

With that emotional scene behind him, anticipation to begin the long-awaited journey built with each whistle blow.

"Ow, you stepped on my foot, Rennie." Veronica's complaint carried three seats back to John, and he craned his head into the aisle.

Right against the hard stomach of a passing stranger. A farmer, by the looks of his plaid shirt, suspenders, work pants, and the bit of mud on his well-worn boots.

"Sorry about that." John rubbed the side of his head.

"Didn't bother me none." The man paused. "You all right?"

"Yes, thank you." Only humiliated. The man passed on toward the men's passenger car, and John peered ahead to determine how the girls fared.

Seats faced forward in this car, and all he could see was their straw hats decorated with ribbons and a single white flower each. He could, however, hear their hushed bickering—though he couldn't make out the words—and they had barely left the depot.

Not a promising beginning. It might be a good thing there hadn't been enough room for the four of them to sit together.

Bracing himself against the rocking motion of the train, he made his way to them. "Well, ladies, we're on our way." The very words lifted his spirits. The beginning of his dream.

Veronica looked mutinous. Livie clutched her doll. Frustration shot sparks from Rennie's blue eyes.

Oh, boy. If this was a sign of things to come, they were in for a difficult journey. "Why are the three of you on one seat?" Even two trim women weren't going to be comfortable for long with a little girl between them.

"Livie is nervous." Rennie put her arm around the frightened child.

"I don't like the black smoke." Her eyes were on the wispy gray mist coming in through the open window. Her grip tightened on the doll in her lap. "It smells bad."

It did, indeed. Like charcoal and soot. "Nearly every window in this car is open. That will clear most of it out."

Unfortunately, it would also allow more smoke in with each stop. He glanced toward the back of the women and children's passenger car. Men traveling with them also could ride in it. Hopefully, they were far enough from the engine that little cinders wouldn't fly inside. Best not to mention that possibility.

"There. You see?" Rennie patted her hand. "It will soon be better."

"We'll make many stops in little towns on our way. Passengers will get on and off. I'd suggest one of you moving to an adjacent seat when it opens." Better to put some space between the sparring sisters.

"Happy to." Veronica crossed her arms. "My toe still hurts where Rennie stepped on it."

"It was an accident." Rennie rolled her eyes. "Good suggestion, John. Sorry there's no room for you around us."

"I'm only three rows back." He gave her an encouraging nod. "Not far if you need anything."

"Thanks."

The train jerked, and John clutched the back of the seat to steady himself. "Keep your tickets handy. The conductor will ask to see them."

"I'd forgotten." Rennie patted one of the valises hanging on hooks below the window. "Did I put those in my bag?"

"They're in the lunch basket at your feet." Veronica shook her head. "I don't know what you'd do without me."

Probably be a lot less distracted. But Rennie's sister *did* tend to be more organized.

"Right." She tried to bend forward. "I can't reach it with three of us in the seat. I'll get it when the conductor asks for it."

John studied Livie's tense face. "Feel that breeze. The windows have let in some fresh morning air, don't you think, Livie?"

She sniffed. "I think so. Thanks, Mr. John."

"My pleasure." His smile included Rennie. "We'll stop for a lunch break later." They had all eaten an early breakfast in order to catch the eight o'clock train. "I'll check on you in a little while."

He picked his way back to his seat. No doubt he'd learn to walk on the rocking car before too many miles passed. Maybe by the time they reached Chicago later this afternoon.

The bigger question was, how soon the sisters would quit bickering.

~

*A*s they had a couple of hours to wait before boarding their next train in Chicago, they ate an early supper. The restaurant's specialties were salmon and trout from Lake Michigan and largemouth bass and carp from the Chicago River. Everyone wanted to see Lake Michigan, so they walked there after a delicious meal. Rennie held Livie's hand.

"George has seen the lake." Veronica halted as they rounded a corner for a view of the smooth waters, which stretched to the horizon with no land in sight. "Why, it does look like the ocean, just as he said. I thought he was fooling me."

Livie's mouth formed an *O.* "Is that what the ocean looks like, Miss Rennie?"

"Can't say. I've never seen it."

John dug his journal and a pen from his knapsack. A moment later, he began to write furiously.

That was right. This was all a big adventure for him. Rennie's gaze returned to the first of the Great Lakes she'd ever set eyes upon. Why, the photos and sketches in books didn't do it justice. How much more would they experience?

"See that pretty gray bird on that branch?" Veronica knelt beside Livie with an arm around the child's shoulder.

"It has a yellow head." Livie held her doll up to see it.

"And splashes of yellow in its wings." Veronica smiled. "I've never seen one like that."

"Me neither." Livie placed her fingers on her lips as she looked up in the tree.

"That's probably a golden-winged warbler." John's gaze followed Veronica's pointing finger. "I read about them this spring."

Rennie blinked, astonished not only at her sister's altered

mood—for the better—but also that John's preparation for the trip had included wildlife he might see along the way.

Livie pointed out more birds in the trees to Veronica. As they walked back to the depot, the pair continued to discuss the sights.

Rennie exchanged a wondering look with John.

"Don't question it," he whispered. "Just be thankful that your sister dropped her sullen attitude long enough to help Livie forget her worries."

"Agreed." Rennie raised her eyebrows when the little girl giggled at a squirrel circling an oak tree. "Why, I haven't heard Livie laugh all day. And she's barely eaten."

"You'll need to change that." John's brown eyes filled with concern. "We've got a lot of miles ahead. She must eat or she'll get sick. The tour guide warns that the folks who skip meals are the ones who suffer most."

"I'd forgotten your advice." She'd packed apples, canned meats, and crackers in her basket. "Perhaps we can find her a bit of cheese to eat as a bedtime snack this evening."

"I'll get enough for all of us. Not sure how comfortable those berths will be, but it's a sight better than trying to sleep sitting on hard benches."

~

*T*hey were miles from Chicago when the sun began to sink to the western horizon. Rennie was content to sit beside John on this part of the journey. The car was less crowded. One seat ahead of them, Livie sat on the aisle with Veronica beside the window, open to allow a hot breeze to stir the stale air inside the car. The pair watched for animals on farms they passed.

Rennie handed out a snack of cheese and crackers. They all

shared a bottle of milk. Thankfully, Livie ate better than she had all day.

"You bought four berths in the sleeping car, right?" Rennie settled back in her seat beside her handsome beau.

"Even with twelves sections with four berths each, they can sell quickly, so I'll always secure them right away." John shifted toward her with a sleepy grin. "No worries on that score."

He carried the money for everyone's tickets and for his own meals. Rennie and her mother had both worried about her carrying all those bills. Daily money was stored in her reticule. The rest was in her valise. Not that she didn't trust her fellow passengers, but one never knew. And there were also train robberies—

No. She musn't dwell on those rare occurrences. She brought her mind back to the task at hand. "I had half wondered if I should share a berth with Livie. She doesn't seem as afraid now, but once I pull the privacy curtain closed...well, I don't know how she'll react."

Veronica popped her head around the seat. "I'm taking Livie to the convenience."

"Thanks." Maybe her sister was trying to get along. This was the first time she'd offered to help their young charge.

"We'll move to the sleeping car when you return." John waited until the girls picked their way down the aisle before turning back to Rennie. "I understand your concern. I'm just not certain there will be a choice. From what I've learned, those berths are pretty narrow. I doubt either of you will sleep a wink all night if you share one."

And he'd be somewhere in the same sleeping car because there wasn't a separate one for men and women. She blushed to think of him being so close in the night.

*W*ithin a few minutes, John and his companions followed several others to the sleeping car, where the berths had been lowered and prepared with sheets, pillows, and blankets. As if they'd need blankets on the hot July night. But John was pleasantly surprised to note the open windows between the upper and lower beds through the aisle. He'd try to get a lower berth where he'd enjoy a greater share of the breezes.

The girls selected three berths.

"You're right, John." Rennie put her hands on her hips. "Far too narrow for comfort."

"What do you mean?" Veronica placed her valise on the bottom one. "You're not much bigger than me. I doubt you'll hang over the sides."

Rennie, who had a trim, womanly figure with curves in all the right places, sputtered.

John was hard pressed not to laugh. This scene was going in a book someday. With fictional characters. "You misunderstand. She was trying to discern whether she and Livie could share the space."

"Of course not, Rennie. What a hare-brained idea."

Rennie shot her a look that should have silenced her.

But Veronica continued. "George told me all about sleeping on trains. You should have asked me."

When two matronly women glanced their way, Rennie's face turned crimson.

"Livie," John asked quickly, "did you want the top or bottom?" With a hand on her shoulder, he drew her closer.

"I think the top. Except...what if I fall off?" She clutched her doll.

"More likely, you'll sink into the middle and stay there all night." Veronica patted her sleeve. "Leastways, that's what George said happened to him."

Her beau outweighed John by thirty pounds, so the extra

weight might've had something to do with it.

"And if you need to visit the convenience during the night," Veronica said, "jump down and wake me up. I'm sleeping below."

"I thought to stay close to her, Veronica." Rennie spoke mildly.

Veronica glanced over at the gray-haired woman already settled on the lower berth beneath the one Rennie claimed for them. "I'll take care of her in the night and wake you if need be."

A reasonable offer made in reasonable tones. And thank goodness, for folks casting glances their way finally turned to tend their own bedtime routines.

John lifted Livie to her bed and then went off to claim his own spot. Of the few still open, he chose a berth above one where a man in the working clothes of a laborer sat. He exchanged a brief greeting with his bunkmate and put his valise on his bed. He'd remove his coat, string tie, and shoes after the long black curtain was closed. How much more convenient it would be if only men slept in here. No doubt the ladies in the car shared that desire in regard to their own privacy.

He turned his head at the sound of Rennie's voice. She sat beside Livie, her head bowed and her hands folded. Livie emulated Rennie, her feet dangling over the side. On her own bunk, Veronica bowed her head as Rennie prayed aloud for their safe trip and Mrs. Sherman's health.

What a special moment. Included in his dreams for Rennie and himself were that they'd pray together with their children at bedtime. Watching her now was like glimpsing into the future.

It was personal. Sacred. A privilege to witness.

Overcome with emotion, he turned and stared out the window in the gathering dusk. Watching the stars from his berth would be almost like sleeping outside. Well, maybe not.

He'd been homeless after his mother's death, but he'd always managed to find shelter for himself and his sister to sleep away from the elements. Fortunately, that had only lasted a few weeks before he and Cora were hired at a restaurant—a train meal stop, no less—where they'd slept in kitchen pantries.

Difficult days in Bradford Junction, the railroad town of their birth. How life had changed when he and his twin met Mama Rosie. She and Pa had adopted them. Raised them on a farm right next door to Rennie.

John had much to be grateful for. He never would have guessed he and Rennie would be traveling west together—even temporarily.

Most folks were in their berths with their curtains closed, though a few mothers were still talking with their children who lay abed. Rennie was storing her valises in the empty space at Livie's feet. She secured the black curtains to ensure the child's privacy and glanced down the aisle at him.

Their eyes met. That old feeling, the love that had grown in him since they were children, stirred in his chest.

She gave him a sweet, self-conscious smile. "Good night, John."

"Good night, Rennie." His heart melted. "Sweet dreams." *Dream of me.*

Veronica poked her head out from behind her curtain. "Rennie, get to bed, for goodness' sake. I'm supposed to be chaperoning you two, and I need my rest."

Her voice had caught the attention of everyone still in the aisles and, likely, everyone settled behind the curtains.

Face flaming, Rennie climbed onto her berth and snatched the curtains closed.

A mother bending over her son's berth straightened, her eyes piercing John. She wagged her finger at him as if she'd be watching him too.

John jumped onto his bed and closed the curtains, humiliated to think he needed a fifteen-year-old chaperone to protect Rennie's reputation.

CHAPTER 5

*W*aking up two days later on Saturday morning, Rennie could barely believe that they were in Omaha, Nebraska. Why, if someone had told her she'd ever step foot in the state, she'd have laughed. But here she was, enjoying her second sponge bath since arriving at the bustling city. Why not? The girls were still sleeping and, oh, what a joy to have room to bathe and dress without bumping elbows with strangers in the train's dressing room.

John had telegraphed ahead for two rooms, and he told Rennie he'd mentioned there were ladies in the party. Seemingly, that had made a difference, as the hotel offered amenities far superior to the sleeping car. Rennie, Veronica, and Livie shared a room but each had their own bed with space to turn from side to side—a luxury compared to the berths. And that beefsteak last night! Why, it had rivaled her mama's. She'd have to remember to tell her about it.

Yet the money John paid from the Shermans' expense account rankled. What her family back home could do with such a sum. Papa had often teased Mama that she could make a silk purse from a sow's ear. Her parents were losing her income they used to pay rent for her trip's duration, something they could ill afford. However, Mr. McMahan had hired Zach to deliver telegrams for the rest of the summer. Hopefully, that would help.

This trip alone—their hotel rooms, the cost of various train tickets along the way, the meals that had cost a dollar every time for each one of them—added up to more money than she'd ever seen in her life. The cost of John's upcoming travel caused Rennie a surge of resentment as they ate breakfast in the noisy hotel dining room.

Diagonal rays of sunlight glinted across men in coats and string ties bent over their hearty servings. Others sported the plaid shirts and trousers of working men. Ladies wore lighter summer fabrics of various quality. Waitresses in ruffled aprons over black skirts and white shirtwaists scurried around the room.

"We didn't get to see much of Omaha last night." John munched on his last slice of bacon, a vast improvement over the corned beef hash at yesterday's early morning train stop. "Do you all want to explore the town for a bit?"

"I do." Livie scooted from her chair, jarring Veronica's elbow.

She frowned. "Wait just one minute, young lady."

Rennie placed a hand on Livie's arm. "She's right. Finish your poached egg first." The child didn't eat enough to keep a bird alive. Or was Rennie just used to seeing how much her own family consumed?

Livie shoveled the egg into her mouth, clearly eager to explore.

"I sent a telegram to Mr. Sherman last night that we arrived here safely," Rennie said. One of his requirements was a daily telegram about the trip's progress.

"Good. I'll arrange for the hotel to deliver our trunks and valises to the depot while you finish up." John guzzled his coffee.

They had nearly two hours to explore the city. The brisk walk in the early morning air should help work out Livie's fidgets. Rennie needed the exercise herself. She wasn't accustomed to sitting for hours on end. Her job at the telegraph office allowed her to be up and down all day. She didn't look forward to the confinement of the train cars that awaited them.

Veronica, holding Livie's hand, stared as if enthralled with the sights of the bustling city.

"You know all those railroad depots we saw?" John, *The Pacific Tourist* in hand, strolled with them past tracks going in several directions. "This city is the most important railroad center west of St. Louis and Chicago. It's unsurpassed as the greatest railroad center on the Missouri River."

"Impressive." Rennie was only mildly interested. She'd rather look at the beautiful river and buildings like the general offices of the Union Pacific Railroad, the four-story post office, and the four-story high school with its steepled tower. The Grand Central Hotel, where they'd spent the night, wasn't as pretty in her eyes as the school. Who knew all this could be found in a state not yet twenty years old?

She stopped at a grocer to replenish her empty lunch basket and left with apples, oranges, crackers, cheese, and lemons. All the trains coming into Omaha must provide goods from many areas of the country. She wouldn't ask John about it. She'd rather not listen to him read from his guidebook again.

All too soon, John announced that they'd best hurry to the depot so he could check the baggage. He had to be there at least thirty minutes ahead of departure in order to ensure their trunks were loaded.

They were soon settled on the train. The seats in this

passenger car faced one another, a nice change that made it convenient to sit together.

"Ladies, we're finally on the Union Pacific Railroad." John's grin encompassed them all. "This is truly where our western adventure begins."

His sense of expectancy somehow sliced through Rennie's despondency over the goodbyes ahead. He really was excited. She'd try to be happy for him.

"Is it an adventure to go see my mama and papa?" Sadness crossed Livie's features as she settled her doll between her and Rennie.

"I'm sorry, Livie. That was insensitive of me." Compassion filled John's eyes. "I didn't mean it that way. We'll continue to pray for your sweet mother, that she gets better every day just knowing you're on your way to her. But I think we can try to enjoy the journey, the new sights along the way. Will that be all right?"

Two long whistle blasts pierced the air.

"Is it bad of me not to think about her every minute?" Livie directed the question to Rennie as the train left the station.

"Not at all. I think your mama will want you to tell her what you see."

"Oh, she will." Livie rested her fingertips on the window's metal ledge. "I'll tell her everything."

Rennie met John's eyes in shared compassion. They'd tried not to talk about Mrs. Sherman to distract Livie's thoughts. Perhaps that had been the wrong choice.

They settled into the familiar motion of the train as it approached a bridge over the Missouri River, leaving Omaha behind them.

"George has been to Chicago, but he's never been this far West." Veronica stared out the open window at the bridge and the river beyond it.

"This bridge is quite impressive." Rennie smiled straight across at John.

"Pretty." Livie, her nose pressed against the windowpane, spoke from beside Rennie. "The top reminds me of a pie that Cook makes sometimes."

"That must have been a mighty fancy pie." John grinned at her.

"She'll make more when I get back with my mama and papa." Her brow furrowed. "No one will tell me when we'll come back. Do you know, Miss Rennie?"

"I don't, Livie. But the most important thing is, you'll be with your parents." Seeking a distraction for the little girl, Rennie looked over her shoulder at the see-through covering over the structure. "I see what you mean about the lattice pattern. In fact, I'll try to remember to use it for my next cherry pie."

"Hope I'm around to eat it." John stared out over the valley outside the window.

Rennie's head jerked toward him. Why did he have to go and remind her that he was leaving her at the end of this journey? Couldn't he give her a few minutes to forget? But how could she? He constantly referred to the thick guidebook in his knapsack, showing them sketches of places they'd see up ahead. Why, he was like a boy catching his first fish. He wasn't sad to be leaving her at all.

No, he was filled with wonder. Meanwhile, she dreaded reaching California, knowing she'd be leaving him there.

Veronica gave a snort. "Oh, don't take on so, Rennie. You knew he wasn't coming back with us."

John's attention swerved to Rennie.

"Of course, I did." Her cheeks flamed. Veronica knew she didn't want John to notice her distress. Rennie had been careful not to refer to his plans since they'd left home. "I just look forward to cooking for you again, John."

"I look forward to that, too, Rennie."

She strained to hear the soft-spoken words over the clatter of the wheels on the tracks. Mama had warned her not to give John grief about continuing his adventure without her, and he'd been more his old self since leaving Hamilton. Probably because Rennie had refrained from saying a negative word about his plans to write for a living.

But, oh, it was difficult to keep it bottled inside.

～

*J*ohn had begun to imagine that Rennie accepted his decision to write novels for a living, allowing him to enjoy the journey. As much as one could enjoy a trip with the sisters bickering, though that tension had eased since Chicago. Rennie was holding her tongue—quite possibly biting it at times.

But it couldn't last. Her very nature demanded she speak her mind. No thought that ever entered her head stayed there for long. She was honest to the point of bluntness. Considered honesty an act of friendship and love.

Maybe she wasn't only biting her tongue with Veronica. Maybe she was fighting the desire to convince him to forget his dreams, to accompany her home.

Since Veronica's comment about chaperoning them, he'd sat beside Veronica or Livie and maintained a respectful distance in the sleeping car. It was awkward for him to sleep yards away from the woman he intended to marry. All in all, he was grateful for Mr. Hill's foresight in sending Veronica.

At the moment, though, Rennie's blue eyes shot sparks at Veronica. The sisters probably needed to talk without himself and Livie.

"Want to explore the train with me, Livie?" John smiled at her.

"Oh, boy!" She jumped down from her seat.

He held out his hand to the little girl. She bounced in the aisle as she clasped it. "Ladies, we'll return shortly."

And hopefully, the girls would resolve any remaining tension before then.

CHAPTER 6

ennie waited only long enough for John and Livie to leave the car to speak. "What are you doing?"

Veronica lifted her auburn eyebrows. "What do you mean?"

She slid across to the window to face her sister squarely. "I'm trying not to mention *anything* to John about him staying in California."

"Why? I know you'll try to talk him out of it."

"Not yet. I want him to have an enjoyable trip. You saw him." Rennie swept her hand toward the small depot they were passing. "He's excited about everything he sees."

"Could end up in a book."

"Far more likely we'll hear about these places around the supper table."

Veronica leaned forward. "He wants his stories to amount to more than entertaining his family and friends."

"Given time, he'll sell more short stories. He's never written a novel." Rennie looked down the aisle. No sign of them. "He can work on it in the evenings."

"When he's relaxing in front of the fireplace while you darn socks?"

"Sounds heavenly." Rennie lifted her chin.

"Will he feel that way?"

Why would Veronica ask such a thing? Her sister had seen Mama struggle to purchase food at the grocers, meat from the butcher, after Papa lost his small savings when his bank closed in 1873. Eleven years had passed, and still they'd not recovered. Hard work was the only thing that pulled them through.

"Of course. By then, he'll know what it takes to make a living, to feed his family."

"I don't believe that will satisfy him, Rennie." Veronica stared at her clasped hands. "He craves your support. He's got a big dream. You should be careful how you speak to him about it."

"I will. Just do me a favor, will you? Say nothing about John leaving me at the end of our trip."

"Rennie, he's traveling for a few weeks. He's not leaving you." Her brow furrowed. "Is that how you feel?"

Yes. "No. And I don't want John thinking I have a problem with it."

"But you do."

"All right." She snapped and glanced at the two women across the aisle whose heads had turned their way. "I do," she whispered. "That doesn't mean John needs to know."

~

*J*ohn took Livie all the way to the front of the train to the Box Express Car and met an armed messenger who whittled a long strip from a piece of wood.

John crouched down beside Livie. "This is where passengers keep their valuables locked away."

"That ain't all." The shaggy-bearded officer of about thirty set down his knife and stood. "Most folks don't know the half of it."

"I'm certain." John glanced around the cramped space. Boxes of various sizes flanked two safes, one nearly as large as an icebox and the other just bigger than a hatbox. "Tell us."

"Young lady, all kinds of valuables might be guarded in here." The man rested a booted foot on one of the boxes. "Gold from the mines farther west. Coined silver. Payroll en route to miners' camps. Bullion on its way to banks, where it'll be held as gold reserve for bank notes." John blinked as the man enumerated the valuables in a slow drawl. "Could also be bank notes or precious stones or expensive jewelry."

"So much as that?" No wonder bandits sometimes attempted to rob a train carting such bounty.

"That and more." The express messenger scanned the boxes and crates scattered around the room. "Or, at any given stop, all of it together might only amount to a thousand dollars."

Only? John gave a low whistle. There was inspiration for a novel here. At least a short story. He'd jot the details in his journal tonight.

"But don't you worry, little lady." The man patted his gun. "I'll keep the valuables safe, or my name ain't Wade Bailey."

Livie shrank against John's leg as if uncertain if the officer intended to turn the weapon on her.

John placed his hand on her shoulder and guided her out the door they'd entered. "Well, thank you kindly for giving the lesson, Mr. Bailey."

"Come again. Or not." The man picked up his wood block and knife. "Don't make me no never mind."

A bit of an odd fellow. Perhaps he'd been too long confined in express cars.

It was a relief to get Livie out of there and into the mail car, where two men sorted letters and packages into heavy canvas bags of various sizes. "Good evening, gentlemen. My name is John Welch, and this is Livie Sherman."

A brown-haired man of perhaps forty introduced himself as Lester Sprinkle. His companion, a short, stout fellow, gave only a quick nod of acknowledgement and continued his work.

"Are you folks stretching your legs, or did you want to learn about our mail car?" Mr. Sprinkle peered at them over spectacles perched on his nose.

"Both." John liked the man's cheerful demeanor. Nothing there to scare a timid little girl. Thankfully, judging by her expression, her fear had changed to curiosity.

"Well, then, you came to the right place." He rubbed his hands together. "We're a railway post office car. Like a post office on wheels. Have you ever been to one in your town?"

Livie nodded, enthralled. "I go to the telegraph office, too, with Miss Bennett. My governess."

"Telegrams are mighty important to railroad folks. There are telegraph stations all up and down through here. See those telegraph wires?" He pointed out the window at the wires attached to poles spaced sporadically. "They run parallel to the tracks the whole way."

She stared out at them as if noticing them for the first time.

"Now this is really a converted baggage car, but we're big enough to take up the whole space." He explained that the mail car was always placed just behind the locomotive unless there was an express car. "You see we have racks to hold these heavy canvas bags. Here, see if you can lift it."

Livie wrapped her arms halfway around the large bag and heaved. It didn't budge.

"I ain't surprised. There are packages along with letters. Some are heavy."

Mr. Sprinkle picked up a package about the size of a stovepipe hat. "This one's light, see?" He put it in her outstretched arms.

"I can pick up this one." She shook it. "I'll bet there's cookies in here."

"Might be. Folks sure do like getting baked goods from back home." He took it from her and placed it in a hanging bag. "This one's going all the way to San Francisco."

"That's where we're going."

"Oh? Why are you going so far?" Mr. Sprinkle sorted another letter.

"Mama and Papa are there. My mama's sick and she needs me." A shadow crossed her face.

John's heart went out to her, but he didn't interrupt. The two of them seemed to have a rapport already.

Mr. Sprinkle squatted in front of her. "You'll be the best medicine she can get."

"I will?"

"For sure." He ran a finger down the bridge of her nose. "My wife gave me something this morning. She said to me, 'Now, Les, if you see a little girl today who misses her mama, give her this cookie for me.'"

Livie's eyebrows went up. "She did?"

"Sure as the world."

"I miss *my* mama."

His eyes lit up. "Well, I reckon you're the one then." He stood. "Do you like ginger snaps?"

She nodded, and he rummaged through a bucket and extracted a cookie the size of John's palm. Amazing what the kindness of a stranger could do for your soul.

"Thank you." John checked his pocket watch as they left the mail car. He'd kept Livie occupied for thirty minutes, significant on long travel days.

"Feels like we're standing slanted." Livie steadied herself against the door.

"You noticed." Grinning, he tweaked one of her pigtails.

"We're heading into the mountains." Cooler temperatures would follow.

It had been a nice reprieve, but they'd best head back to their seats in the middle passenger car. As they entered the first one, a strong odor of smoke wafted into the open windows. Not the kind he'd grown accustomed to on the locomotive. Then he noticed the hush of voices as all heads turned toward the southerly windows.

Livie gasped. "What's that, Mr. John?"

Something he'd never wanted to see. "It's a fire." About as long on the horizon as their train.

CHAPTER 7

"*V*eronica, wake up." Rennie nudged her sister's shoulder while staring at the ominous black cloud to the south. Something about it didn't look right. If it was an impending storm, it was a bad one.

"What's that?" A boy in the next seat pointed out the window.

His frightened voice seemed louder in the sudden quiet.

"That's a prairie fire, sonny." A gray-haired man stood from the opposite aisle. "I've seen many of 'em from my farm."

A prairie fire? Rennie had heard of the devastation caused by some that burned for days.

"Miss Rennie." Livie, eyes wide and terrified, ran down the aisle and threw herself into Rennie's arms. "Did you see it?"

"Yes, I saw it. We're safe." But were they? She patted the girl's shoulders while seeking John's concerned gaze.

"That fire might be twenty miles from us." John sank into the seat beside Veronica, who rubbed her eyes with a yawn.

"I'd say you've got the right of it, son." The old man in gray trousers with brown suspenders over his red-plaid shirt darted a glance at John. "As to whether we're safe or not, it depends on the way the wind blows. Why, I've seen a fierce wind push a fire twenty miles in an hour."

Rennie's gasp mingled with those of several other women.

"The wind is blowing the prairie grass," Vanessa whispered, her gazed fixed on the wide valley in front of them, where indeed, shoulder-high grass bent toward the west.

John offered them a faint smile. "It's probably not common for fires to spread that fast."

$\sim$

*J*ohn joined the farmer in the aisle and shook his hand after introducing himself.

"Name's Gus Nuxhall. And I agree. I've sat up all night watching a blaze not twenty miles distant." He glanced at other passengers looking his direction. "By morning, the wind had changed direction toward another farm."

John lowered his voice. "So there is little cause for concern?"

"'Course, sonny." The farmer rubbed his gray whiskers. "Always cause for concern under such conditions."

A boy of perhaps twelve crept closer. Blond hair stood up in a cowlick on his crown. "What conditions, begging your pardon?"

"What's your name, son?"

"Wes Tucker, sir."

"Wes, grass starts drying out in the heat of summer." The train jutted over rough track. Mr. Nuxhall widened his stance. "Then all it takes is someone not putting out their campfire all the way...or a lightning strike or even a cinder spark from a passing train to get the trouble started."

John's heart still beat the steady but elevated rhythm it had begun when he'd first spotted the black smoke with a bit of orange blazing on the ground. The prairie sounded like a dangerous place to live.

The train stopped to refill the water tender and the coal hopper.

Gus, who had a bit of a storyteller in him, began to talk to Wes about fighting the flames. Settlers built fire guards—several feet of plowed grounds around the homestead itself—for protection.

John stepped away to peer out the window. Depot workers hurried to assist the crew. They all glanced over their shoulders occasionally at the black horizon beyond a few town buildings and homes.

"John?" Rennie gestured to the seat opposite hers. Livie sat by the window clutching her doll. "What are you thinking?"

"I'm concerned." After learning how fast the fire *could* reach them, he couldn't relax until it burned itself out or it was well behind them. "The crew outside seems wary, yet they're going about their business."

Rennie glanced at Livie, who stared up at them. "Perhaps we should do the same."

Compassionate. Practical. Now that was the woman he loved. She hadn't been acting like herself lately. "Agreed."

The train chugged away from the depot. The orange flames against the golden grass and black smoke headed west ahead of the train. The frightening scene filled him with a strange sense of excitement.

"Want to read the ABC book with me, Livie?" Veronica lifted a valise off the wall hook.

"All right."

Rennie gave her sister a grateful smile.

John rose to allow the girls to sit beside one another. Sinking onto the seat next to Rennie, he clasped her hand. Her fingers tightening around his felt as it had from the first day he's held her hand...just right.

The terrible destruction to the south drew his gaze again. Was the blaze closer, or did he imagine it?

~

"*N*ext stop, Fremont, folks." The conductor, in the top hat and frock coat worn by those of his profession, walked down the aisle, seemingly having no trouble negotiating the frequent bumps that had nearly plummeted Rennie into the burly shoulder of a complete stranger yesterday. "An eating station. You'll have twenty-five minutes at this one."

"Pardon me, sir." Rennie leaned around John to catch the trainman's attention.

"Yes, miss?" The man paused beside her.

"Are we really stopping to eat with that raging fire so near?" Rennie could scarcely believe it was safe to stop so long.

"I guarantee that all the farmers, ranchers, townspeople—all men in the vicinity—dropped every task to fight it." The man near her father's age gave a reassuring nod.

"I'm certain that's true." Brow furrowed, John stood. "But we've learned that these fires have been known to travel twenty miles in an hour. I'd wager it's closer than that to this train."

"Our last report was eighteen miles." He scanned the horizon. "We've got telegraph wires along the tracks, and we check with our station masters at each depot."

The conductor seemed more watchful than scared. He checked his pocket watch before moving away. "Be there in five minutes."

"Miss Rennie, is that fire going to get us?" Livie's chin quivered.

"No, child." Rennie reached to scoop the frightened girl into her arms. "Let's pray for safety and for all those fighting the blaze." She'd been doing that silently since spotting it.

John gave up his seat for them to sit together and joined Veronica as she stowed the book in the valise.

"In the middle of the day?" Livie asked Rennie.

"Yes, you can pray to God anytime. Especially when you're scared." Clasping Livie's hand, Rennie whispered a prayer for everyone's safety and added a request for rain to douse the flames.

～

*J*ohn still felt uneasy about the stop as they followed other passengers toward the restaurant set amidst a surprising number of buildings. The orange-and-black backdrop gave the town an eerie atmosphere. Undoubtedly, the crew would seek the latest reports.

He tried to push away his concerns as he selected an unclaimed table for four. He offered a biscuit from the bread basket in the center to Livie first. All of them were munching when a man wearing brown trousers and coat with a patterned yellow vest stopped at the table.

"It'll be four dollars for the meal, sir." He held out his hand.

Rennie quickly placed three bills on the man's open palm. John paid the last one, but she ought to allow him to pay for all their meals from Mr. Sherman's fund. He'd been taught that the man paid for the meal. On the other hand, toting the money for tickets and hotels was a hefty amount already. Perhaps splitting it had been best.

Two girls around Veronica's age brought bowls of onion soup. He had barely tasted the watered down but flavorful soup when a plate of hot beefsteak, three cubes of boiled potatoes, and a generous spoonful of corn was placed in front of him.

"We have coffee or milk to drink." A girl with blond braids waited respectfully. They gave their preferences, and she left the table quickly.

"When I worked at a meal stop restaurant," John said, "my boss demanded we have the food on the table when customers arrived."

"I'd forgotten you and Cora had that job." Rennie's gaze darted toward the back window that framed the prairie fire.

She was worried, but he didn't want to call attention to her fear and scare the girls.

"This is too much food." Using her fork, Livie poked the steak larger than her hand as the waitress delivered their drinks.

Indeed. It was feast or famine at these places.

Rennie eyed the large portions. "Eat the soup. Or the potatoes and corn. And drink your milk."

John tried again to distract Rennie's uneasiness. "Fremont has a new hotel called the Occidental." He spoke between bites of steak. "Along with smaller ones. Two newspapers. The opera house here is supposed to be the finest one in the West. This town also has the biggest dry-goods store in all of Nebraska."

"Ten-minute call, folks." The conductor's voice carried over the room's chatter.

John checked his pocket watch. The crew had shortened their lunch break by five minutes. Not cause for alarm, surely, but it heightened his concern.

Their waitress hurried over with a tray filled with slices of walnut cake. "Sorry this is so late." She placed one small dessert plate in front of each of them and scurried to the next table.

John forced himself to relax. "It's best to eat whatever you most want at this point."

Veronica attacked her cake with her fork.

"Cake?" Livie's eyes beseeched Rennie.

"That's fine. You ate your vegetables."

The conductor returned with a two-minute warning,

although he hadn't been gone more than three minutes. John met Rennie's wide-eyed gaze.

"Let's wrap up our food and take what we can with us." Rennie picked up her basket from the floor. "We'll eat at our seats."

~

he train led them into The Great Platte Valley after lunch. Rennie studied the fire that appeared to her frightened gaze maybe a mile long, licking up dry grass...and surely, homes and barns and fences. She prayed for the families, the children in its path.

Across from her, John was writing in his journal. She was glad he hadn't strayed far from them since spotting the danger. His presence always calmed her, no matter what was happening.

"Want to read your *Aesop's Fables* book?" Veronica smiled at their young charge and fished inside one of their bags.

"Not right now." Livie stared out the window as if mesmerized.

Seeking a distraction for the child, Rennie looked out the other side of the train. "What's that?"

John followed her gaze. "That's sod house."

Livie turned to look. "A house made out of dirt?"

Veronica grimaced. "Imagine trying to clean it."

"And trying to keep mud off your clothing." Rennie shook her head.

Suddenly, the brakes began to squeal. John, clutching his journal, smashed against Rennie. Livie was thrown backward. Veronica fell on her knees as the locomotive continued to slow down. Screams and thuds told Rennie their fellow passengers suffered the same dilemma.

There was a thump, and then the train stopped completely

in the middle of the prairie. For a moment, there was aston-ished silence.

"Why'd we stop in the middle of the prairie?" A woman's voice.

"No depot in sight." A man near the front spoke.

"What did we hit?" another man asked.

Then conversation became indistinguishable as everyone began to talk.

"Sorry, Rennie." John pushed away from her. "Are you hurt?"

"No, just surprised."

"Anyone hurt?" John placed a hand on Livie's shoulder, who shook her head.

Veronica groaned. "I'll have bruised knees, but I'm all right."

John helped her back into her seat. "I wonder what we hit."

"What are those?" Livie pointed toward the front of the train.

Rennie looked out the window and gasped. "Are those... buffalo?" A herd of the massive animals crossed the tracks in front of the train.

"Sure enough." John shook his head. "I'll bet we struck one."

Remembering the thud, Rennie couldn't argue. It was doubtful the poor animal survived.

"It's like nothing I've ever seen before." Veronica stared as if memorizing the strange sight.

"Animals are smart. They're fleeing from the prairie fire. North." John stood behind Rennie. "Wonder if it's safe to get off."

"Not until the herd passes." Those humped backs and massive bodies coupled with some mighty scary curved horns inspired both fear and awe. How could he consider leaving the car's safety?

"Folks, we'll have a delay while the buffalo herd passes." The conductor's voice cut over the conversations, and everyone turned to listen. "We hit one of them. We'll stay inside until they move out, and then we'll take the one we killed with us. Could use some help with it."

John's hand shot up, along with those of a few other men.

How long would that take? The smell of the prairie fire permeated the car. They were a little ahead of it, but what if they sat here long enough for it to reach them? Rennie said another prayer for the men fighting the blaze. The sunny sky belied her prayer for rain, yet she requested it again.

~

Dried grass crinkled under John's boots. It felt good to leave the confines of the car.

"Men, we've lost nearly three-quarters of an hour already." The conductor led a dozen men to the front of the train. "Let's get this done quickly."

Gus Nuxhall nudged John. "Do you see the prairie fire?"

"Can't see much except the dust from about three hundred buffalo." John, walking beside him, strained his eyes.

"The men fighting the flames have attacked its center." He pointed. "Now there's two smaller blazes. Could be promising."

That Mr. Nuxhall thought so comforted him. "Sure hope no one lost their homes."

"Some probably did." He sighed. "Crops were surely destroyed. These fires are common. Most happen in the fall."

"It's a bit gruesome, folks." The conductor halted.

John looked over. He wouldn't be describing this in his book.

"That bull weighed close to two thousand pounds." Mr. Nuxhall surveyed it. "How you figure on moving it?"

The conductor grimaced. "Didn't expect it to be taller than me. I'm six foot."

"Let's butcher it," Mr. Nuxhall suggested.

Others nodded agreement.

"Anyone ever butcher a buffalo?"

No one spoke. John's pa paid to butcher his cows and pigs. John had never even been this close to such a massive animal. Such a pity it died in this manner.

"I've butchered many a cow." Mr. Nuxhall pulled a knife from a sheath on his belt. "Let's give it a try."

~

*R*ennie stepped outside with the girls when other families alighted from the train. The wind tried to snatch her hat, and she clamped her hand over it. Though secured by a hatpin, it seemed too precarious to release.

Dust stirred up by the herd dissipated in the breeze. The smoky odor wafted closer.

"We're going with the other girls to look for wildflowers." Veronica touched her arm.

Three sisters, the youngest one around Livie's age, waited on the fringe of about a dozen women and children. Some of them Rennie recognized as passengers she'd exchanged pleasantries with them in line for the dressing room. "Don't wander far." A short walk would do them good, especially Livie.

"We won't." Veronica grinned. "I'm not going to chance missing the train."

"Livie, you stay with Veronica."

"I will."

The group headed toward a patch of yellow about a hundred paces distant.

"We can see them from here. They'll be all right." A young

woman walked up beside her. "Those are my sisters that your sisters are talking with. I'm Beth Carlson. Please, call me Beth."

"And I'm Rennie. Rennie Hill. How nice it is to meet you." She gave the friendly woman a nod. "Veronica is my sister, but I'm acting as governess to the younger one, Livie Sherman."

"My mistake." Her short blond curls blew in the wind. "I left my hat on my seat. The wind that's stirring up that fire makes it difficult to retain one's hat."

"True." Rennie kept her hand over hers to keep it from blowing away. "Are we safe from the blazes?"

"If we don't stay here long. What we need is for the wind to shift. Or rain." Beth studied the horizon, her blue gingham skirt flapping against her boots. "The fire's smaller, likely thanks to local men fighting the flames. Once we get another twenty miles farther up the tracks, we should be safe."

That was a relief. "I keep praying those dark clouds in the distance hold rain and not just smoke from the fire."

Beth laughed. "Me too."

"What's your destination?"

"Cheyenne. That's where we live. We spent a month with my aunt in Omaha. How about you?"

"San Francisco." It was good to know that someone familiar with the area was more watchful than fearful of the distant blaze.

"California. I've never been there." She looked toward the front of the train. "It appears the men will be a while. Do you want to join the others?"

Rennie glanced at two distinct, smaller fires on the horizon. She could relax a little. How pleasant it was to talk with another woman her age. "Let's do."

A rumble of thunder sounded in the distance.

"Wait." Beth gestured to the south. "I thought I saw lightning."

"I didn't." She studied the gray horizon. "I thought those were smoke clouds."

"So did I. Lightning can start a fire somewhere else."

Rennie began to understand dangerous prairie fires were far too common. "So lightning started this."

"Could have. Most are caused by hunters or farmers clearing their field." Beth patted her arm. "I'm easier in my spirit now that blaze is divided. Those fighting the flames will soon have it under control."

As long as it burned, Rennie wouldn't rest easy until they were no longer trapped on the prairie with it.

CHAPTER 8

The train resumed its journey a half hour later with two barrels of buffalo meat stored in the refrigerated car. Rennie had enjoyed meeting Beth and made plans to eat supper together. Her new friend's siblings were well-behaved with a touch of shyness, a reserve Rennie understood. She looked forward to introducing John to them.

Livie fell asleep clutching a bouquet of Black-eyed Susans. John had taken his knapsack, and murmuring something about writing, left them for the men's car after the rain started. No doubt he wanted to pen his thoughts about the fire, which was now more gray smoke than flames. And thank heavens, the train was finally in front of it.

Veronica soon nodded off, her head against the windowpane.

Outside the rain-splattered window, the wind made waves in the prairie grasses in the beautiful valley that varied in width. A river—she overheard someone say it was the Platte— captured her eye with its untamed beauty. It hugged the bluffs in sharp contrast so that she didn't know which to look at first.

The water moved over boulders in the river bed, creating tiny waterfalls here and there.

Who knew such beauty existed? Sketches, photographs, and even paintings didn't capture the wild magnificence she'd encountered so far. According to John, the best was yet to come.

The rain stopped. Sun broke through the clouds. She lowered their window, turning her face toward the fresh breeze. For the first time, she could understand why John wanted to see their country with his own eyes, witness its stark beauty, which affected one so deep down inside that words didn't do it justice.

At least, no words she knew. John would find a way to describe it.

The train chugged to a stop. Chatter faded as folks looked around. The station they sat outside appeared little better than a barn. A man wondered aloud if he might get out and smoke a cigar in the afternoon sun. No one opened the doors, though.

Rennie craned her neck at a water tower. Looked like a huge bucket on stilts, to her way of thinking. This one was made of wood. She'd seen other, larger ones made of steel. Steam locomotives stopped at almost every station to replenish their tenders with water. The train's foreman shifted the spout for the liquid to flow into the tender.

As the train dumped ashes into a stone pit, she watched carefully so she could describe the process to her father and brothers. Then the men shoveled coal into the train's hopper from a pile near the tracks. Coal was replenished less often than water, every few stations. She'd actually learned quite a bit on this trip—and not all of it was from John's guidebook.

"Hi, Rennie." John whispered, sliding in next to her.

She jumped. "You scared me." She kept her voice low.

"Sorry. How long have they been sleeping?" The train chugged into motion.

She shrugged. "Half hour."

"Good."

"What did you do?" She shifted from the window to look at him. The chatter that had been fairly loud before the water and coal stop hadn't picked up. Folks must be trying to nap, or perhaps they'd run out of things to say to their companions.

"I wrote about the prairie fires. That will make it into a novel someday." He patted his knapsack. "Read a couple of newspapers, one from Omaha and one from Fremont. I can't buy one in every city that prints them because I can't tote them around. But I'll save some as a memento of my trip."

"I won't have much to remind me of my trip." She sighed. "I didn't even think to bring my knitting needles and yarn. Why, can you imagine how many scarves and mittens I could have finished on a trip this long?"

"I can. I've watched you knit many evenings at your mama's fireplace."

"Those were good times." How long before they'd sit around that fireplace again? No telling. Best change the subject. "The girls and I made some friends while you carved that buffalo."

"I saw you talking to a pretty blonde about our age. Is that her?"

"Yes, her name is Beth Carlson." John found her pretty? "She's traveling with her three sisters in another passenger car. We'll eat supper with them."

Livie sat up and rubbed her eyes. "Is it time to eat? I'm hungry."

"We ate a very early lunch. That's why you're hungry in the middle of the afternoon. We've picked up speed to make up time lost. I expect supper will be late. How about an apple? Or a bit of cheese and a cracker?"

"What?" Veronica straightened, her red curls awry. "Are we eating now?"

"Just a snack." Rennie reached for her basket. With the

knife she stored inside, she sliced a thin sliver of cheese and put it on a cracker, which she gave to the little girl.

"I want one." Veronica held out her hand for the next slice.

Rennie obliged her, then glanced at John. "How about you?"

"Thought you'd never ask."

His eyes crinkled with that teasing glint she loved. His hand covered hers as she gave him a generous apple slice. She leaned against his side for a brief moment, comforted that the earlier danger had started to mend the torn bonds between them.

~

John had an idea for a short story related to prairie fires. After enjoying their snack together, he sat in the men's car and put together a few ideas for it. Thoughts of Rennie kept intruding.

Memories of their courtship had flooded over him when she mentioned knitting—happy times with her and her family. He'd always gotten along with her father better than anyone else in her family, even Zach. Rennie's oldest brother was only four years his junior, but their differing personalities kept their friendship on a superficial level.

Not so with Mr. Hill. Perhaps that was because Rennie felt such a kinship with her father. Perhaps it was because Trent Hill reminded him of his own father, his first one. Regardless of the reason, he had built a rapport with him.

He leafed through his journal—half-filled, and this was only the third day. But the detail helped him flesh out the points for an article. It was after six o'clock when he went to check on his ladies.

Rennie pressed a wet cloth against Livie's forehead.

"What's wrong?"

The child's face was red, but that could be from the heat. Rays of sunshine beat down on this half of the car.

"Her stomach hurts."

"Train sickness?" The air was stuffy. Perhaps that was causing the problem.

"Maybe." Rennie raised concerned blue eyes to his. "Or possibly she's hungry."

John saw her eat two slices of cheese with crackers. "Has she eaten anything else?"

"She asked. At first, I refused so as not to ruin her supper. After that, she didn't want anything. Do you know when we'll stop?"

"I'll ask the conductor." John looked up in time to see the man's frock coat disappear into another car and took off after him.

He caught up with him in another car and quickly explained.

"Try to feed her. Traveling on an empty stomach isn't good."

"Right." He'd tried to warn Rennie. "Where's our next meal stop?"

"Grand Island. Eat the mutton chops. Stay away from the prairie hens. Another thirty minutes."

John hurried back and told them what he'd discovered. "How about a dipper of water? It's cold. I saw ice in the barrel when I passed."

"Yes, please."

Livie drank half the water. Veronica finished it.

A cold breeze stirred wisps of reddish-brown hair around Rennie's pretty face.

"We're climbing into higher altitudes. Wear warmer clothing starting tomorrow."

"Just three days into our trip?" Veronica's eyes sparkled as she rubbed her hands together. "George is sweating back home, and I'll wear wool in the morning."

The corners of Rennie's mouth pulled down. Cold weather wasn't her favorite.

Eyes closed, Livie leaned against Rennie's arm for the next few minutes. Had she fallen asleep?

One long whistle blast. Good. They were approaching Grand Island.

Once they stopped, he carried Livie down the steep steps and set her down. Fresh air might revive her.

"Twenty minutes, folks!"

"This is a bigger town." Rennie's gaze darted to the stores, shops, and houses. "See if they have a lunch counter. Livie can't eat a big meal, and I don't want one either." She extracted three dollars from her reticule. "Buy us each a sandwich, biscuits, and fruit. Milk might settle Livie's stomach."

"Want tea." Livie rested her head against Rennie's waist.

"All right. Tea for me too." She pointed to a bench outside the restaurant. "We'll sit and wait. Veronica, help him carry it. I left my basket on the train."

John hesitated. "Aren't we supposed to eat with your friend's family?"

"Oh, I'd forgotten." Rennie looked beyond him. "Beth, you found us." She quickly introduced Beth and her sisters.

John greeted them. Jillian appeared to be around Veronica's age. Hannah was perhaps twelve. Annie told him proudly that she was eight. Livie needed someone her age to talk to—when she felt better.

"I'm sorry, Beth. Livie's feeling poorly." Rennie sat, and Livie scooched to lean against her. "We're going to buy a sandwich from the lunch counter and eat out here."

"That's fine by us." Beth pointed. "Do you mind if we sit at the bench beside yours? My sisters have been excited about eating with you."

"Not at all."

"Good." Beth gave a relieved smile. "Annie, you and Hannah stay out here, but don't bother Livie."

When they returned with the food, Livie took a bite of a

roasted beef sandwich and refused anything else. She turned her face away. "Don't want to get back on the train."

A different conductor strode past them. "Five minutes, folks! You've got five minutes."

Rennie turned to him. "John, will you send our daily telegram to Mr. Sherman? Mention the prairie fire, I guess, but tell him we're safe. In less than ten words."

It was a flat charge up to ten words. The telegraph office was in the next wooden building over. "Shall I say that Livie's sick?" He stood.

"No, let's see how she is tomorrow."

CHAPTER 9

"*L*ivie needs the bottom berth tonight, Veronica." Two hours later, Rennie pulled back the blankets to claim three berths for them near the women's dressing room. "Livie, take this one."

The little girl curled up on the berth and closed her eyes. Rennie arranged the sheet and blanket around her and kissed her cheek. A little warm. Had standing outside on that windy prairie brought on a cold? She'd been cranky. Veronica and Beth had combined their efforts with Rennie's to coax Livie back on the train. Rennie wasn't certain she could have got her on without physically carrying her otherwise. Beth was in another sleeping car, but she'd come by in the morning to check on Livie.

"And you're sleeping on the top one." Veronica placed her bag on the adjacent top berth, the bottom one already being occupied by a woman with a cap covering her hair. "I'm not getting up in the night if she gets sick. I need my sleep."

"Fine." Rennie rolled her eyes at John, who gave her a sympathetic shrug. "I'll only wake you if necessary."

"I'll claim a berth at the other end." John placed her valise on the lower berth at Livie's feet.

Rennie ran the back of her wrist across her forehead. "I'll pray she sleeps."

"Me too." He looked away. "Good night."

Rennie remembered well when a warm kiss accompanied his goodnights. Even though this wasn't the time or place, she wished for one all the same. Wished she at least saw him longing for one as she did.

"Sweet dreams." That was what she always said to him when he left her at the end of an evening together.

He turned back. Something sparked in his eyes. "Let me know if you need help."

She watched him amble away with the car's rocking motion and then turned back to Veronica's knowing glance.

"Just remember what Mama said." Veronica climbed onto her bed for the night.

Mama said a lot of things. She talked more than all of them combined.

"Good night." Veronica closed her curtain.

Rennie needed to focus on Livie. She hadn't emptied her stomach—a blessing, for sure—but had been nauseated. She bent over her. Already asleep. She removed the child's shoes and then kissed her cheek. She'd pray for the little girl's family herself.

She climbed up, closed the curtain, and removed her shoes, ready to be alone with her thoughts. Beth's friendship meant she didn't only have Veronica and John to rely upon. It was a comforting feeling. No other passengers had spoken much more than polite greetings the whole journey.

The window was closed against the night's chill. She touched the pane. Cold. She pulled the blanket up to her chin. The only advantage to sleeping fully clothed because of the men in the car was the added warmth.

And the fact that she'd be ready in an instant should Livie awaken in the night.

The stars seemed more numerous in this western sky. Prettier too.

Pine torches interrupted the serene sky as the train chugged into a station. Another water stop. Between water stops every few minutes, the coal stops, the bells, and the whistles, it was difficult to sleep through the night.

She situated herself as comfortably as possible on the narrow berth that swayed with every movement. It reminded her of the only occasion she went horseback riding with John, hoping to impress him. Instead, she'd screamed when her horse took her to the middle of a creek and took a long drink. John had told her family that night at supper with many embellishments. She'd laughed until her sides ached.

She turned on her side facing the window when the train left the depot. Soon everything was black again outside, though the moon and stars cast a shimmery sheen over treetops.

The locomotive was never quiet, but she'd become accustomed to that particular noise. The coal fumes, the black smoke, the smells—that was another matter entirely. No wonder folks got sick while traveling.

That reminded her to pray for Livie and her mom. Rennie said a prayer for her family too. And she prayed for John, that he'd find his way in this world before losing every last penny he'd saved.

~

*M*ovement in the car awoke Rennie at dawn on Sunday. Livie had slept through the night, thank the Lord.

She scratched at a thin line of frost that clung to her

window. The porter had built a fire in the heat stove last night. The warmth didn't reach this far—and John had warned it was only going to get colder. Time to don the second set of under-clothes.

Perhaps that guide *had* been worth its price.

Pushing aside the curtain a few inches, she climbed down in her stockinged feet and peeked at Livie, who stirred and then went still again. Her forehead was warm but not feverish. Rennie pushed back the top blanket and straightened, pondering what to do.

Perhaps it was better that she and Livie stay on the train. John and Veronica could bring some breakfast back for them... toast or biscuits or apples. And ginger tea, if available, to soothe the child's stomach. Yesterday had taught her a lesson. If she could prevent train sickness with crackers or fruit, Livie wouldn't be sick again on this trip.

A man headed to the men's dressing room. A mother leaned over her son to nudge him awake. One woman, her gray hair askew, ambled toward the women's facilities.

Good. Not many people were up. Rennie would get dressed before awakening Veronica to take her turn in the washing room. Then Beth had promised to visit.

Rennie stepped inside the small room, grimacing at the single dirty brush fastened to the wall with a chain. After brushing her teeth and taking a quick sponge bath, she donned a wool dress. Three women and two little girls had entered the small room by the time she brushed her hair. It was difficult to find enough arm room to fashion her hair into a single braid and pin it up.

Fearing Livie was already awake, Rennie eased her way into the aisle where several women and children waited. Among them was Veronica.

"Thanks for waking me up so I could be at the front of the

line." Sarcasm colored Veronica's angry tone. "You got my towel?"

Rennie ignored the tone and laid a towel in her outstretched hands. "Livie awake?"

"No, but no one's being quiet. She'll be up soon." Veronica gestured to the line as someone exited the dressing room. "No need to hurry."

In her bunk, Livie lay on her side with her hands folded under her face, crying. "Honey, what is it? Does your stomach hurt?"

"I want my mama." A tear slid down her cheek.

Rennie's heart broke. "You miss her more when you feel bad?"

She nodded.

"You'll see her in less than a week."

Beyond an overnight stay in Ogden, Utah, delays weren't likely. But after that prairie fire, who knew what might happen?

"It's already been a long time."

"It surely has." Rennie smoothed the child's hair back, brown tendrils wet with tears. "Does your stomach hurt?"

"I feel sick. Can I keep lying down?"

"You can lie there until the porter comes to make up the beds." Which usually happened before the breakfast stop. "Do you want a cracker?"

"Sleepy." She closed her eyes.

"Good morning, ladies."

Rennie stood too quickly and struck her head against the upper berth. "Morning, John." She rubbed the back of her head.

His clean-shaven face and freshly combed hair showed him ready to face the day.

"She still sleeping?"

"Trying to rest. It's her stomach." Rennie touched the girl's forehead. "No fever to speak of."

"Good morning, everyone. How is she?" Beth hurried toward them.

Rennie offered her a welcoming smile. "She wasn't up during the night. But her stomach still hurts. She wants to lie down."

Beth's blue eyes filled with compassion. "Maybe the porter can take up her berth last."

"That will help." If her illness continued, would they have to stop overnight? "John, I'll stay with her while you and Veronica eat. Bring us back something that's easy to digest."

"My sisters and I will help him." Beth patted her arm. "I'll see if the eatery can make her ginger tea."

"If not, they might sell ginger cakes or cookies." John clasped Rennie's hand.

"That would be wonderful." What a relief to share her concern with her beau—and her new friend.

"We'll see how she feels at noon."

Rennie met his eyes. He must also be wondering if they should find a hotel for the night. "Yes, let's see if she feels better after eating."

∼

*J*ohn alighted the train in the brisk morning breeze and turned to help Veronica, Beth, and her sisters down the steep steps in Sidney, Nebraska. It didn't feel right to eat in the dining room with Rennie's new friends that he barely knew, but she assured him that's what she wanted. Watching her compassionate manner with Livie evoked visions of her caring for the children he dreamed they'd have one day.

"Thank you." Beth held her skirts with one hand and clasped his with the other.

"My pleasure." He released her to lift the youngest one, Annie, onto the landing.

"I'm cold." Veronica shivered.

"Feels normal to us." Jillian, Beth's sister closest to Veronica's age, secured her blue shawl around her shoulders. "We live about a hundred miles from here."

"You do?" John blinked. Rennie hadn't told him much about Beth and her family. "Where's that?"

"Our father's ranch is near Cheyenne in Wyoming Territory." Beth's eyes sparkled. "In fact, we'll get off there. It's the next meal stop."

"Cheyenne? That's one of the cities where I hope to spend a few days."

"I'm certain my parents would welcome all of you to stay with us while you're in town." She smiled. "Let's get inside. They're giving us thirty minutes this stop, but we'll need it to eat and get something to soothe Livie's stomach."

They couldn't stop now unless Livie was too sick to travel—and he'd be alone when he came back, so he couldn't accept the invitation.

Veronica frowned at him and then scurried after the sisters.

The crisp air was as invigorating as the scenery to John. The grassy plains leading up to the mountains were beautiful with rugged bluffs that jutted close to town. He could scarcely take his eyes off them. He'd study them and describe them in his journal this morning. He turned away from the grandeur reluctantly.

A loud gong made him forget the scenery.

"Your feast awaits!" A man stood at the doorway by the resounding gong. "Come inside for the spread within."

"Thank you." John nodded, a little uncomfortable at the overzealous welcome.

He followed the others inside to neatly arrayed tables. They had no sooner seated themselves when ladies brought them plates of thin buckwheat hot cakes, hot beefsteak, cold roast antelope, cold chicken, ham and poached eggs, boiled potatoes, sweet corn, and stewed tomatoes. The fellow hadn't exaggerated. John could give Veronica some chicken, hot cakes, and potatoes to wrap up in her basket for Rennie and buy something lighter for Livie on his way out.

He sat between Beth and Veronica. He asked the blessing, and then they all began to eat as the younger girls talked about their ranch. Too bad that Rennie was unable to join them.

Partway through the meal, Beth patted her lips with her napkin and rose. "I'll go to the counter while the line is short and see if they'll make ginger tea for us."

It was more his responsibility than hers. He joined her as the lady behind the counter hurried away.

Beth turned to him. "She'll make the tea so it will be ready when we leave. They also have ginger cakes. I asked for two portions and unbuttered toast."

"Excellent." Hopefully, Livie could eat it. "You didn't pay for it, right?"

She shook her head. "We're to come back when we finish eating."

They reseated themselves at the large round table, and John gave his attention to the still-hot steak. A boy of perhaps fourteen, the same age John had been when working at a meal stop, delivered a biscuit the size of John's fist. Was he an orphan as John had been?

"Is there milk or coffee?"

"I'll bring milk for the young'uns." The boy's gaze swept the group. "Coffee for the rest. Be right back."

Beth glanced at him. "Rennie told me you want to write novels."

Had she spoken of it with pride? Or shared her disapproval? "That's my plan." If only he had more to show for his dream. He'd tossed every page of his novel he'd written so far into the fire as the rubbish it was. What if her fears were true? What if he couldn't write a novel?

"Congratulations on getting your short stories published." She sliced into her chicken without taking her eyes off him. "I'll ask my father to find those magazines. We both enjoy reading."

"You do?" A hearty bite of eggs spilled off his fork. "What to do you read?"

"Anything I can find. Romance novels. Adventure novels. Western novels. My father's library is the most extensive in our area." She clasped her hands together, ignoring her nearly untouched meal.

He turned to face her. "Who's your favorite author?"

"My father has read *Moby Dick* every year since he purchased it. Herman Melville is his favorite. Mine's probably Mark Twain."

"Twain is my favorite." He stared at her. How heartening to meet an avid reader in these parts. "Which books?"

"I certainly enjoyed *The Adventures of Tom Sawyer* and *The Innocents Abroad*." Her eyes glowed. "My favorite has to be *Roughing It*."

"About his years in the West." His jaw slackened. "Mine too."

"I'll look for your writings, too, as they come out."

"Thank you." She seemed sincerely interested. In contrast to Rennie who was bent on changing him.

"Ten more minutes, folks." The conductor stood at the open door. His voice carried to the back of the room the size of a barn. "Ten minutes."

The warning brought John back to his surroundings. He resumed eating at a faster pace. They must take food back to Rennie and Livie.

"Eat your eggs and vegetables first." Beth picked up her fork. "Put your favorite meat on your biscuit. We'll take it with us if we don't finish our meal."

Practical suggestion. She was a lot like Rennie. Except his girl wasn't interested in books or writing.

John gestured toward his potatoes, chicken, and biscuit. "Veronica, will you carry this with yours back to our car? I'll see if our food is ready at the counter."

The triumphant look Rennie's sister shot at Beth puzzled him as long strides took him to the lunch counter.

CHAPTER 10

*R*ennie gave Livie a sponge bath and helped the listless child don her warmest dress while the others were in the dining room. The porter had graciously agreed to make up Livie's berth last. He regretted that this train didn't have an invalid car where she could rest all day. Although Rennie shared his regret, that sounded expensive.

Livie drank a dipper of icy-cold water before they moved to their seats in the passenger car.

"They'll be here soon, don't you fret." Rennie patted Livie's hand. "Are you hungry?"

"A little."

"Good." As she looked up, what a comfort to see John's broad smile.

"We have a bottle of ginger tea." He gave it to Livie. "Sip on that, sweetheart."

She complied and made a face.

"I'm so glad they had the beverage." Rennie looked beyond him to her friend. "Oh, Beth, I'm sorry we weren't able to join you for breakfast. Can we try again for lunch?"

"That's our last opportunity." Beth raised her hands, palms up. "We'll eat lunch in Cheyenne, where we'll disembark."

"Let's see how Livie feels in an hour or two." After eating. If she still needed to lie down, Rennie planned to talk to John about spending the night at the next bigger town. Presumably, that was Beth's stop, anyway.

"We'll come back then." Beth covered Livie's hand with her own. "We're praying you feel better quickly, little one." Her sisters also spoke with Livie.

After they left, Livie ate a piece of toast. A few minutes later, she ate another while sipping the tea. Rennie ate her chicken biscuit sandwich with a lighter heart. If Livie continued to improve, there was no need for an emergency stop.

$\sim$

The train stopped to refill its water tank at Bushnell, the last station in Nebraska, and then was on its way. The sense of excitement and adventure was growing in John again now that Livie felt better. "Ladies, we're about to enter the Wyoming Territory." A *territory,* for goodness' sakes. Likely to become a state...one day. This trip was something to describe to his children and grandchildren.

"Where are we now?" Livie turned from the window. Her doll was positioned between her and Veronica. She'd perked up after eating ginger cake.

That gave him pause. "We're in the state of Nebraska." They'd never mentioned what state they passed through to the child? Rennie had brought two books to read her on the trip. Besides that and the tour he'd taken her on, they'd done little to entertain her. An oversight he'd fix starting now. "It became the thirty-seventh state to enter our Union in 1867."

"It did?" Curiosity sparked in her eyes.

"Sure enough." He grinned, happy to see color back in her pale cheeks. "You remember the sod houses we saw?"

She nodded.

"There are big ranches here too. You saw a buffalo herd yesterday. You'll see or hear coyotes. And I imagine that station we passed a few miles back wasn't named 'Antelope' for nothing." The High Plains with the mountains far in the distance was a sight he'd only dreamed of seeing.

"We're in Pine Bluffs." Veronica returned from visiting with the Carlsons and pointed out the window at stunted pine trees before sitting beside John. "I heard someone say this is the first station in the Wyoming Territory."

"Who knew it'd be so pretty?" A deep desire stirred within him to explore this beautiful new country.

"I'm glad you like it."

He looked up at the now-familiar voice. Beth and her sisters crowded around their seats.

"What's not to like?"

"Agreed." Beth laughed. "We came to see how Livie feels."

"Much better, as you can see." Rennie patted the child's arm.

"That's wonderful. We—"

"We want you to eat with us." Annie, the youngest, wiggled into the seat between Rennie and Livie. "Our pa and ma will take us to the hotel for lunch."

"Yes, let's do." Rennie clasped her hands together. "Livie and I were sad to miss breakfast with everyone."

The Carlson sisters described the hotel where they'd dine. It had the reputation of being one of the country's finest. The girls mentioned the town's several new churches and a school.

John intended to see what he could while he was there today. Perhaps his travels would bring him back. And now he had friends here.

~

*R*ennie was delighted to meet Beth's parents outside the two-story hotel. Mr. Carlson ushered them into the elegant dining room where they'd reserved two round tables, one for the adults and one for the five younger girls.

"Beth sent us a telegram yesterday. We sure were happy to hear that the danger from the prairie fire passed." Mr. Carlson, a husky man with broad shoulders, hung his Stetson hat on a wall hook before sitting between his wife and Beth. "She told us to plan on four more for lunch."

"We're thrilled that our daughters made new friends on their journey." It was obvious Beth inherited her blue eyes and curly blond hair from her gracious mother, whose green gingham dress showed a still-trim figure.

The waiter brought their plates full to the brim with lamb chops, an omelet, green beans, and freshly baked bread. Beth's father asked the blessing, and they all began to eat.

"If a herd of buffalo hadn't stopped the train, I doubt we'd have met." Rennie glanced over at Livie, grateful to see her sister slicing the meat for the child.

"If you want to break your trip, we'd be happy to host you all for a night or two." The short motherly woman gave her a gracious smile. "No doubt you are tired of traveling."

Rennie met John's gaze. He gave a slight shake of his head. Sadly, she agreed. "Thank you for the invitation. How I wish we could accept. Unfortunately, Livie's mother is ill. We're taking her to be with her parents in San Francisco."

"We understand, of course. We'll say a prayer for her." Mr. Carlson turned to John. "Am I to understand that you're an author?"

"Not yet." Regret crossed John's features, as if he wished he were able to answer differently. "It's my life's ambition to write books. Adventures."

"Ever read anything by Mark Twain?"

"He's my favorite." John straightened. "Beth said that you're both avid readers."

They began discussing Twain's various works. It was a good thing for John that he'd found someone to talk with about his books. Rennie ate her lamb chop and tried to keep her eyes on her plate, but it was difficult with those animals staring down at her from the wall.

Or just the animals' heads, actually. Buffalo, deer, mountain sheep, elk, and antelopes. Why, she'd never seen such a ghastly sight. Animals looked so different when...not alive. But they gave the unnerving *appearance* of being alive.

"Dear, I believe that Rennie will enjoy a change of topic." Mrs. Carlson gave her an apologetic look. "Their discussions of books can last hours."

"Of course, dear." Mr. Carlson patted his wife's hand. "My apologies."

"My sisters feel the same, Rennie." Beth smiled at her. "May I tell you a bit about our town?"

"I'd love that." Rennie's cheeks burned that her face had revealed her boredom with talk of books. After all, her hosts had paid for their meals before they arrived.

"Cheyenne is east of South Pass, a wide gap between the northern and southern Rockies." Beth sipped her lemonade. "That's why we can only see the highest mountains in the distance. But you'll soon ride into the Rocky Mountains. Isn't that exciting?"

"It is." Rennie sensed her love for the land. She resolved to look for the beauty from the train window.

"People concerned for their health use our town as a resort," Mr. Carlson added before finishing his lamb chop.

"It's over six thousand feet above sea level with a dry atmosphere." Beth's face shone with pride. "Visitors can purchase ponies cheaply here and ride over the hills and enjoy the scenery."

"You ride on our ranch nearly every day, Beth." Mrs. Carlson gave her an indulgent smile.

"You do?" John looked at Beth. "It sounds like an amazing life."

"It is." She held his gaze. "I don't want to live anywhere else."

John swallowed visibly, then began eating as if he were about to miss the train.

What had just happened? Perhaps it was a good thing they weren't staying overnight. How could Rennie compete with a beautiful woman like Beth who shared two of John's loves, books and horseback riding?

$\sim$

*A*fter leaving Cheyenne, John sat in the men's car. Rennie and Beth had promised to write one another while the younger girls hugged each other beside the train's steps. John had pumped Mr. Carlson's hand, thanked him for their meal, and tipped his hat at the ladies.

There had been something in the way Beth looked at him that shook him to his core. Perhaps it hadn't indicated an interest in him. Her fascination with his writing coupled with her living on a ranch had piqued his interest...but not as a potential wife. Rennie had secured that place in his heart.

But oh, it had felt good to discuss books. Were Rennie to display a modicum of interest in his writing, she'd surely, slowly, begin to understand his dreams.

Rennie needed to make friends. Hopefully, she hadn't noticed the way Beth looked at him. A momentary lapse of judgment for such a well-bred young lady, certainly, and not to be repeated.

Still, he was unsettled for Rennie's sake. And it didn't feel appropriate to talk with Rennie about such a fleeting concern, something so minor now that they'd never see Beth again.

Thoughts in turmoil, he pulled out his journal. His spirit began to calm as he wrote of the high prairie that sloped to the west. Yesterday's short rain was long gone. There wasn't a cloud in the sky.

They'd be in the Laramie Mountains, a rugged range in the eastern Rockies, later today.

The Rockies. Seeing such sights had been only a dream in a young boy's heart when he listened to his father's stories. Pa had worked as a brakeman on a train. His route had been from Bradford Junction, where they lived in Ohio, to Chicago. John had listened to his pa's stories about what he'd learned of the land out West. They'd even planned to go to California after John graduated. That dream died with so many others when Pa fell off the train's roof on an icy December evening. Broke his neck in the fall. Shattered John's life and splintered his mama's heart. Cora had wilted like a flower in the hot sun. John became the man of the house when he was far from ready for the responsibility. When Mama died, they were truly orphans. And homeless until Mrs. Saunders hired them at the restaurant. They'd slept there, though he never considered it a home.

John had forgotten his desire to see the West, experience it, until dissatisfaction with his job at the newspaper convinced him to reach for his writing dreams. Like Mark Twain had. Twain held a myriad of jobs before learning to his astonishment that publishers wanted to pay him for his stories. His novels delighted readers all over the country.

Such would be a dream come true for John. Twain originally came West by stagecoach. John didn't expect to replace his hero as America's favorite author—that place was sufficiently filled—but he prayed daily to build a successful living in writing.

He had a feeling somewhere in his soul that there was a story set in Wyoming Territory because the beauty of the High Plain prairie setting inspired him.

Stuffing his journal in his knapsack, he headed back to join Rennie and the girls.

"It was fun to travel with others for a while. We'll all miss the Carlsons, right, John?" Rennie gave him a searching glance as he stopped beside their seats.

"I'm certain you girls will all miss them." He gazed at her steadily. "Are you bored now?"

"I suppose. Too bad there wasn't room in our valises for games or puzzles." Rennie shrugged. "Besides, where would we play tiddlywinks?"

A game her family played at least weekly and all excelled in. "Agreed." John sat beside Rennie. "The winks could fly across the seats and strike someone on the nose." He gave Livie's nose a gentle tap.

She giggled. "Then what can we do, Mr. John?"

He looked down into her trusting green eyes. After her illness, she deserved something special. He had only his stories to offer. "I can tell you something about the land we're traveling through."

"Please tell me, Mr. John." Brown pigtails bounced as she straightened in her seat.

"It will be my pleasure, little one." Leaning forward to tug on a pigtail, he wiggled his ears, a talent he'd discovered when entertaining his youngest siblings.

She giggled and tried to emulate him to no avail.

John laughed at her antics. Then he began telling her about square miles of sunflowers in Kansas and Nebraska that grew to be nine feet tall. Those same sunflowers were only nine inches in Colorado, a wonder to him. And to the girls, if Veronica's mesmerized look was an indication.

When Livie asked what a sunflower looked like, he took his

journal from his knapsack and drew a sketch of one for her. It was rough—he never claimed to be an artist—but she seemed satisfied.

"Tell me something else, please."

John studied Livie's rapt face. The little girl was starved for stories. Something he had in abundance. Talking about coyotes might scare her. Same with the slaughter of buffalo herds. He told her of events that happened in the area. Finally, he shifted to talk about his younger brothers and sisters.

Livie rested her elbows on her knees with her chin against her open palms. She didn't take her eyes off him.

As he told story after story, folks around him stopped talking. They were looking at him.

They were *listening* to him.

He'd never told his stories to anyone beyond his family and friends—unless one counted the couple he'd published.

Then he heard a man chuckle at a fishing adventure John had with his brothers. Someone else tittered when he told of Rennie's brothers chasing the neighborhood girls with garden snakes. He'd never thought of that as funny, but now saw the humorous side.

Or was it the way he told it?

A little boy walked up and stopped by his seat. A woman, presumably his mother, followed him. Instead of ordering him to return to his bench, she remained silent behind her son. Apparently, John was helping pass the time for a dozen passengers, maybe more.

A bearded gentleman ambled down the rickety aisle. "I'm too far away to hear, son. Hope you don't mind if I listen a spell."

"Not at all, sir." Whether everyone was simply bored and grasping for any available entertainment or they actually *liked* his stories was difficult to discern.

But their attention felt good. Really good. Making others laugh satisfied a need in him.

As long as they wanted to listen, he was happy to talk.

~

*R*ennie reminded everyone to wear their overcoats to their supper stop. The train had passed through snow sheds that day. Heading through the long, dark tunnels had frightened Livie the first time. Luckily, John had been entertaining the entire car with his stories, which she'd heard time and again—why, the conductor had even paused to listen to one of them—and that had distracted Livie's fear.

"Thirty minutes to eat, folks!" The conductor's top hat slipped as he turned to look at them.

"Well, there's a mercy." Rennie sighed. "We'll have time to consume our food." And only two cans of meat remained in her basket. She'd have to replenish supplies.

"Agreed." John carried the basket for their leftovers. Seemingly, he was all talked out when they pulled into the station because he hadn't spoken much after the crowd around him dispersed.

"It's cold out here." Veronica's breath came out in hazy puffs as they stepped onto the platform.

"I'm cold too." Livie held Rennie's hand as they walked on the loose floorboards leading to the eating station.

A cheerful fire in the wide fireplace warmed the big room, more welcoming than those animal heads in that fine dining hall in Cheyenne, to her way of thinking. Except that meal had been free. She'd enjoyed lunch with the Carlsons until Beth displayed a little too much fascination with John. Or was Rennie being too sensitive? Beth had been kindness itself when Livie was sick.

She followed John to a round table.

"There's cornbread on the table." John took a piece. "That's what I like to see." He passed the basket to Rennie.

A girl of perhaps thirteen brought two plates of antelope steak, hominy, and applesauce. "Be right back with the last two. I'll bring more cornbread."

Once those were delivered, she brought glasses of cold milk for the girls and coffee for the adults.

Rennie had never eaten antelope, but thankfully, it had been cooked all the way through. The meat at one station had been nearly raw, and none of them had eaten it. It was a shame there wasn't a cookstove in the ladies' car, for she was certainly not the only woman who'd wanted to heat those steaks longer.

"I just want hominy, tomatoes, and applesauce." Livie looked at Rennie for permission.

That didn't sound like enough to stay with her until breakfast. "I'll share my applesauce." Their midday meal had been hours before. Best not risk the child getting a queasy stomach. "Eat your cornbread too."

"I'll take your steak." John speared it and put it on his plate. "I'm starved."

"I can't believe I'm eating antelope." Veronica sliced off a piece. "What's George going to say about that?"

Rennie's thoughts returned to Beth and her attentiveness to everything John said at lunch. Had he noticed? And was she supposed to listen to him talk about books and the Wild West with the same fascination?

~

John wrote in his journal after lunch on Monday in the men's car. He didn't seem able to write around Rennie. Whether it was the distraction of her pretty face or her lack of belief in his abilities, he couldn't say.

Probably, it was because she interrupted him every few minutes.

It was easier to write here, in his lone seat, with no one to bother him.

"You the fella who was telling them stories yesterday in the ladies' car?" A grizzled, gray-bearded man plopped onto the seat opposite him.

John blinked. Passengers in other cars had heard about him? "I am."

"Hey, Will, it is him." He crooked a finger at someone behind John.

A man wearing a plaid shirt and suspenders that barely held up his gray pants sat beside his friend.

"I told you this was that fella what was writing in his book." He slapped John on the leg. "How 'bout you tell us them stories?"

John closed his journal. "Which one do you want to hear?"

CHAPTER 11

*L*ate Tuesday afternoon, Rennie breathed a sigh of relief as they disembarked in Ogden, which was in the Territory of Utah. This was the end of the line for the Union Pacific Railroad. Mr. Sherman had provided extra money for a hotel. The opportunity to sleep on a bed that didn't sway with the locomotive's motion was a luxury, even if it would delay their arrival in San Francisco.

The train on the new railroad, the Central Pacific, didn't leave until tomorrow evening. On Wednesday, they'd eat supper here and then embark on the next leg of their journey. They all needed a day of relaxation. She'd make certain that Livie got a good, long rest and then get her out for exercise in the morning.

My, but it was warm at five o'clock. They'd come out of the mountains into the hot valley, and Veronica's face turned the color of ripe cherries. Poor Livie looked as though she'd wilt away like a flower in the sun.

They'd have to find their hotel immediately after their meal to bathe and change out of their wool dresses.

John kicked up a dust cloud as he carried their valises

across the road. "I sent a telegram back in Omaha to secure hotel rooms for us. I've arranged for our trunks to be delivered there."

"Thank you." Her beau had done an excellent job seeing to their comfort throughout the journey. "Eating a leisurely supper will be a treat." She'd almost forgot how that felt.

"Sure will. Is everyone hungry?" John peered down the street at a two-story frame building where their former fellow passengers entered.

"I guess." Livie stopped and watched two cowboys ride by on the dirt road.

They tipped their hats at Rennie and Veronica before passing at a slow trot.

Since John's hands were full, he gave them a cordial nod. "Let's eat supper before we go to the hotel." He flicked a glance at Livie.

"Good idea." Rennie shared his concern for the little girl, who had been dragging all day.

"We won't ride a train again until tomorrow evening." Veronica grinned.

"No fooling?" Livie's face brightened.

"The passengers have an hour to eat *and* buy tickets for the Central Pacific. *And* check the baggage." Veronica did a little skip, her boots stirring up more dust. "Glad that's not us."

Rennie coughed and covered her mouth and nose with a pink handkerchief, the only clean one left after four days of travel. She'd launder them all tonight.

"They'll have to take the omnibus to the depot to get there in time." John nodded at a family passing by in a buckboard. Two little girls waved at Livie, who grew more animated at the friendly gesture.

The dining hall was cheerful with lively conversation. Rennie fanned her face. It wasn't noticeably cooler inside, even with every window open, but being out of the hot sun was a comfort in itself.

They were soon seated. John paid for their meal that included beefsteak, buttered parsley potatoes, spinach with sliced, hard-boiled eggs arranged on top, pickled beets, and rhubarb pie. And thank goodness, Livie ate bits of everything for the first time the whole trip.

"I have a surprise for all of you." John's glance lingered on Rennie's face.

"What is it?" Rennie's spirits lifted at his enthusiasm. There'd been such little opportunity to speak privately this entire trip. This respite in Ogden might provide some quiet moments together.

"How do you feel about exploring a canyon?" John's glance darted to them all and then settled on Rennie.

"A canyon?" Veronica stared at him. "I'll bet George has never visited one of those."

Livie's eyes lit up. "Will it be fun, Mr. John?"

"Very much fun, Miss Livie." His grin broadened.

Sounded expensive to Rennie. "But I don't understand. How can we—"

"I arranged an excursion for the four of us by telegram." His legs knocked together in his excitement. "This is my treat. I talked with Eleanora after my job ended and I moved my things to Hamilton. She sent a telegram to Mr. Sherman, who gave his consent. He believes it will be a nice change for Livie after the monotony of the train."

Rennie fought against feeling left out of the decision.

John laughed as if he read her mind. "How could I tell you in advance when the surprise was for you too?"

"True." Feelings of rejection melted. He must still care for her to take on the trouble and expense of an excursion. An *excursion.* She'd never been on one of those. How did one dress?

"We'll leave right after breakfast and return no later than

midafternoon. Wear light clothing and bring a wrap." John ate his last piece of beefsteak. "Weather in this part of the desert varies. It's hot now but may be chilly inside the canyon."

Rennie gasped as she thought of their filthy clothing. "I must wash our clothes tonight so they'll dry. Will the hotel allow me to borrow their washtub?" There had been no need to wash clothes at their earlier hotel stay.

"Pay the maid to do it. Mr. Sherman provided extra money for such expenses." John sank back in his chair. "Let's not waste a minute of our stay in Ogden. Do you want to take a walk and watch the sun set?"

"I'd like that."

Livie clapped her hands. "I want to go."

"Me too. I know George never watched the sun set in the desert." Veronica's eyes gleamed with satisfaction.

Rennie suppressed a sigh. Apparently, she'd need to put a bug in Veronica's ear to arrange a long-overdue moment alone for herself and John.

~

ohn gave up any idea of keeping up with the younger ones. Livie pulled Veronica along toward the western horizon. As long as he kept them within eyesight, they were safe. Veronica kept turning around to make certain he and her sister were still in view.

A few couples strolled about the small town. A half-dozen horses stood with their reins looped over the hitching post in front of a saloon on the opposite side of the dirt road. He coughed as a wagon full of crates and burlap sacks passed, stirring up dust clouds. Did it ever rain here?

Since they ate an early supper, they'd all had time to bathe in the bath room and change into lighter clothing. He felt like a new man after donning a cotton shirt and summer jacket.

Rennie must feel the same, for she hadn't looked this relaxed in days. And mighty pretty in that pink frock. The sunlight glinted off her long brown hair, which was still damp, her braid pinned to her hairline like a halo. Such a hairstyle suited her perfectly.

"What made you think of an excursion?" Rennie tucked her hand onto John's arm.

"I had planned a stop in Ogden when I was coming alone." John loved the feeling of her small hand pressed against his side, the way her steps matched his ambling stride. "When I knew you were coming and Mr. Sherman approved an overnight stay, I modified those plans."

Her head went down. "My apologies."

Did she realize how much he'd changed to be able to escort her? He'd wanted to stay in Cheyenne for several days and then stop farther into Wyoming to enjoy the Rockies for the first time. A week or two drinking in such views couldn't fail to inspire a story. Maybe he'd head up to Oregon and the Territory of Idaho from California. He'd best make the most of this journey, as it was likely the only one he'd ever take.

But he didn't want her to believe he didn't want her here, especially since she'd quit berating his ambitions. He stopped beside the twisted trunk of a juniper tree at the edge of town and turned to her. "Everything is more fun with you."

"Oh, John." She inclined her face up to his so that she was mere inches away. "You don't know how good that sounds."

He caught his breath. There she was, giving him that tender look, impossible to resist. He remembered to check on the girls, who had seated themselves on a boulder facing the sinking sun.

She leaned closer. He caressed her soft cheek. Things had been so unsettled between them that he hadn't kissed her since her birthday in May.

Her gaze dropped to his lips. He lowered his mouth to hers, reveling that the moment had been worth the wait.

Her arms crept around his neck as he deepened the kiss. Her fingers entwined in his hair as she leaned into him. He drew her close and kissed her again. How long it had been, too long—

"Mr. John." Livie tugged on his arm. "Veronica sent me to get you."

He stepped away, humiliated that the child they were supposed to be chaperoning turned the tables on them.

"You and Miss Rennie are missing the sunset." Livie frowned.

"So we are."

Rennie's face had turned the color of a ripe strawberry. John offered an arm to each of his companions. Livie placed her hand on it, giggling at the grown-up gesture.

Rennie gave him a shy smile. The warmth of her hand on his arm reached all the way to his heart. Perhaps she was beginning to accept his decision about his life's work.

Perhaps, someday, she'd actually be proud of him.

CHAPTER 12

*R*ennie awoke the next morning with a sense of expectancy. Her rift with John was on the mend, and she was about to spend the day in a western canyon. It'd be something else to tell her family.

She chose a white dress with blue cornflowers. Mama had said the color enhanced the blue in Rennie's eyes. She sure hoped John agreed with her. She was determined not to say anything derogatory about his writing today.

Maybe Mama had been right to advise her not to nag him about it.

"What do you think we're going to do on our 'scursion, Miss Rennie?" Livie squirmed as Rennie tied the white sash around her lemon-yellow dress.

"Stand still a minute so I can tie this bow." Her fingers fumbled so that the satin didn't cooperate.

"Let me do it." Veronica snatched the fabric from her. "Good thing I'm already dressed."

"Don't act like that." She looked quite fetching in her gingham the color of blueberries, but that didn't mean she should treat her sister rudely.

"Sorry." Her apology seemed sincere. "I'm hungry."

"It's time for breakfast. John's waiting for us in the lobby by now." They'd waited in line for the ladies' washroom that morning, though it hadn't been as bad as on the train.

Nothing was as bad as the train. She was ready for the journey's end.

"Miss Rennie," Livie said. "You didn't answer me."

"I'm sorry. What did you—oh, about our excursion." Rennie pinned on her blue hat. "I don't know much because it's a surprise."

Livie, face flushed with excitement, clapped her hands.

"We'll see a canyon," Veronica reminded her.

"But what will it look like?"

"Probably a bit like what we saw on the way out here."

Rennie only half listened to Livie's chatter about their coming adventure as she gave one last visual sweep of the room. Everything was packed except the clothing the maid was washing. The woman had assured her the clothes had been laundered last night and would be pressed and folded on the bed by lunchtime.

She and Veronica carried their reticules as they followed Livie downstairs.

Rennie met John's appreciate gaze.

"Good morning, ladies." His glance lingered on Rennie. "How pretty you all look."

He looked fine himself in his brown coat and trousers, red-and-tan plaid shirt, and black string tie.

"Our guide will meet us at half-past eight, so we'd best get to our breakfast." He offered his arm to Rennie.

She'd missed that courtesy since their argument on Independence Day. A smile tugged at her lips as she laid her hand on John's muscular arm.

"For crying out loud," Veronica grumbled, "we're only crossing the lobby to the dining room."

Rennie glared at her sister.

"I'm chaperoning you two, remember?"

"How could we forget?" Rennie gritted her teeth.

John smothered a chuckle.

Rennie's frustration evaporated at his laughter. One thing she loved about John was his ability to see the funny side of things. She could be too serious at times. Apparently, this was one of them.

They were quickly seated and paid the waiter. "Lottie will bring your meal shortly." He picked up the money and left.

"I hope we're getting eggs." Livie squirmed in her seat. "And milk. I'm thirsty too."

"I smell bacon." The corners of John's mouth turned up.

"That reminds me." Rennie turned to him. "My food basket is empty."

"I saw a store down the street." He looked up as a girl younger than Veronica set two plates in front of him and Rennie and then scurried back to the kitchen. "Baked eggs. Your wish is granted, Livie."

"And applesauce." She studied his plate. "Is that strawberry jam with that toast?"

He nodded.

She bounced in anticipation. "I like jam."

The rest of the food arrived with milk for Livie and coffee for the rest.

After John asked a blessing on the meal, Rennie leaned closer. "You did say that our lunch was included in the price of today's adventure, right?"

"Everything is included." He sighed. "Must you always be so concerned about every penny? None of this expense comes from your purse."

Rennie straightened. "Try going without necessities and then talk to me about worrying over money."

He met her eyes without speaking.

Heat rushed up her face. Of course. John had been a home-less orphan. He understood poverty better than she did yet didn't stress over what he lacked. He simply worked hard and saved what he could for unforeseen troubles.

Yet here he was, planning to throw away good money on his Wild West adventure, money they could use toward the purchase of a future home.

After last evening's embrace, she wanted to get married sooner rather than later. Didn't he want that too?

She didn't understand him at all.

~

*T*heir guide for the excursion, a thin, bearded man, introduced himself as Jeb. John liked Jeb right away. His floppy black hat hid his hair. He seemed ageless, as if he'd lived his entire life outdoors.

Their conveyance was a modified wagon. Two benches with backs had been nailed to the bed of the vehicle. Even this prim-itive wagon in the midst of a western town fit John's expecta-tions as he helped the girls onto the middle seat. He sat with Rennie in the back.

When she smiled up at him, the lingering concern he'd felt at breakfast at her compulsive worry over money melted. He didn't want her to know that today's outing cost as much as his train journey to California, so he hadn't saved a nickel by escorting the girls. Still, the cost was worth it, for the opportu-nity to give Rennie this treat might never come again.

Jeb jumped onto the driver's seat, released the brake, and drove away from their hotel. "Now, most folks ask me to take them by the Mormon Tabernacle. It ain't the big one. That's in Salt Lake City some forty miles from here, so I can't show you Temple Square unless you folks will be here at least four days. Five is better. Cost is reasonable."

"We leave this evening, so we'll hold you to the promise of returning by three o'clock." A snail could move faster than this wagon. John leaned forward. He had made that plain in his telegram. "Just the one-day excursion, please."

"That's what I got paid for. Didn't know if you changed your mind. Lots of folks do once they get here." Jeb turned sideways in his seat as he talked. "Folks always ask me to tell them about it, so here's what I know. Brigham Young decided that Temple Square was to be the spot where the Salt Lake Temple was to stand. That was back in 1847." He spat tobacco juice over the side. "You folks ever seen a sketch of it?"

Rennie shook her head.

"What folks like so much about the tabernacle is the dome. And it's also famous for the organ, which has seven hundred pipes."

"Seven hundred?" Rennie squeaked.

"Ah, now, that caught your attention, didn't it, little lady? Joseph Ridges built it the sixties. Sounds right prettyful. I can take you back to the hotel and wait while you pack a valise." He looked at John. "Sure you won't change your mind?"

"We're interested in seeing Weber Canyon." Hopefully, John's firm tone put an end to the matter. If they stuck to their plan, they'd return in time to take another quick bath. Even he was looking forward to one more dip in a tub. Taking sponge baths in the train's dressing room left a lot to be desired.

"The canyon, it is." He loosened the reins, and the horse picked up speed. "By the way, that building yonder is our courthouse."

Livie craned her neck to study the brick building.

"Impressive." It was the nicest building John had seen in Ogden so far. Wood frame houses and shops made up the majority of the town's buildings. Rennie remained silent. Probably nervous about leaving the safety of town. Hopefully, she'd contribute to the conversation now and then.

Come to think of it, Jeb probably wouldn't notice if *no one* commented.

"Ought to be." Their driver stared at the building as if counting the bricks. "Cost twenty thousand dollars."

The horse turned to the right without Jeb ever looking forward. Who was driving, the horse or Jeb?

"We got three churches along with our own Mormon tabernacle. Reckon I shouldn't say it that way since I ain't a Mormon. Got one wife. Don't need another naggin' woman."

Rennie's lips twitched. She shot John a glance. Oh, boy. She was about to laugh out loud.

He looked away quickly. Bit his tongue to keep his own laughter at bay. He couldn't wait to write about Jeb in his journal tonight.

∼

*R*ennie blinked rapidly at the beauty of the clear waters of the Weber River. Its rich blue contrasted with patches of deeply green grass dotting its banks. Bushes taller than she was along with a few mature trees were scattered in vivid color near the bottom of the canyon around the low banks. Aquamarine-colored shrubs no higher than her knees grew in patches up the sides of the riverbank like balls of fluff. Perhaps they weren't quite as small as they appeared from a distance of some hundred yards.

Rocky bluffs jutted out here and there in a nearly horizontal pattern, predominantly the color of clay with lines of white. Parts of the bluff were smooth with no vegetation. On the rest, small pine trees seemingly grew out of the rock.

It was a wondrous sight. She memorized it to describe to her pa.

Cool air, no doubt stirred by the rushing river, was welcome after the drive of four or five miles in the hot sun. She arranged her shawl over her arms.

"Them pine trees in the middle and up to the top are bigger than you think." Jeb pulled back on the reins, and the wagon stopped. "We've got big ol' cottonwood trees. You'll see aspen groves as we continue on after our picnic. 'Course, you'll find oaks and maples like them over there."

Rennie had seen plenty of those in Ohio. "Did you say something about a picnic?" Her empty stomach might give an unladylike rumble if they didn't eat soon.

"Yep." Jeb threw back the brake. "Included in the cost." The wagon creaked when he jumped down. "You'll find privacy behind that patch of bushes over there."

Though happy for the information, Rennie's cheeks heated like fire.

He extracted a basket and a colorful quilt from behind Rennie's seat and set off in the direction of tall cottonwoods near the river.

"Guess he expects us to follow." John jumped down and then lifted Livie and Veronica to the ground. They scurried to the bushes. He held out his hand to Rennie. "Thanks for sharing this day with me."

She tucked her hand in his, loving the look in his brown eyes, as if she were the most precious woman in the world. She couldn't move. It had been a while since he'd looked at her that way.

His gaze didn't waver from hers as he released her hand and lifted her down.

Rennie stared up at him. Her feet were on the ground, but he didn't release her. All she could think of were his kisses the previous evening. "I don't mind if you kiss me right quick. Nobody's looking."

He laughed. "I don't mind that either." He pulled her close, tilted her chin, and covered her mouth with his. Kissed her once. Twice. Then his lips grew more insistent.

She wrapped her arms around his neck, shivering at his touch. That disastrous day when she'd called his trip a foolish idea seemed far away. Maybe he had forgiven her—

"Hey, John."

They pulled apart at Jeb's shout. The man had come back into view.

"Bring the canteens under the seat, will you?"

Rennie's face must be as red as John's. She stepped away, and her back struck the wagon. The horse whinnied and looked around.

"I'll bring the girls over in a minute." Rennie ran for the bushes.

But she couldn't be sorry for John's kisses...even if that old nosy Jeb did see it.

CHAPTER 13

*T*oday was progressing even better than he'd dreamed. Not only had he found a private moment with Rennie—how could he resist kissing her among the beauty of the canyon?—but something deep in his soul responded to the scenery. He praised God for the untouched beauty of the bluffs, the aspens, the water splashing over boulders in reckless abandon.

This was what he'd come to see. To show Rennie. He had seen the awestruck wonder in her expressive blue eyes for the first time this whole journey. Perhaps she understood now why he'd want to put such experiences into future novels. His desire for this trip had steadily grown from his prayers for guidance. Maybe she was beginning to realize the reason for his path.

As for Jeb's stories, they didn't run out while they munched on cold fried chicken, corn on the cob, and long fingers of boiled potatoes. It reminded John of himself around his family's dinner table, putting a colorful spin on events that he or others around him had experienced. Most of John's yarns were true. Others started out with a true event and spiraled away like a spinning top when his imagination caught hold of them. How many of Jeb's stories were simply told for entertainment?

"Ouch. I'm sitting on a rock." Livie shifted on the quilt.

"I'm sitting on a cushion of grass. Move over here by me." Rennie wiped her fingers on a cotton napkin and then reached for the child's plate.

Livie scooted between her and John, who moved over.

Veronica tilted back the canteen, then shook droplets from it. "I'll refill this." She sauntered toward the rushing river.

"I'll help." Livie ran after her.

"You girls be careful." Rennie's brow furrowed as she watched them bend over the low bank.

"That's good advice, miss." Jeb gave a sage nod. A kernel of corn fell from his beard. "If they was to fall in, the current might take them a good ways before we could fish them out."

Rennie paled. Pushing herself to her feet, she hurried after them. "Stay back from the edge."

"How can we stay back and still get water?" Veronica called back in an exasperated tone.

"Sure can tell them two are sisters." Jeb picked up the last chicken leg. "Your girl is like a mother hen with her brood."

"That's a good description." It was how she'd always been with her siblings...and now Livie.

"Her sister don't want coddlin'. Figures she's too old for it." Jeb dropped the picked-clean bone into the basket.

John stared at Jeb, who, after spending one morning in their company, had struck upon the crux of their troubles. He'd tell her as soon as they got another moment alone.

"You girls hurry on back." Jeb leapt to his feet. "Finish up. I got more to show you." He wandered away, probably to find a private bush.

John reached for the dripping canteen when the girls returned. "I'd rather drink this than eat another bite." He took a

SANDRA MERVILLE HART

long swig. Deliciously cold water refreshed his mouth and throat.

"It's your turn to refill it." Veronica ate the last potato slice from her wood plate.

"I shall"—he offered the canteen to Livie—"when it's empty."

Livie took a drink and then gave it to Rennie. A yellow-and-black butterfly flew over her head. "Look at the pretty butterfly. I want to catch it."

"All right. Stay away from the river." Rennie gathered up their plates.

"I'll go with her." Veronica hurried after her.

John stacked the empty serving bowls. The opportunity for privacy came more quickly than he'd dreamed. "Jeb figured out the cause of the problem between you and your sister." He explained the westerner's observation.

"Well, I'd like to know how a man who just met us thinks he's figured us out." Rennie's blue eyes snapped.

Oh, boy. Perhaps he should have eased into it. "He's not claiming to have you figured out. Just told me his observation."

"Where did those girls go?" Rennie, hands on hips, peered in every direction.

"Around that bend." John pointed.

"I'm going after them." A few steps and she turned back. "And I'll thank you not to discuss me and my family with strangers." She flounced away, her shawl slipping down her arms.

A mother hen, indeed. Even though she might chastise her sister, no one else better do it.

*R*ennie was still fit to be tied—as Mama always said —when she returned with the girls, who had chased the elusive butterfly farther than intended. Outrageous that a total stranger stuck his nose into her trouble with her sister—and to think John had encouraged the man's opinions.

It ruined her pleasure in the excursion. Now she just wanted to go back to the hotel, refresh herself with a quick bath and have the other girls do the same, and then resume their journey.

Jeb loaded the wagon while John and Livie refilled the canteens one last time. There was a bit more splashing than necessary, but Livie's giggles were a tonic to Rennie. There were other reasons to be grateful to John for providing this adventure. Both Veronica and Livie had lost their pale, listless looks brought on by the inactivity and monotony of the train. And Livie hadn't asked if her mother was still sick all day.

John ran with Livie back to the wagon. He said something that made her laugh again. Rennie smiled.

With a lighter heart, she took John's hand for support into the wagon. His touch warmed her skin and cooled her anger. After all, he'd only repeated what he'd heard. That didn't mean he agreed with the man.

"I always save this part for last." Jeb half turned but kept his attention on the trail ahead. "This canyon is in the Wasatch Range. Weber River is forty miles long. It runs toward the Great Salt Lake to the west."

Rennie settled back to enjoy the soothing rush of the river. Perhaps she wasn't ready to hurry back to the hotel, after all. Especially not with John sitting so close that his leg brushed against hers.

"I'm about to show you the railroad that runs through Weber Canyon because Brigham Young convinced the Union Pacific Railroad to come here. They had some kind of agreement." Jeb faced forward to navigate a narrow passage by the river. "That's why they built the Transcontinental Railroad through this canyon. Breathed new life into the area, the way I see it. I can drive visitors around the countryside for days on end, iffen I want to."

"How about in the winter?" John leaned forward, his wrists resting on his knees.

"Not many folks come then. Cain't say as I blame them. They take a chance on traveling through snow on the way here. You folks noticed those sheds built over the tracks in the mountains, right? Them tunnels you went through?"

"I did." Livie gave a little shiver, though the shade from the bluff was pleasant rather than chilly.

"Sure, you did. You notice things, don't you?" Jeb spoke over his shoulder.

"Yes." Livie nodded.

"If folks want to know something, they should ask you, right?"

She gave him a pleased smile.

"Anyways, them snow sheds ain't there for no reason." He pointed. "See the railroad tracks ahead?"

Rennie craned her neck to see where the tracks ran away from the river.

"I'll show you our Thousand Mile Tree."

"Thousand Mile Tree?" Peering ahead, John angled to get a view.

"Seems Union Pacific Railroad workers figured out they'd come one thousand miles away from Omaha. Them fellers found a tall pine tree on the exact spot and hung a sign on it."

They'd come one thousand miles since leaving Omaha—more since leaving Ohio. No wonder Rennie's back ached. One night in a bed that didn't move had eased that pain.

The special tree snagged her interest. Three or four yards of flat land flanked the tracks, then sloped upward in a steep, rocky grade on both sides. There was a bit of grass along with cottonwoods, aspens, and shrubs in the valley and up the sides, but she didn't see the sign Jeb had mentioned.

Dust rose as the wheels jutted over a rock on one side or the other almost constantly. The way alongside the tracks grew narrower. Why, this wasn't a wagon road at all. Might one of those rocks split a wheel? Was the sign worth this trouble?

"Well, folks, ole Hank cain't get us no closer." Jeb applied the brake. "It's around the corner a ways. Shouldn't be a train come through while we're walking—if it does, stop walking, stand beside the canyon wall, and hold onto the little lady." He jumped down. "I'll tie Hank here to a tree so he'll be safe if one passes."

Rennie wondered at the wiry man's fount of energy, for the wagon's jolts were taking a toll on her. She swiped dust from her face.

John lifted her down first. "I'll feel better if you hold Livie's hand on this rocky ground even if no train passes by."

"I plan on it."

While Jeb tethered the horse to a tree, John fished his journal and a pencil from his knapsack.

"I'll go first. A lady slipped on a stone last week." Jeb smothered a grin. "Let's just say the back of her fancy skirt was more brown than orange when she got back to the hotel. So watch your step."

Rennie held Livie's hand and checked that Veronica was behind them.

"You don't need to watch out for me, Rennie," she grumbled. "I'm not going to fall."

"That's likely what that woman thought."

Veronica scowled at her.

"There it is." Jeb rounded a corner as he pointed ahead.

"Let me see." Livie tugged on Rennie's hand to hurry her along.

A pine tree forty to fifty feet high, its lower branches sawn off, stood proudly ahead of them about ten feet from the railroad tracks. A sign reading *1000 Mile Tree* had been tied to its lowest branch.

Jeb strode closer, but John passed him for a better look. "I'll write about this one."

"What's that? You an author, son?"

"I hope to be." After peering up at the tree, he opened his notebook and began to write.

"Knowing that," Jeb said, "I got a few more stories to tell you on the way back. I'll write my name down for you on your paper."

"I'm obliged to you." John looked back at the tree and then scribbled again. "Wish I could sketch it. Folks like them in novels. Never was an artist, though."

"I'll do it." Veronica took his journal. "Good. This one doesn't have lines." She accepted the pencil from him while studying the tree, the tracks, and the walls on both sides that sloped upward in an angle.

"I didn't know you could draw." Rennie stared at her, dumbfounded.

"I got some sketches at home." Her tone was hesitant. "Been doing it for years."

"Why didn't you say something?"

"Mama doesn't even know. Just George."

This seemed important to her sister. "I can't wait to see your drawing."

Her eyes lit up. "All right." She perched on a flat rock. Her pencil raced across the page.

Livie crept over to watch, mesmerized by the image taking shape.

Rennie met John's shocked gaze. John wanted sketches for his book. If Veronica was good enough, he might want her to draw a few scenes. After all, she'd been on the same journey, had seen the same things. With a few descriptive words to remind her of a setting, she should be able to produce good images.

If she was talented enough.

Rennie couldn't do anything special, possessed no particular talent.

For the first time, that truth bothered her.

CHAPTER 14

*B*ack at the hotel, John parted company with Rennie and the girls for last-minute preparations. They met again for an early supper. He couldn't contain his excitement as he ate fried trout, pickled beets, and salad. "Veronica, do you realize how talented you are?"

Veronica blushed but looked pleased. "Do you really think so? I can do better if I have more time."

"You can?" He shook his head, amazed. "It already looks just like what we saw today. Don't you agree, Rennie?"

She nodded. "It was very like the real scenery, Veronica. I could scarcely believe my eyes."

"Really?"

"Absolutely. I'm stunned." She raised her hand, palms up. "I can't draw worth a lick, but you possess amazing talent."

Rennie looked proud of her sister but also a little sad. Obviously, Veronica's confidence needed bolstering, something he understood well. Was his talent good enough to support their family? Rennie's doubts had pierced what little confidence he'd found in publishing his stories. Yes, he understood her sister's need for praise.

"How long have you been drawing?"

"I drew in the dirt when I was little." She stared down at her plate. "I stole Rennie's slate sometimes after she started school. Then one day, she got upset when it wasn't where she left it. I knew I'd done wrong, so after that, I waited until I had a slate of my own."

Tilting her head, Rennie studied her.

John gave her a gentle smile. "You had no idea."

"None." Rennie's gaze shifted to her plate. "I wish you'd told me, Veronica."

"I bought a sketchpad with money Mama and Papa gave me for my thirteenth birthday. I was afraid my drawings weren't as good as I thought, so I hid them behind a loose board in the loft while practicing. It's my favorite thing to do...as though my fingers fairly itched to find a quiet place to sit down and draw."

"I understand." Boy, did John understand that longing. His spirits became depressed when something prevented him from writing daily.

Rennie's eyes darted at him. She toyed with a radish in her salad.

"I reckon it's the same way with your writing, right?" Veronica tilted her head. "I've wanted to draw so many things while on this trip. Livie leaning her head against the window-pane while taking a nap, the tall Rockies in the distance I saw from a depot, even the snow shed tunnels we rode through where it was dark as night inside the cars." She looked up at her sister. "Can't you understand, Rennie?"

"I'm trying." Her forehead puckered. "George knows about it?"

"Don't be mad." Veronica tucked a stray curl behind her ear. "He saw one of my sketches and asked me to draw him." She smiled at the memory. "I drew him sitting on a hollow log in the copse of trees between our house and John's."

"I've crossed through on that dirt path many times to see

Rennie. I know that log well." He'd kissed Rennie for the first time on that spot. Her self-conscious look showed she remembered too.

"Can you teach me how to draw, Veronica?" Livie paused with a forkful of salad midway to her open mouth.

"Don't see why not. Let's buy sketchpads on our way to the train—one for you, one for me." Veronica looked over at Rennie. "We have enough extra money for that, right?"

"I'll buy them." A wild idea was growing. Publishers often wanted illustrations scattered throughout novels. Perhaps John could coax Veronica to illustrate his book—if the publisher agreed. He'd run the idea by Rennie first—and her parents, of course. Why, Veronica had even drawn the telegraph wires that resembled a tall, skinny letter *T* in her sketch that John had all but ignored since he was now so accustomed to seeing them. "Then you can begin lessons tonight until it grows dark."

"Wonderful."

It was difficult to tell who looked happier, Livie or Veronica. Having someone recognize her artistic talent must be so new to her that she didn't know what to think. Her cheeks were flushed. The sparkle in her eyes reminded him of her sister.

The waitress delivered slices of blueberry pie. The aroma convinced John he had enough room for the dessert, and he attacked it with renewed appetite.

"It will be good to have something to occupy Livie on the train." A blueberry fell off Rennie's fork on its way to her mouth.

Ever practical. Always sensible. Of course, that was where Rennie's thoughts went. For the first time, John felt more sympathetic to Veronica than Rennie. His spirits deflated. Rennie didn't understand folks like him and her sister, the ones who needed to express their creative bents.

"Let's hurry so we can make our purchases and still board

on time. Good thing we ate early." Rennie's tone was reserved. "I'll replenish supplies for our food basket while we're there."

She spoke in almost a monotone. Wasn't she excited for her sister?

~

*R*ennie followed her group to a general merchandise shop down the street, her head reeling. Had Veronica told her she wanted to open a bakery or design houses for a living, she couldn't be more surprised. She was creative, like John.

The pair had something in common, something she didn't share.

Why couldn't she be more like her sister? Perhaps then she'd understand John's decisions that pushed their marriage ever more into the future.

When she stepped inside the store, they were all gathered in front of a display of slates, writing utensils, and pads of paper.

Rennie went in search of crackers, which went into her basket. Then a block of cheese and four hard-boiled eggs. When she had enough for the next two days, she joined the others.

"Here it is." Veronica snatched a book that resembled John's journal, only it was longer and wider. "Look, Livie. They have more."

John selected two pencils and a pen. "Do you want a slate, Livie?"

She nodded. "I can practice my letters."

A slate and slate pencil were added to the pile.

"Anything else?"

"Can I have a book to read? They have *Little Red Riding Hood*." Livie pointed to a colorful children's volume.

"I'll purchase it." Rennie took the book from Livie, who practically glowed. After paying for their excursion—he'd refused to disclose the cost—and now Veronica's materials, John had bought more than enough. "I have funds from your father." From her governess pay for the trip, greatly dwindled now because of the continual need to replenish snacks.

"Thanks, Miss Rennie."

"My pleasure." She raised her eyebrows at both girls and indicated John with a jerk of her head.

Veronica gave her heartfelt thanks. Livie hugged his waist.

"The pleasure is mine, ladies." John smiled at them. "I always enjoy encouraging talent when I see it." He carried their purchases to the counter.

"Did you hear that?" Veronica sounded in awe. "I never thought I'd be this happy when Papa ordered me to go with you to the Wild West."

"The omnibus just passed." John stuffed his purchases into his knapsack. "Our trunks and valises are at the hotel. I'll run ahead and get them loaded. Follow as soon as you can."

"We'll hurry." She needed to pack the laundry waiting in their room and lock the trunks. Familiar tension caused by the strain of traveling on a strict schedule tightened Rennie's shoulders. She scurried to the counter to purchase the food and Livie's book. That done, she met her sister's anxious gaze and gave her a quick hug. "I'm glad you're happy."

"Thanks, Rennie." Veronica returned her embrace almost convulsively. She reached for the food basket. "Reckon we'd best get to the hotel."

Following her sister outside into the bright sunlight, Rennie wished she shared her happiness.

She'd always thought John's desire to write for a living would pass, but maybe that wasn't how it worked with people like him—and now Veronica. Maybe they needed to be creative. And if that were the case, what did that mean for Rennie, for her future? Would he be able to support her financially?

Would she be able to support his dreams?

❧

*J*ohn smiled at Rennie's gasp of surprise over their accommodations. "This is our home the next two days." He stepped aside to allow the girls to enter the luxurious silver palace car. They stared, open-mouthed, at the chandeliers spaced throughout the car and the oil-clothed, patterned carpet. "This is Mr. Sherman's surprise. We have a section for four."

He maneuvered around Rennie to lead them to their high-backed, cushioned benches that faced one another for ease of conversation. Half the sections were already occupied with folks hanging their bags on hooks under the windows and settling in for a long ride.

"I should have known the inside would be quite something when the outside is painted canary yellow." Rennie blinked as she touched the cushion. "Well, look at that. Covered with velvet. Our backs won't hurt at the end of each day."

Livie ran her hands along the back. "So soft. I like it. My papa got this for us?"

"We'll have to thank him." Rennie gave her a quick hug. "I won't mind traveling in such luxury."

"We've never been so pampered." Veronica claimed a window seat. "I can't wait to tell George."

"Draw him a picture." Claiming the other spot by the window seat, Livie stared outside at folks milling around on the platform.

"Great idea." Veronica looked at John's bag.

"You want to draw this palace car, and I want to write about it." John grinned, extracting the new sketchpads and a pencil for both of them.

Veronica murmured her thanks and opened the pad immediately. Livie showed more interest in the emptying train platform.

Rennie gave her head a little shake. "Why did you keep this a secret, John?"

"In case something unplanned happened. We had that prairie fire...and we struck that poor buffalo. Unexpected delays. What if there had been trouble with the locomotive or Livie hadn't gotten better, forcing us to pay for another hotel stay? Look around." He grinned. "Did you notice there's more room? Fewer passengers in these palace cars. We'll sleep in here too."

"Really?" Rennie looked at the upper berth, secured against the roof.

"That berth is large enough for two. These seats draw out and join in the center to make a bottom berth that sleeps two." John marveled at the design. Trying to rest in the sleeping cars on the earlier part of their journey had been challenging.

"What did you say, John?" Veronica's pencil stilled on the page. "There isn't a separate berth for you in another section?"

Rennie blanched.

Why hadn't he considered that this area would belong to Rennie and the girls alone? "I'm sorry...I didn't realize..."

"It's my job to chaperone you two." Veronica eyed them. "Papa sure will be glad he sent me to keep an eye on things."

Rennie waved her off, her face turned the color of cooked beets. "Where will you...?"

He hid a sigh. "After the train leaves the station, I'll find the conductor to inquire if there are any unclaimed berths in the men's sleeping car." Else he'd get what sleep he could sitting upright in the passenger car. He kicked himself for not realizing each section was its own private area after the long black curtains were drawn.

Within a few seconds, the car was in motion. John took the opportunity to steer the conversation away from his blunder. "We're on our way to California again."

"Where Mama is." Livie's face brightened. "When will I see her?"

"On Friday." John tugged on her braid. "Less than two days."

"Will Papa meet the train?"

"Miss Eleanora said we have to ride a boat from Oakland to San Francisco." Rennie looked at John as if for confirmation. "He'll meet us at the wharf."

Livie's brow furrowed.

"That's right." John's guidebook had come in handy on this trip. "It's a twenty-minute ride across the bay."

"Good." Her shoulders relaxed. "I don't know how to find our house."

"We'll get you there." Even if something delayed Mr. Sherman, John would deliver the little girl to her ailing mother at the soonest possible minute. He whispered a silent prayer for Mrs. Sherman's speedy recovery.

"Can Veronica take me to see the train?" Livie looked at Rennie with pleading eyes.

"I don't mind." Rennie spoke absently, as if her thoughts had wandered.

"Come on, Veronica." Livie tugged on her hand.

"All right." She stored her drawing pad in the valise hanging under the window. "I'd like to see the other palace cars too." They headed away from the front of the train.

Once they were gone, John settled next to the window to study the beautiful canyons. He'd never forget that Rennie had accompanied him on an excursion to explore one of them.

"Where will I find the sheets to make the beds?"

His eyes slid back to Rennie. She wouldn't relax until she understood the new routine of the palace car. "The porter will take care of everything. Pay him twenty-five cents a day for his trouble." For he'd not be around to do it. The less said about sleeping arrangements now, the better.

"I have enough to pay the porter."

Rennie never ceased to worry over expenditures, even when the money wasn't hers. He tried to instill a cheerful lilt into his voice. "There's also a dining car where we can enjoy leisurely meals."

Rennie's eyes widened.

"What's troubling you?"

A family passed and settled themselves in another section farther on before she leaned closer. "I have three dollars per meal for me and the girls in my valise," she whispered, "with enough for the porter's fee. I spent all but a dollar of the pay Mr. Sherman gave me."

John struggled to keep his face smooth. Where did that money go? The extra snacks and the daily telegrams? Not good, but they didn't have far to go. Ticket fares for the ferry and the final train of their journey were hidden in his knapsack, not to be spent for anything else. "Let me know if you run out. I can buy a meal." But that was the limit. Paying for their excursion ate away at the extra bills stored in his boot. He kept a generous amount for his daily needs in his coin purse. What he required for his journeys around western towns had been sewn into his brown vest—at his mama's insistence—and that was packed in his trunk.

"Maybe it's best we keep buying meals at the meal stops." Her tone softened. "So we don't overspend."

"Mr. Sherman sent enough to cover our expenses." He'd been looking forward to leisurely meals to pass the monotony of the train.

"Well, I didn't know about the expensive meals." She lifted her chin. "Since you kept this fancy car a secret."

It had been meant as a surprise. Frustration settled in his gut. Must they always argue about money? "We're several miles from the station. I'll see if I can find the conductor." John was suddenly looking forward to the privacy of a sleeping berth.

CHAPTER 15

*R*ennie took a leisurely walk through the other palace cars when the girls didn't return. She discovered them standing outside one of them, enjoying the breeze.

"You girls hold onto that railing." Her heart fluttered. If one of them fell down the steep stairs on the side...

"We're already doing that. Don't be such a mother hen." Veronica sighed. "We decided standing outside was more fun than exploring the cars."

Rennie leaned against the iron railing. Even in the breeze, it was pleasant to be outdoors. "Our linen dusters should guard our clothes against the dirt blowing around."

"Doesn't it feel good just to relax?" Veronica studied the horizon. "Stop worrying about everything. We have to trust God because some things we just can't control."

When did her sister get so wise? "I'll try."

They passed into the shade of a lonely desert canyon. As Rennie stood quietly with the breeze blowing tendrils of hair across her face, some of the tension in her shoulders released.

It was Wednesday evening. They'd cross into Nevada and

then be in California Friday morning. Her job was nearly completed. Veronica was right. Time to stop fretting.

~

"*C*are for a drink, miss?" Back at their seats, the conductor passed a full dipper to Rennie.

"Thank you." Icy water soothed her mouth and throat. "Nice and cold."

"I want some." Livie pouted.

"I'll bring two dippers next time." The conductor touched the rim of his top hat. "And it'll stay cold because we have ice in an ice house to keep drinks cold." He accepted the empty ladle from Rennie and hurried away.

Hot breezes drifted through open windows along with dust, occasional sparks, and the ever-present smell of smoke. Rennie pushed her duster's flaps closed to keep as much of her blue gingham dress clean as possible.

"Here you go, little ladies." The trainman gave handles of ladels to both girls, who drank thirstily. "The barrel's at the back of the car. Help yourselves anytime. Can I see your tickets?"

Rennie snatched them from the top of her basket and gave them to him.

He glanced at the tickets. "Going all the way to Oakland, I see."

"To San Francisco." Livie spoke in a firm voice, surprising in one so young. "To see my mama. She's sick."

"Well, I sure am sorry to hear that, little lady. Remember to pray for her." He gave her a nod. "You all had your supper?"

"In Ogden."

"Good." He gave them a stub that showed the distance between stations. "I'll come around early in the morning with bills of fare for breakfast. You tell me what you want, and I'll see your orders make it to the kitchen."

"My beau, John Welch, is traveling with us. He'll eat with us. He left to find you." Rennie lowered her eyes to her lap as she explained why.

"Haven't seen him, but I'll save him a berth. I'm almost finished checking tickets, then I'll walk the train."

"Thank you."

After he moved to the next group, the girls went to the convenience. It was a good time to replenish the money in Rennie's reticule for the following day's expenses. She rummaged through their bag. Where was the envelope containing the rest of their money?

She pushed everything aside and took a second look. Not there.

Sweat broke out on her forehead. Maybe it was in the valise with their towels and toiletries. She snatched it from its hook and fished through its contents. No envelope.

Had it fallen out at the hotel? But that was miles away.

Wait. Had someone stolen it? They'd left their bags unattended at the hotel and also on the train.

What was she to do? She had twenty-five cents in her reticule and at least twelve meals to buy.

Remembering Livie's train sickness, she swiped her forehead with shaking fingers. The child must eat.

"Rennie, your face is as white as that towel in your hand." Veronica sat beside her. "What's wrong?"

"I've misplaced something." Her voice was faint in her own ears.

"What? Did you leave something back at the hotel?"

"No." She had checked all their bags before leaving on the excursion. When they'd returned, all she did was add the laundered clothes to the trunk and lock it. Rennie's conviction grew that someone had taken it. Someone in this fancy car?

She looked around. The family of four sitting opposite them played a word game. A gray-haired couple next to them dozed with their heads against the window. A pretty woman in another section met Rennie's gaze briefly and then spoke to her husband.

"Well, what was it?" Veronica opened the other valise. "I'll help you look."

"Me too." Livie set her new book aside.

How Rennie regretted purchasing the book. It would have provided a meal for the little girl. "No, I think I'll ask John."

"That's right. He might have it."

He didn't, but Rennie wanted to shield the girls from the terrible news as long as possible. "Will you read to Livie while I go find him?"

"I have a better idea." Tilting her head, Veronica studied Livie. "Shall I sketch you until the sunlight fades? You can keep the drawing or give it to your parents as a gift."

"Oh, boy." She bounced in her seat. "I'll have a present to give Mama and Papa."

"What a lovely idea, Veronica." Despite her fears over the lost money, Rennie was touched by her sister's thoughtfulness. Was it the discovery of her talent that changed her? Or the journey itself?

"Mr. John's not in the palace cars, Miss Rennie."

"Thank you, Livie." Impulsively, she bent and kissed the girl's cheek. "I'll return soon."

Her reticule dangled from her wrist as she hurried down the aisle. Where was John?

omeone slammed into John as he opened the outside door. "Rennie? Are you all right?"

"John." She clutched his hands. "My money...it's been stolen."

"What?" He led her to the landing's sturdy rail in the hot desert sun. "When did this happen?"

"I don't know." Her hands within his quivered like leaves in the wind. "Perhaps at the hotel. But I also stood out here with the girls for half an hour. I left our bags at the seat."

This was a blow. "You couldn't know." John released one of her icy hands so she could hold onto the rail. Money had become a form of security for her. Clearly, the robbery had shaken her to her core. "We've left the bags unattended many times—at every meal stop—without a problem."

What were they to do? There was ticket money and four dollars extra in his boot. He couldn't get to the money hidden in his locked trunk until they disembarked.

"I should have carried it all in my reticule. The most important thing is to take care of Livie and Veronica." Her shoulders slumped. "How am I to do that now?"

"You bought some food in Ogden."

"Enough for one small meal."

"It's something." More like a snack. "I have enough to buy us another meal. Too bad I already paid for my berth."

"I'm responsible for taking care of Livie. What have I done?"

He put his arm around her.

She snuggled against his side. "Thank you for not being angry at my stupidity."

"Later I'll be angry with the dishonest person who put you in this predicament." He kissed her cheek. "Right now, let's focus on what we must do to take care of the girls in our care."

"Let's pray about it."

"The best way to handle any problem." John bowed his head and prayed for help and guidance.

~

*a*fter John's prayer, a measure of peace allowed Rennie to enjoy the beauty of the sunset with her beau.

"That view inspires me, just like The Thousand Mile Tree did." John adjusted the brim of his hat over his eyes. "Veronica gave me permission to use her sketch. I don't know how these things are handled. I didn't have sketches on the other stories. If they don't pay her for it, I will."

"How much?" A paying job? That would be good for her sister. Bad for John. He couldn't afford to pay much. Bad for her too. Wedding bells were too far distant as it was.

"I don't know. From what I hear, book publishers will pay me *and* the illustrator. Do you think she'll draw sketches for my book? She's got talent, Rennie."

Right, but what would their parents think? "Hold off on asking her about it." She touched his arm. "As you say, neither of us knows how such things work."

"You're against the idea?" Direct light from the sunset cast an orange glow on his best brown suit. And his frown. He turned and her hand fell from his forearm.

"Not if the publisher pays her. You said they probably will." Rennie stared at his stiff back. "I'm against you covering the expense. Hard to tell how much that will be. You need to make money from your writing and not keep spending it as though your savings will never run dry."

"Even if the publisher pays, neither of us are famous. I don't know how much we'll make under those circumstances."

"Veronica won't mind whatever they pay. She doesn't have a job."

"I've prayed to find someone to illustrate scenes in my book...someone who deserves recognition but is unknown like me. I'd want sketches here and there where it benefits the story. Like Mark Twain does." His head went down. "I was overjoyed to find someone so close to me—to you—with not only the ability but the desire to work with me."

There he went again, talking about that Twain fellow. It was as if the author could do no wrong. "You don't have to do everything Mark Twain does."

"It works for him."

"Yes, it does." Though she had no idea if it worked for the famous author or not. She didn't read his books. Or any other books very often. Her information came from John, *her* favorite writer. "But you're not him."

His indrawn breath told her she'd said the wrong thing. But maybe not. *Someone* must tell him the truth.

He rubbed his forehead, dislodging his bowler hat so that it tumbled to the dusty platform. The breeze carried it against the railing. He bent to brush it off. His fingers curled around the brim.

"I'm not saying that's a bad thing. I like you the way you are."

Smoky brown eyes held her gaze.

"Dreams aren't bad. You have to mix in a good dose of reality, to my way of thinking."

A couple in their thirties exited the palace car. The brunette woman was the same one who'd been watching Rennie when she'd discovered her money was missing. A ring on her left hand showed the couple was married. Rennie flushed, but John gave them a cordial nod.

"Looks like we missed the sunset, darling." The man, in an ordinary coat and trousers underneath the linen dusters nearly everyone wore, scanned the horizon where only a small dome of the sun remained.

"There'll be others, dear." The woman rested one hand on the railing and the other on her husband's arm. She smiled at Rennie but spoke to her husband. "Let's go back inside and wait for another day. Not every day goes as we plan."

Wasn't that the truth? Rennie looked away from the couple. Watching the sunset had been like an oasis from her money worries. And then she had to go and say those things about John's hero. The truth had hurt him.

Reality descended with twilight. She had more immediate concerns. Their money had been stolen. What was she to do now?

At last, the man opened the door and allowed his wife to enter the car first. The door closed behind them as the train slowed.

Whistles screeched. Rennie covered her ears.

"Hold on." John reached an arm around her waist and clutched the railing to secure her.

She gripped the railing and also leaned into John, desiring the comfort of his closeness.

"Must be a water stop." John released her when the train came to a halt.

The crew was already on the ground. Two men in work clothes exited the depot, which looked more like a small barn or a shed. A water tank built on stilts was located along the tracks.

"I need to let the girls know what happened." She felt almost ill over the loss.

"Want me to come with you?" Compassion lit his eyes.

"No. It's nearly dark. The porters will be preparing the sleeping berths."

"True." He watched the fireman move the spout from the water tank and set it so that the water gushed into the tender. "I did want to mention to you that I've got a bad feeling again."

"Like the one you had before the flood last spring?" Rennie had learned to trust John's intuition. "And before the riots?"

He nodded. "The same."

"Is it the robbery?"

"No. That's already happened. It's something else."

As though they needed something worse. A terrible possibility made Rennie's breath catch in her throat. "Not...not Mrs. Sherman..." Had Livie's mother taken a turn—or worse?

"I don't know. I'm praying for her, that's for sure." He scratched his head. "Funny thing is that the premonition didn't start until this evening."

"What does that mean?" She'd pray extra hard for Livie's sweet Mama that night.

"No telling. Just pray for her. For us and our protection. And for God providing food for us after the robbery."

"I sent the Shermans a telegram from Ogden. That all was well and we'd arrive Friday morning."

"That's all we can do." He clasped her hands. "I'll come to the palace car before breakfast." He opened the door for her. "Try to get some sleep."

"Good night." She entered the car, and the door shut behind her.

Taking a deep breath, she headed toward her seat. Veronica needed to know what they faced.

CHAPTER 16

*B*eneath the glowing chandeliers, Rennie returned to her seat. Neighboring passengers had gathered in small groups to chatter. The fact that she and the girls had kept to themselves saved her from making polite conversation now. A nod, a cordial greeting was about as much as she'd exchanged with most of her fellow passengers.

"What's wrong?" Veronica straightened.

Rennie sat beside Livie. She studied her clenched hands. How she wished the loss of the money affected only her.

"Where's John?"

"He'll come by for breakfast." John wasn't only upset about the robbery. Emotions had got the best of her, and she'd spoken too bluntly just now.

Livie pouted. "I wanted to show him my picture."

"Show him tomorrow. It will be a nice beginning for his day." Rennie had forgotten the sketch Veronica started as she left. "I must tell you something." Taking a deep breath, she explained about the missing money.

"That's not good." Veronica emptied the first valise onto the seat. And then the second.

Hope rose in Rennie that her sister would find the money. A vain one.

"Someone stole it." Veronica's face paled.

"Looks that way." She helped her sister repack the bags.

"But why?" Livie's lower lip protruded.

Rennie put her arm around her. The little girl looked as shaken as she felt. "I don't know." Hopefully, the person took the money because he—or she—needed it and not out of meanness. At the moment, they all needed a distraction. "Will you show me the sketch?"

Veronica extracted the top page from the sketchpad beside her and held it aloft. Livie took it from Veronica, who lowered her head.

Remembering the hurt in John's eyes when she told him he wasn't Mark Twain, Rennie decided she'd praise the sketch no matter how it had turned out. John had often called her honesty refreshing. It was doubtful he still believed that.

Beaming, Livie held up the sketch. "Here it is."

The pencil drawing had captured the child's longing for her parents, which often lingered in the droop of her mouth. Veronica had also captured her hope, her childlike faith that her mother would soon recover.

"Why, it looks just like you, Livie." Taking it from her, Rennie tilted it toward the light of the closest chandelier. "You look so beautiful. Are you giving it to your parents?"

She nodded, eyes shining.

"Veronica, this is very, very good." She stared at her sister. "To me, this is even better than your drawing of the canyon."

"You think so?" Tears filled her sister's eyes. "You *really* think so?"

"It's exceptional. Amazing." Words failed her. Pride in her sister welled up, pricking the back of her throat in unaccustomed tears.

"Do you mind if I look at your drawing, miss?"

Rennie jumped at the strange woman's voice behind her. She turned to see the couple who had missed the sunset. "Not at all. I'm Rennie Hill." Her glance slid to her apprehensive sister, who joined her in the aisle. "This is my sister, Veronica. She's the one who sketched our young friend here, Olivia Sherman." Rennie drew the suddenly shy girl to her side. "We're accompanying her to her family in San Francisco."

"A pleasure to meet you all. My name is Iris Birchfield, and this is my husband, William."

They murmured their *how do you do's* while Rennie tilted the drawing so the couple could see. Her astonishment at the detail Veronica had managed to create in the half hour she'd been away expanded into a pride she'd scarcely felt for her sister. But why did this evidence of her talent change her view? It shouldn't. Realization struck hard.

She should have been proud of her sister all along.

"Such detail. Quite lovely." Mrs. Birchfield covered her open mouth with a gloved hand.

Her husband shot Veronica a stunned look. "You drew this on a moving train?"

Nodding, she exchanged a look with Rennie. "It jolted a couple of times." She pointed to Livie's jawline and the shoulder of her print dress. "I added strands of hair to cover the mistake."

A few others gathered to peek over Mr. Birchfield's shoulder. Gasps and exclamations of praise convinced Rennie of the sketch's quality. These strangers recognized her sister's talent immediately.

Veronica, red-faced, nodded her thanks.

"Quite extraordinary." Mr. Birchfield studied it. "It's not signed. You must always put your name on your work, Miss Hill, because you are an artist. If someone wanted to purchase this, would ten dollars be enough?"

So much as that? Rennie felt as stunned as her sister looked.

"No, it's mine." Livie reached to snatch it from Rennie's hands.

"Of course, it is." Rennie looked at her sister. But, oh, how they needed that money. Why, that was one day's worth of meals at train stops with enough left over for sending the daily telegram to Mr. Sherman.

"I'm sorry, Mr. Birchfield." Veronica took it from Rennie and gave it to Livie. The little girl huddled over it as if someone might yet steal it from her. "That one is a gift to my friend, which she plans to give to her parents."

"I'm certain they'll treasure it." Mrs. Birchfield placed a gloved hand on her husband's arm.

"Perhaps we can commission you to sketch my wife for twenty dollars?" Mr. Birchfield raised his eyebrow.

"What a lovely idea." Mrs. Birchfield pressed her hands together. "Will, how about a drawing of the two of us together?"

"Excellent idea." He clasped her hand.

Twenty dollars? Rennie's heart thudded at the offer. The amount covered their expenses to San Francisco.

Mrs. Birchfield turned a beaming face toward Veronica. "My dear Miss Hill, we'll offer twice that amount if you draw both my husband and me together."

Forty dollars? Rennie's knees shook so badly she grabbed the seat to steady herself. Such an amount would help with their expenses while in California. She trusted the Shermans to front the cost of the return trip.

"I've only drawn people I know." Veronica wrung her hands. "What if you don't like it?"

"I'm quite certain we will." Mr. Birchfield rubbed his bearded jaw. "But I understand why it would be good for you to study our expressions in a relaxed setting. Why don't you join us in the dining car for breakfast? Your meals will be our treat."

"The young man you saw me with this evening is John Welch," Rennie said, "my beau and our escort. Is he included in your invitation?" It was a bold request reminiscent of her mama. She didn't care. He had little money left after paying for their excursion.

"Of course." Mrs. Birchfield gave her a calculating look that quickly turned into a smile. "It will be our pleasure."

The porter entered to ready the car for sleeping.

"Ladies, we will talk with you in the morning." Mrs. Birchfield gave them a nod. "What a blessing to meet a talented artist in our car."

~

*J*ohn slumped on an otherwise vacant seat in the men's passenger car, his forehead on the cool pane beneath the open window. The train rumbled over a rough bit of track, jostling his valise, which hung on a hook. Thank goodness he'd possessed the foresight to claim this seat by storing his belongings here after securing his berth for the next two nights.

The theft of Rennie's money weighed on him. If he hadn't treated the four of them to that canyon excursion, he'd be able to pay for all their meals, the telegrams, and porter fees all the way to California. He'd be Rennie's hero.

Instead, he felt like a failure. She'd said he was no Mark Twain, and though the words stung, he agreed. But she'd also called his desire to support them through his writing foolishness at the picnic. Now he wondered if she was right. Was he tossing his meager savings to the wind? Should he forget this dream?

All of his loved ones had always come first for him. He'd shouldered responsibilities for his mother, Cora, and the rest of his siblings. This journey was the first thing he'd done in years specifically for himself. No, that wasn't completely true. Finding subject matter for future novels benefited not only himself, but also Rennie and the family they'd raise.

Had he been selfish? Maybe, because he couldn't even come to her aid now.

Rennie was right. He couldn't afford to continue splurging on excursions and gifts for the girls.

A finger tapped on his shoulder. "Young fella, the berths in your sleeping car are prepared." The middle-aged conductor rested a hand on the back of the seat. "You look like you lost your best friend, if you don't mind me saying so."

"Yes, sir." The cost of his dreams weighed heavy tonight.

"Got a son about your age. Want to tell me about it?"

Maybe it was best to report the theft. He explained what happened.

"Figure it happened on the train or at the hotel?" The trainman rubbed his whiskered jaw.

"Can't rule out either place."

"Reckon I can't, either, but I'll keep my eyes open for trouble." He patted John's shoulder. "Seems like you got a heavy burden. A good night's sleep might help. Lots of worries that keep us awake at night don't look so bad in the light of day." He straightened. "Pray on it and get some rest, son."

"I will. Thank you, sir." John grabbed his bag as the conductor approached another man two seats away. He'd pray for God's provision for them the rest of their journey...and guidance for his footsteps.

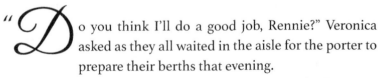

"*D*o you think I'll do a good job, Rennie?" Veronica asked as they all waited in the aisle for the porter to prepare their berths that evening.

"Having seen displays of your talent twice today," Rennie

said, putting her hands on her sister's shoulders, "I'm certain of it. The money you earn will not only provide all we'll need the remainder of our journey, but also our expenses in California. I used all my pay on things not covered by Mr. Sherman. Like snacks and such."

"Look how my hands are shaking." She held one out, and, indeed, it trembled.

The porter, a smile lighting his dark face, stepped back respectfully. "It's ready for you ladies."

"Thank you." Rennie gave him her last coin. He'd earned the fee, and Veronica would be paid tomorrow.

"I believe you'll do just fine." Livie yawned and stretched.

"Me too." Rennie grew tired of offering reassurances. The theft had stolen something from her. She was too emotional to decipher it. She closed the privacy curtain in the dim car. Shadowy pines outside the lone window suddenly became clearer. "It's time for bed. There's room for two on each berth. Where do you want to sleep?"

"Top. It doesn't have windows in this car." Veronica climbed up. "Maybe lantern lights at the stations won't awaken me."

Best not mention the whistles, shouts from trainmen, the rush of water filling the tender, and bumps when coal was shoveled into its bin. "How about you, Livie?" Rennie thumped both pillows on the lower berth, anticipating a more comfortable sleep on the cushions.

"The top. I don't like the lights either."

Rennie gave her a boost.

"We can't forget to pray for Mama."

"No, we won't. Fold your hands." Remembering John's premonition, Rennie prayed for Mrs. Sherman and then encouraged both Livie and Veronica to voice their prayers. Straightening, Rennie silently echoed Livie's prayer for "God to make Mama all better."

Moments later, Rennie was alone on the lower bed—the

solitude she'd craved since glimpsing the pain she'd caused in John's eyes.

It was her statement about his not being Mark Twain that did it. Didn't he realize she thought it a compliment? She loved John. He wasn't the same man as his hero.

He was infinitely better.

Twain might be America's most beloved author—a phrase she'd heard from John time and again—but there were plenty of other authors writing worthy books. She didn't have to read them all to understand that truth.

John would be one of the good ones. Someday. She'd laughed at too many of his stories not to know he spun a good yarn. But that was for the future.

She'd nagged at him for months to quit his job at the *Times-Star* in Cincinnati to work at a newspaper in Hamilton. He'd only been in the big city to watch over his twin while she finished kindergarten training school. That stuck like a burr in Rennie's stockings, even now that Cora was engaged and teaching in Hamilton until her wedding next summer...because it had meant Rennie only saw John about once a month.

Cora finally understood how much Rennie had missed John those two years because now she was separated from Ben, her fiancée. That brought Rennie some comfort, for she'd been jealous. There. She'd finally admitted it to herself. She'd been jealous of John's protective care for his sister. She was certain John would have been established in a good job in Hamilton long before now if not for Cora. They'd be married. Combining his pay with hers to save toward their family home.

His choice to guard Cora had put a wedge between them that deepened every time she was mentioned. Mama had even told Rennie to stop nagging him about it. She had finally listened. Patience wasn't her virtue. Their relationship slowly mended after Cora announced her intention to move back to the family farm.

Thousands of stars captured Rennie's attention. She turned on her side for a better view. The West had its own desolate beauty. She understood John's desire to see it, but why did he have to do it now, when it delayed their starting their lives together? He could have waited. When their children had grown up, after he'd established himself in a career, she'd have suggested taking a trip to California, Colorado...wherever he wanted.

Her feet were firmly planted on the ground. John's head was nearer to those stars lighting the sky.

She'd lost some friends over the years, ones who didn't understand that her plain speaking bespoke caring. It had made her a loner. Growing up, she'd kept to herself until the Walkers adopted John and Cora, changing her life forever.

How she loved her dreamer. Had she been too blunt, ruined everything? Had her words finally crossed the line?

~

*J*ohn lay on an uncomfortable top berth in the men's sleeping car, staring at the starry sky. He should be grateful to have a bed at all—the conductor who sold it to him said there were only two left at the time he reserved it—but it was difficult to feel gratitude for anything right now.

The knife thrust of Rennie's words sliced to his core.

Of course, everyone knew he wasn't as talented as America's most beloved author. That went without saying. Why had Rennie felt the need to hammer that reality into his heart?

His hurt went too deep for words. Too deep for prayer.

She knew John better than anyone—even Cora. No doubt Rennie had the right of it.

He turned on his side for a better view of the stars. His

dream of becoming an author was as out of reach as any of them.

Even as a boy, he'd dreamed of writing books. His pa was the only one in the family who understood. Pa had encouraged him to learn all he could in school and never stop telling his stories.

And then Pa died. It had been a bitter blow. It was bitter still, because John never got over missing him.

The man of the house at twelve, John had pushed aside his dreams. His ma wouldn't allow him to quit school, so he'd worked odd jobs after school and on Saturdays. Ma took in extra washing. They scraped by until she took sick with a lung ailment the following year. He didn't dwell on those dark days if he could help it.

Survival had been his focus. Dreams had had no place in his life.

Apparently, dreams still had no place in his life.

CHAPTER 17

*D*ue to the fewer number of passengers in the palace car, conversation was not as loud when John stepped inside the following morning. The mood felt relaxed as he exchanged greetings with other passengers on his way to Rennie and the girls, who pored over the bill of fare for breakfast.

"Aren't we eating a boiled egg from your food basket this morning?" John asked after greeting them. He could only buy one meal for them.

"The Birchfields are buying our meal." Rennie indicated an attractive woman and a swarthy man sitting across the aisle and down from them. "That invitation happened after you left last evening." She looked at Veronica. "Go ahead. Tell him."

With eyes that fairly glowed, Veronica shared astonishing news about how she'd been commissioned to draw the couple.

Some of the burden slipped from his shoulders. This was an answer to their prayers. "May I see the sketch of Livie?" John could scarcely take in the fact that Veronica had been offered forty dollars for a drawing. He'd received fifty for *two* of his stories.

Livie opened a sketchpad and handed him a sheet.

Heart pounding, John gave a low whistle. "Veronica, this looks very like her. It's even better than the one of the canyon."

"Mr. Birchfield wanted to buy it. For ten dollars."

Her expression might have been smug with such success. Instead, her eyes were filled with wonder.

John's glance slid to Rennie. Pride was mixed with reserve, as if she feared the good fortune wouldn't last.

So like Rennie to look at the practical, sensible side of every success.

"I'm listing our orders for the kitchen." Rennie handed him the menu. "We're each ordering an omelet with ham, toasted bread—"

"I want a biscuit." Livie took her sketch from John as he sat beside Rennie.

"That's right. With strawberries. And chocolate to drink. All that is ninety-five cents, so we can eat here tomorrow again." Rennie's eyes shone. "Maybe for other meals, too, if we order carefully. I don't want to spend too much of my sister's earnings."

"I don't mind paying," Veronica said.

John scanned the offerings. "I'll have poached eggs with bacon and fried potatoes. Coffee. And I hope their rye bread is as good as your mother's." He returned the menu. "Feels good to have choices."

Rennie studied the prices. "Yours will be one dollar and twenty-five cents. That shouldn't be too great a cost for our hosts."

"If they can pay forty dollars for a sketch, our meal costing just over four dollars isn't likely to be a problem." John's head spun at the offer.

He hated himself for envying Veronica's good fortune.

◈

*W*ith only four people per table, Rennie sat beside Livie and opposite John across the aisle from the Birchfields and Veronica. They all talked as a group until the food arrived. Rennie kept an eye on her nervous sister, but she needn't have worried. Mrs. Birchfield, her pleasant looks enhanced by a lemon-yellow dress, encouraged her to talk about George, her favorite topic. The couple seemed delighted when they heard about her beau's quiet support of her abilities.

"Rest easy." John glanced at Rennie's untouched plate. "She seems happy."

"True." Rennie ate a bite of omelet. "Delicious. Can you believe all this food was prepared on a moving train?"

"In a fully-stocked kitchen. I glanced at it yesterday." John spread his hands. "Every appliance a cook might need was stuffed in about an eight-foot-square room."

"Really?" Livie speared a slice of strawberry. "A kitchen on a train?"

John had probably already written a description in his journal. This was a safe topic...until Rennie found a moment to apologize. John was more relaxed after learning their money problem had been solved, but he'd steered clear of personal topics all morning.

"Surprising, isn't it?" John grinned at the little girl. "A full range, pots and pans. I even spotted a pantry with china, glass, and silver. Oh, and there was an icebox."

Why, her parents didn't even own an icebox, though John's parents did. Rennie winked at him. "I'd happily prepare a meal there."

When John only offered a halfhearted smile in return, Rennie's stomach knotted. John hadn't teased her or said anything beyond the commonplace. She owed him that apology.

Veronica was still talking about George. Hopefully, she was

also paying attention to her host's and hostess's expressions, the reason for dining together.

"Will I see Mama tomorrow?" Livie asked.

"Yes." Rennie patted her hand. "One more day."

"Seems like we've been riding forever."

Rennie met John's eyes with a silent question. Did he still have his premonition?

His expression darkened.

An uneasiness washed over Rennie. They had asked God to watch over the Shermans when blessing the food. They couldn't come this far only to deliver the worst possible news to this sweet child.

"Mr. John?"

"Yes, Livie?"

"You seem sad. Did someone hurt your feelings?"

At Rennie's gasp, his gaze shot to her. Sorrowful eyes held hers captive.

Her spirits plummeted. "John, I have an unfortunately blunt manner. I'm sorry—"

"No need to discuss it now."

Livie patted his hand. "I'm sorry, too, Mr. John. I hope you feel better soon."

"I shall." He gave her a genuine smile. "Nothing will make me happier than to take you to your parents tomorrow."

Her expression brightened as she ate with more appetite.

Rennie tried to catch John's eye, but his attention had returned to his meal. How was she to apologize when her only regret was the way she'd delivered her message? She didn't regret what she said. Not when, in her mind, John stood head and shoulders over his hero.

*J*ohn found a vacant seat in the palace car to write in his journal after breakfast. There'd been some discussion about the Birchfields posing on the car's platform where he and Rennie had watched the sunset—and had their most painful conversation to date—but Veronica had said she couldn't draw while fighting the windy conditions.

Instead, the pair stood in the aisle, opposite one another with hands entwined, like a newly wedded couple might. Mrs. Birchfield wanted the chandelier over their heads in the sketch, and Veronica was to fill the view outside the window with a valley leading to mountains in the distance. "Perhaps a herd of cattle or buffalo back near the slopes. Whatever's easiest."

Demanding couple. They wanted their money's worth.

"Neither of those is easy." Veronica took a seat in the opposite aisle.

"Trees, then. And a stream would be lovely."

Their voices easily carried to where John sat by an open window. No river, lake, or brook within sight. Nor cattle, for that matter.

"All right. I'll imagine that later." She drew with Livie peering over her shoulder. Rennie sat on the edge of her seat, eyes darting from the couple to her sister's flying pencil.

Veronica seemed to gain confidence as she continued.

Taking that as a good sign, John allowed his gaze to drift to the mountains. In this part of Nevada, they weren't tall like the Rockies but seemed attached to one another in an extended ridgeline that was rounded here and in a sharp peak just beyond. They were brownish-green in color, as if grass didn't cover the whole where the dirt peeked out.

Would he have the heart to continue his journey after Rennie returned home? It was difficult to write with her lack of faith in him uppermost in his mind.

~

*J*ohn trusted that the Birchfields would pay Veronica that afternoon and bought their noon meal at an eating station. It had a lunch counter, so they ate sandwiches and apples on benches outside with the bright, hot summer sun beating down on them.

John sat beside Livie. Her childish chatter lifted his spirits somewhat. She seemed to understand he was feeling low.

Most passengers ate inside. A handful of the train crew strode about the platform. No doubt those paying for meals in the dining car were enjoying a leisurely lunch.

"Veronica's drawing isn't done," Livie confided between bites of her ham-and-cheese sandwich. "You didn't see it yet, but it looks pretty."

"I'll put in a mountain with trees and a stream in a valley." Veronica leaned over to look at him.

John scanned the nearly barren mountain. "What was it like to draw strangers?"

"Not as easy as sketching George or Livie." She sighed. "I hope they're pleased."

"It looks like them." Rennie wiped crumbs from her calico dress. John liked her in blue, for it deepened the blue of her eyes. "Don't fret, sister. You'll make more in a few hours than I make in six weeks."

"Really?" Veronica's cheeks flushed. "They said they'll pay me when we get to Oakland."

John didn't like the sound of that. He had only enough money to send their daily telegram and purchase their train tickets. The Birchfields needed to reimburse her today. Did they plan to steal away without paying her? "Don't give them the drawing until they pay. I'll stay with you when they come for it."

"I will too." Rennie's face tightened as if she sensed his concern. "Perhaps you can keep it in your knapsack."

"Agreed." He didn't like to think ill of anyone. The couple had paid for their breakfast. However, their demands afterward had flustered Veronica. Perhaps they didn't realize it.

It reminded him of his duty as their escort. He mustn't allow his desire for distance from Rennie to prevent him from protecting them should the need arise.

~

*J*ohn stayed close while Veronica made her final changes to the drawing after lunch. They all sat together and allowed her to work in silence. Livie drew her home back in Hamilton to remind her parents what it looked like, and John jotted a few notes about lunch counters because he'd neglected to do it at other stops.

"Hello, everyone." Mrs. Birchfield clasped her hands together. "I stopped by to see if our sketch is done. I'm dying to see it."

"I just finished it." Veronica studied it with a critical eye as she rose. Then she looked at John.

He stood as well. "Mrs. Birchfield. How wonderful to see you again. We think you'll be pleased with it."

She tried to peer around him. "You can imagine my excitement. May I see it?"

"One moment." He glanced at the sketch, which clearly showed Veronica's talent. "Did you forget to sign it?" He couldn't find a name.

"I did." She sat and remedied the omission. "I'm going to name it *The Birchfields on a Western Journey.*"

"The perfect title. William will love it." Mrs. Birchfield looked over her shoulder at her husband, asleep with his head propped against the window. "I'll awaken him, shall I?"

John agreed with a smile.

They were back before Veronica finished titling the piece. She gave it to John.

"What do you think?" He held it up for them.

Mrs. Birchfield scrutinized it. "May I hold it?"

John gave it to her reluctantly. The couple sat four yards away. They weren't going far.

Veronica paled as the Birchfields whispered together behind her gloved hand.

John didn't take his eyes off them. Would they try to back out of the deal?

Their smiles had disappeared when they returned. John braced himself.

"We're sorry to point this out to you, my dear," Mr. Birchfield said, "but this sketch isn't up to the same quality as the one you drew earlier. Certainly not worth the original fee for an unknown artist. We'll pay you ten because we like you so well."

Veronica burst into tears.

Rennie said, "Now just one minute—"

John took one look at Rennie's outraged face and knew the couple was in for it if he didn't intervene. "No, sir. The agreed-upon price is forty dollars. She made it clear that she's never drawn strangers before this. You insisted."

"Ten's my price." He folded his arms.

"Nope." John widened his stance. "Forty or we'll sell it elsewhere." His insistence was risky because they needed the cash, but they weren't going to tread over the feelings of a weeping girl. Rennie's sister deserved better.

Mrs. Birchfield gasped. "Well, I never."

"All right. You'll have your full price." Her husband turned away. "We'll pay tomorrow."

"Fine." John reached around and took the sketch from him. "We'll make the exchange then."

Mrs. Birchfield tilted her chin in the air and flounced out of the car, her husband at her heels.

Rennie put her arms around her weeping sister.

At least the entitled couple had shown the good sense to leave. Sharing a car after this would be awkward. But how were they supposed to pay for their remaining meals until tomorrow? Empty stomachs would make them all sick.

The worst part was that none of them would ever feel good about something that had at first seemed an unbelievable blessing. He sighed. *Unbelievable* was the right description, for who would offer so much for an unknown artist's work?

"I'm sorry they attempted to lower the price, Veronica." By seventy-five percent. Outrageous. John knelt in front of the devastated girl. "I thought them a well-to-do couple who loved your work...willing to pay a high price to encourage you."

"What if they change their mind? Decide they don't want it?" Veronica rubbed her scarlet face with a handkerchief Rennie pressed into her hands. "I was so happy. I couldn't wait to tell Mama. And George."

"I think it's a good thing Mama wasn't here." Rennie glared at the door. "That man would've had his ears boxed. And I don't like to think what those flowers and feathers on Mrs. Birchfield's hat would have looked like after Mama snatched it off, hatpin and all."

Imagining it, John smothered a chuckle. Mrs. Hill was a fine woman. But no one messed with her children. Rennie possessed the same protective instincts.

Veronica's tears stopped, and a giggle erupted. At her laughter, the rest joined in, even Livie who didn't know Mrs. Hill.

They'd already drawn the stares of everyone in the car.

Then Rennie sobered. "I've only two crackers left. How will we pay for our next meal?"

John had no answer. The offer from the Birchfields had seemed an answered prayer. What were they to do now?

CHAPTER 18

*R*ennie watched the door for the Birchfields' return for the next half hour. John stayed with them, thank goodness, but he'd not prevent her from going after the woman if there were further insults to her sister.

John wrote in his journal. Livie wrote on her slate. Veronica stared listlessly out the window.

The Birchfields' offer of ten dollars worried Rennie. Maybe they didn't have the agreed-upon amount. Then why suggest it? Rennie hated that her sister's first paying job might not end up covering more than the cost of breakfast.

Worse, she was out of money. John had only the ticket fees left and wasn't allowed to get into his trunk stored in the baggage cars for money hidden there. Besides, that money had to cover the next part of his journey. She was still puzzling over what to do when the conductor beckoned to John.

The two of them walked far enough away that she couldn't hear a word. Her beau stood, feet firmly planted. They had a long conversation.

"What's happening?" Veronica craned her neck to see.

"I'll bet that couple complained about us. I've a good mind to go find them."

"I'm coming with you." She started to stand.

Rennie pushed her back as reason took over. "We're not going anywhere." She should be an example of how to keep her temper in check. That's what Papa had always said. Somewhere along the line, maintaining control got to be a habit.

She sure wished Papa were here today, though doubtful even her mild-mannered father would have held his temper as well as John did. He was good for her.

The sadness lingering in her sister's eyes at having her work ridiculed filled her own heart. Was this the bad thing that had prompted John's premonition? By his own admission, he hadn't had the bad feeling on the first leg of the journey.

He returned for his knapsack. "Wait here." He rejoined the conductor and showed him the sketch. They talked back and forth.

The conductor gathered two valises and left.

"What did he say?" Rennie barely waited until John reseated himself.

"A couple of things." Tension eased from his face. "First, it seems the Birchfields complained that we tried to swindle them."

Rennie shot out of her chair.

He slid his fingers around her wrist. "Calm down. Listen to the rest."

The back of her neck burned like fire, but his gentle hand was cool, his words reasoned. She didn't sit but waited. "Go on."

He released her wrist and clasped her hand. "I explained everything to the conductor. Showed him the sketch." He looked at Veronica. "He thinks it's quite a good likeness of the couple. Worth the price, in his opinion."

"He likes it?" Something akin to awe flittered across Veronica's face. "Maybe it's not so bad?"

"It's very good, Veronica," John said. "The Birchfields belittled it to shame you into lowering the price."

"They did that. Shame me, I mean."

"All the shame's on them." Rennie's lips tightened in a mutinous line.

"Agreed. Anyway, the completed work convinced the trainman we acted in good faith and they didn't. He's moving them to another car and giving me their section."

"So you'll be here tonight in case they come back for the drawing?"

He gave a firm nod. "A dozen feet away. I'll hear everything. Besides, I have the sketch in my knapsack. I'll take it with me everywhere until our journey ends."

Until their journey ended. Loneliness was about to become Rennie's constant companion. Again. She'd endured weeks of not seeing him when he worked in Cincinnati, an hour's train ride away. Living for his letters. Months of separation when he was hundreds of miles from her would be pure torture.

John squeezed her hand. "In my opinion, they never intended to give Veronica the forty dollars, yet it was an insult to offer a quarter of that amount. Who knows? They may pay it yet. Regardless, their scheme has been discovered."

"Good." At his touch, some of the anger seeped away. The conductor believed them and had made it right. And John now had a berth in their palace car.

"The second news is far more welcome because it gives us the means to buy our meals and send telegrams to Mr. Sherman." Releasing her, he picked up his knapsack. "Remember when I told stories on the last train?"

Nodding, Rennie straightened.

"A few folks who traveled on it heard me. They've talked about me to train crews who passed it on to this crew." He held out his hands, palms up. "The long and short of it is…I've been asked to entertain some guests from another palace car. They'll pay me twenty dollars."

"Twenty dollars?" It seemed a fortune at this moment. "Oh, John, that's wonderful."

"I'm happy for you." Veronica smiled at him.

"Me too." But Rennie wasn't ready to see the couple who'd given them so much grief. "What if the—"

"The Birchfields won't be placed in that car or this one, and the conductor promised to keep his eye on them. They falsely accused us. He 'don't cotton to no shady dealings' on his watch." John mimicked the conductor's accent. "But it's possible they'll pay in Oakland tomorrow."

"Now that you'll be paid for your speech, I don't care so much." Veronica's face lightened.

This sounded better and better. Her sister's anguish had made the situation doubly hard for Rennie. Her anger seeped away as Veronica recovered.

"It's good to see you smiling again." John patted Veronica's shoulder. "You all are invited to come listen to my stories if you think you can stomach them one more time. Even Livie has heard a couple of them."

"I'll come." The little girl reached for his hand and held on. "Can I bring my slate to practice my letters?"

"I think that's a *very* good idea." He grinned at her. "Little girls and boys need something to occupy their hands when they have to sit and listen to a stuffy old storyteller."

"You're not old until you're as old as my father."

John and Rennie laughed at Livie's idea of an old man.

"I'll come if Veronica does." Rennie had heard all John's stories. Knew which ones were tall tales and which were entirely true. "I'm not tired of them."

"Me either. I need a laugh." Veronica stepped into the aisle.

"You might want to comb your hair first, John." Rennie tilted her head, studying him. "Your curls are starting to come back." His hair was always wavy, but he hated those dark curls that Rennie was partial to.

"There was no opportunity to get a haircut before we left. Never fear—I'll remedy that in San Francisco." He headed toward the men's washroom.

The ladies took the chance to refresh themselves and check their hair. John was drumming his fingers across the back of their seat when they returned.

"Nervous?" Rennie smiled at him.

"Maybe a little. This is the first time someone's paid me to entertain their guests." He seemed distracted. "Just trying to remember some I haven't told."

"What about your time as an orphan?"

He frowned. "Not much that's amusing about being an orphan."

"Maybe someday you'll figure out some funny parts and still remind folks of the orphan's plight without beating them over the head with it."

He gave her an incredulous look. "Maybe I will. Someday."

But that wasn't helping him for this speech. "Why not tell about your customers at the meal stop where you worked?"

A smile crept over his face, lighting his eyes. "Brilliant idea. Thank you, Rennie. You never fail to surprise me."

She liked that look—almost wonder—in his eyes. As though he appreciated her again.

"Are you all ready?"

"Lead the way." Rennie's face softened as she looked into John's compassionate yet strong face. She'd hurt him last night, but that hadn't prevented him from standing by her and her sister.

How she loved him.

*J*ohn had walked through this palace car before and been impressed with its opulence. Instead of the high-backed, cushioned bench seats bolted to the floor like in their car, this one had cushioned armchairs reminiscent of those found in a parlor. Rather than being set in groups of four as they had been earlier, they were arranged in rows facing the same direction.

For a speaker.

Him.

Butterflies skittered in his stomach. He'd envisioned sitting in a partial circle, telling stories. Not this. Yet this setting honored him. People stood in groups of three or four, chatting as one might before a show. He gulped.

Rennie halted beside him. "They prepared it for you."

Judging from the quality of fabric in the men's suits and hats and the women's silk and taffeta dresses, this group lived above his means. Ruffles, pleats, lace, and ribbons on bustled dresses of every color made him dizzy. He'd been far more comfortable weaving his stories in the gentlemen's car on the earlier leg of their journey.

"Don't worry." Rennie placed a warm hand on his shoulder. "You've told your stories almost daily for years. Added new ones weekly for as long as I've known you. Just speak with these folks as you do everyone else, as if they're strangers about to become friends."

Her words put him back together. Restored his confidence. How did she know just what to say? Because she knew him better than anyone else. "Thank you, Rennie." His equilibrium righted.

"You can do this." She gazed at him with those beautiful cornflower-blue eyes. "I know you can."

That was what he needed to hear.

"Mr. Welch?" At his nod, a portly man stepped forward,

hand extended. "I'm Percival Holmstead of Holmstead Furniture. Perhaps you've heard of us?"

"Yes, sir." But only because the conductor had mentioned it. "Pleasure to make your acquaintance."

"Likewise." The curly ends of man's black mustache twitched. "And who do you have with you?"

Pleased with his host's jovial demeanor, he clasped Rennie's hand. "May I introduce Miss Rennie Hill, whom I've courted three years, and her sister, Veronica."

Both girls curtsied.

"And this young lady is Olivia Sherman." He drew her forward.

In turn, Mr. Holmstead beckoned to a blonde in her thirties and introduced her as his wife. The woman's pleasant face was made lovelier by the gracious way she greeted them.

"I'll introduce our guests after your talk." Mr. Holmstead clapped him on the back. "We're looking forward to an afternoon's entertainment."

"I'll do my best, sir." His back smarted from his host's overly zealous pat.

"I expect nothing less." He spoke in hearty tones. "My dear, show these ladies to their seats."

Rennie gave him a reassuring smile before following her.

Mr. Holmstead motioned to his guests. "Take your seats, everyone. We're ready to begin."

Those gathered occupied the cushioned chairs.

The train whistle blew as it entered a station. John cast a nervous glance out the window. A water stop. He swiped beads of sweat from his forehead. The audience might imagine the summer day's heat to be the cause. He knew differently.

"Folks, we're in for a treat this afternoon." Mr. Holmstead rubbed his palms together. "Talk of this young man's storytelling prowess reached our conductor's ears this morning. He waxed so eloquent about it that I knew we must hear this

gentleman for ourselves"—he leaned toward the audience—
"for it's been said by one who heard Mark Twain speak that this
young man has a similar style to that famous author."

John's heart picked up a galloping speed. Did his host just
say...or did he merely imagine it...? Had someone compared
him to Mark Twain? Favorably?

The audience, looking at him with renewed interest,
erupted into applause.

"But he's not only a storyteller. No, today's speaker has
enjoyed success from the written word this very year."

Nods. A few glanced at each other as if impressed.

John searched out Rennie's gaze in the back row. She
beamed at him.

"Friends, we're privileged to listen to a young man before
fame finds him. The conductor assured me you'll tell your
grandchildren about the day you listened to this storyteller
while riding on a train through Nevada."

How was he to live up to such an introduction? His heart
pounded as hard as those hammers that laid the tracks beneath
his feet must have done.

Talk to them as if they're strangers about to become friends.

Rennie's advice returned to him as clearly as if she'd whispered it in his ear. His feet back on solid ground even as the
locomotive's wheels churned forward once more, he uttered a
silent prayer that he would tell his stories as they deserved to
be told.

"Ladies and gentlemen," the man said, "please welcome Mr.
John Welch."

John stepped forward while they applauded. "Thank you,
folks, and thank you, Mr. Holmstead, for that gracious introduction. I pray I can live up to it." Someday. "It's an honor and
privilege to be with you today."

His host took the only vacant seat in the front row. He gave
an encouraging nod.

"As we're traveling across the country by train, I thought it might be appropriate to entertain you folks with some stories from my own time working at a train stop." A few eyebrows raised as the group settled back to listen.

Chin high, sitting on the edge of her seat, Rennie gave him a direct look. She willed him to succeed. That felt good.

"My sister and I were mere babes of thirteen—that's right, folks, she's my twin—when we began working at Mrs. Saunders' Eatery..."

CHAPTER 19

*R*ennie sat on the edge of her chair, as stiff as the binding on a book, and prayed for John to captivate his audience with his speech. Nobody else would notice his nervousness, but she knew him well.

He brushed over the tragic deaths of their parents as if realizing his audience preferred the comic side. However, it was wise of him to mention he was an orphan as he began because the crowd's mood clearly shifted to sympathetic.

His description of his early mistakes at the restaurant invited folks to chuckle at his expense. Then came stories about meeting Mama Rosie, the twins' adoption, and their transition to farm life. He had an uncanny ability to know what to say at just the right time in a way that enthralled his audience. Amazing.

Every titter, every chuckle seemed to energize John, which she had witnessed time without number over the supper table. Why, some of the men sat on the edge of their seats, hands on their knees, mouths ready to smile.

"Pardon me, folks." John sought Rennie's eyes. "Would you mind getting me a dipper of water?"

She hurried to the back of the room to the barrel of iced water and filled two dippers. Skirting around people standing at the back of the seats, she approached the front nervously.

"Thanks, Rennie. Everyone, I'd like you to meet my girl, Miss Renita Hill." He downed one dipper while the audience applauded. "She works at a telegraph office. And gentlemen, don't ask her if she likes your hat unless you're prepared for either a positive or a negative response, for she'll tell it like she sees it."

He drank until the laughter stopped and gave her back the dipper. "Thank you."

"You're giving an amazing talk," she whispered.

His chest puffed out.

As she scurried back to the water barrel, the conductor entered through the back door. "How's he doing?" he whispered.

"Better than I dreamed." She hung the dipper on the wall and turned to face John, who had moved on to another story.

"Don't underestimate that young man. There's something about him..." He chuckled, nodding at the crowd standing behind the chairs. "Those folks are from another palace car. Wonder when they came?"

"I've no idea." Rennie shrugged.

"Still others asked me about standing in the back to listen. Turned 'em down." He put his hands on his hips.

"How did they know about it?"

"Whole train operates like a small town, miss. Most even know about the Birchfields' treatment of your sister."

Rennie's face could surely light a match. How humiliating to learn that fellow passengers knew of the slashed offer.

"Mr. Holmstead is footing the expense for this entertainment. If he don't mind other folks coming in and listening..." He started forward. "I'll ask the host, quiet like."

The conductor moved with sure steps on the moving train. He leaned to whisper in the host's ear.

John glanced over but didn't miss a beat. He'd moved on to challenges in working on the newspaper. From the laughter, Rennie could tell his listeners were just as fascinated with that topic.

The conductor strode back to her. "He won't mind a few more joining in, so I'll go back and invite them in."

Because of the monotony of traveling? Or was John really that good a speaker?

"I'd return to your seat if I were you, miss. Someone might not know it's taken."

Good point. First, an icy-cold drink would hit the spot. Before she finished the first dipper, Livie and Veronica, carrying John's knapsack, were at her side.

"I'm tired of writing on my slate." Livie held it up, filled with sentences.

More like, the little girl was tired of sitting still. Rennie didn't blame her. "Let me get you some nice cold water." She gave her a full dipper.

"We've been sitting for an hour." An hour where Veronica had not only calmed down from the Birchfields' betrayal but also returned to her feisty self. "I've heard most of John's stories. I'd rather draw now."

"Me, too," Livie agreed.

"How would it look if we walked out? We're here to support John."

To leave, they would have to walk around him. It would not only be disruptive, but it might affect his confidence. Under normal circumstances, Rennie would send Livie and her sister back to entertain themselves. That was out of the question with the Birchfields still on the train. However, her support of John seemed more important after she'd hurt his feelings last evening.

Several people came in and surged past them. Three women occupied their empty seats, their husbands standing behind them.

Veronica replaced the empty dipper. "It's a sign we're supposed to leave now."

"Reckon it is." Nothing they could do, anyway, unless they wanted to create a stir. "Follow me."

They hurried forward and passed John while the audience laughed at a joke. Rennie met John's concerned gaze and pointed to Livie, as if the little girl had demanded to leave. Which she had, sort of, though it was mostly Veronica. He gave a slight nod and turned back to his audience like a natural. She was right proud of him.

They scurried through the car and back to their seats.

"Did we leave our valise like that?" Veronica pointed to the bag stuffed into a rack nearly tilted sideways.

Definitely not. A chill went down Rennie's spine.

~

*J*ohn ended his speech when the group began murmuring to one another. Mr. Holmstead joined him in front and congratulated him with a handshake.

Afterward, a few thanked him. Then his host took him aside. "Twenty is the amount I believe we agreed upon."

"Yes, sir." John had to work two weeks at the newspaper to earn so much. It was good for him to see, after what happened with the Birchfields, that most people stuck to their word.

"I'm very pleased with your performance." Mr. Holmstead took his purse from his coat pocket. "So are my guests. You're quite the storyteller." He extracted some bills. "I'm giving you an extra five dollars."

"Thank you, sir," John managed not to stammer. The

money was an answered prayer. And the speech was an answer His Creator gave that John never knew he needed. "This is my first speaking fee, and a generous one."

"I'll wager they'll be many opportunities, should you desire them." He clapped John on the back. "Enjoy the rest of your journey."

John headed back to his own car, his senses reeling. How could this experience be topped?

He found the girls going through their valise, their own dramatic story unfolding. Rennie explained the bag had obviously been moved while they were gone.

"Is anything missing?" John's thoughts flew to the Birchfields, looking for the sketch.

"Not that we can tell." Rennie clenched her fists. "Although Livie's things have been moved around."

Thinking that her sketch would be among them? John's conviction that the Birchfields had searched their bags grew. If so, they didn't have any intention of paying for the drawing.

"They didn't take my doll." Livie clutched it to her chest. "Or my mama's letters. I hope they didn't read them."

Rennie sat beside her, patting her shoulder. "I doubt they did." She looked at the valise he held. "Is anything missing from yours?"

He shook his head. The sketch was hidden in his knapsack, which the girls had carried with them to and from the speech.

"Good thing we'll be in San Francisco tomorrow." Rennie looked at Livie. "We're ready to be there, aren't we?"

Livie nodded, leaning against Rennie's arm.

"We're still in Nevada, so we have miles to go. When we wake up in the morning, we'll be in California." John settled back next to Veronica.

Rennie's face brightened.

"Shall I tell you my good news?" He'd only intended to tell Rennie, but they probably all needed a distraction.

"What is it?" Rennie raised her eyebrows. "I'm sorry we didn't stay the whole time."

"It's fine." Grinning, he told them how he came to have twenty-five dollars in his pocket.

Rennie's mouth formed an O. "John, that's wonderful."

"I'll buy supper for us tonight in the dining car."

Rennie frowned. "Is that too expensive?"

"No." Must she always be practical? "I want to celebrate with all of you because you shared this experience with me."

"If you're certain, then thank you. A leisurely meal on our last evening will be memorable. The conductor brought around the menus."

"Let's look." He gave her a coaxing smile.

She returned it.

Veronica handed out the pages. "I'm happy for you." She spoke quietly. "And thank you for buying us supper. I'm glad you came with us."

"Me too."

If the Birchfields were indeed the ones who'd searched their bags, they hadn't heard the last from them.

CHAPTER 20

*R*ennie enjoyed sitting opposite of John at the table for four and tried not to worry that supper was more expensive than breakfast. It had been challenging to calculate a way to eat for less than a dollar, but she and Livie managed it. The little girl didn't have a big appetite, and corn, mashed potatoes, a biscuit, blackberry jam, and milk were plenty for her. Rennie had the same except with coffee.

John ruined her frugal efforts by ordering antelope steak. When Veronica ordered beefsteak, Rennie didn't have the heart to protest after her sister's rough day.

She tried not to mind the whole extra dollar John spent by adding to their order a slice of blueberry pie for everyone.

It was pleasant to eat a leisurely meal amid the chatter of surrounding diners. Tables were set close together to squeeze in as many guests as possible. Rennie liked that aspect because she was accustomed to eating at a crowded table. When they had guests like John, George, and Cora, Mama simply added chairs, scooting so many together that arms knocked elbows in the cramped space. In the dining car, it was the backs of chairs that knocked against one another when diners stood to leave.

Despite this, dinner conversation was strained. Veronica searched the room every few minutes for the Birchfields. And though Rennie had shown her support for John's speech, residual tension remained between them. What were his specific plans beyond escorting them all to Mr. Sherman's care? He'd enjoyed some adventures, told his stories. Maybe the journey itself was enough to inspire multiple stories.

"How did your speech go after we left?" Rennie ate another bite of the delicious pie. It was hard to blame John for adding the dessert they all consumed with such pleasure.

"They laughed in all the right places. What did you think?"

"That it was a great experience for you. One you won't forget. Why don't you write down the stories you told in case you're asked to do it again? Although folks back home know you too well. Passengers on the train are ripe for entertainment to relieve the monotony."

"So that audience would have been happy with any entertainment." He returned his untouched fork to his plate. "Perhaps an opera singer or a banjo player would have been more welcome."

"That's not what I meant." Rennie tried to meet his eyes, but he didn't look up from his dessert. "I just meant they might not have asked you otherwise."

"True." The response came out clipped. "An audience must be bored to ask an unknown writer like me to tell my stories."

"I can't seem to say the right thing anymore. You're always looking for offense."

He looked at her, his customary smile missing. "I don't know what other meaning your words might have. You're right. They were bored. I relieved that boredom for a while."

"And made them laugh."

"No further discussion needed." Resting his elbows on the table, he pressed his fingertips together until they turned white. "Did everyone enjoy the meals?"

Livie nodded. "The best part was the mashed potatoes."

"My steak was tender and not too pink. Delicious." Veronica gave Rennie a warning look. "Thank you for treating us to supper."

He smiled at her. "My pleasure, everyone."

Rennie started to voice her thanks when a couple stopped by their table. They'd been guests at John's performance.

He stood and greeted them.

"We don't mean to interrupt your supper, Mr. Welch." The gray-haired man rested his hand on an ivory-handled cane. "We'll depart the train in Reno and simply couldn't let you go without expressing to you how entertaining we found your stories."

"I'm happy my simple stories relieved your monotony."

"Oh, it was far more than that, right, my dear?" He turned to his wife, and a pink silk rose on his wife's hat wiggled as she nodded. "You have a gift. You tell a story with a lovely blend of humor and compassion that I've seldom seen."

John seemed rendered speechless.

"Put those stories on paper, and you'll be published, my boy." The man held out his hand. "I'll be watching for your name in print."

"I scarcely know what to say." John shook his hand.

"After listening to you talk for two hours today, my guess is that rarely happens." He chuckled. "In any case, best of luck to you. I hope for an opportunity to hear you speak again. My wife and I are pleased to have been in your first audience." With a nod, they walked away.

"Well, I'll say." Rennie stared after them. "That answers our question. The audience listened not from boredom, but interest."

"*R*eckon so." John shied away from speaking any more about his speech. Why couldn't she see in him what that couple saw? What her friend Beth saw? She'd listened to him with the same fascination his audience had shown. It gave him hope that someday folks would want to read his books. "If you've all finished, why don't we watch the sun set from the platform?"

"Oh, boy." Livie bounced in her chair. "I want to. I'm tired of riding."

"We'll still be riding." He sympathized with her. He was almost as ready to get to their destination as she was...except he hadn't decided his next step. He'd prayed for guidance and was still waiting for it. "We must be very careful. You will stand in the middle of the railing where you can see best."

She smiled. "Then I'll draw it on my sketchpad later so Mama and Papa can see it too."

The simple sweetness of it touched his heart. "Excellent idea."

"I will too." Veronica got a faraway look in her eyes. "I'll give mine to George. I'm sure he misses me."

"I'm certain of it." Rennie stood. "Let's not forget our bags."

They were carrying all their possessions everywhere now. "I'll get them." John waited for the ladies to step away before retrieving the valises from under the table.

In a few minutes, they were standing on the platform with the wind blowing Livie's braids behind her.

"It will be a few minutes before the sun goes down." Veronica stared at the sky. "What is that mountain?"

"I believe that's Elko Mountain. Passengers not eating in the dining car ate at the Elko station." John didn't try to pull out his guidebook in this wind. A herd of cattle grazed in the valley. He searched but didn't see any cowboys on horseback.

"The ground looks almost red." Livie held onto the rail with Rennie's arm securing her.

"That's right. I believe the sunset creates that effect. There's green grass closer to us." Veronica studied it. "The sky is beautiful with those blue swirls, the breaks of white clouds. Almost like a painting with the mountains jutting up like that. A streak of rust too. Do you think I could paint this scene, Rennie?"

"Do you own paints?"

Ever practical Rennie. Couldn't she allow the girl to dream? Especially after the day's disappointment?

Veronica's shoulders drooped.

"Sketch it out this evening," John suggested. "Put the colors as you remember them in notes on the bottom. Like a footnote. Then recreate it in color when you return home."

Rennie looked at him with those eyes the color of the evening sky. This evening's sky. It took his breath away. Now he knew how to describe them.

This journey was ending tomorrow. Being with Rennie again daily after living in another city for two years had been a gift. How he'd miss her, even with her lack of faith in his abilities.

John turned back to study the sinking sun, unsettled. Not only by his own indecision about God's leading but also for the sisters' safety on their return journey.

Truth was, he didn't relish the idea of them traveling back without him after all that happened today. Eleanora had assured them Mr. Sherman would provide an escort for their journey home. John would have to meet the man. If he didn't approve, he'd accompany them. He couldn't allow anything to happen to them, not if it was within his power to prevent it.

∽

"*I* didn't mean that folks *only* listened to John out of boredom." Rennie spoke to her sister in a low voice. John sat in his new seat out of earshot, scribbling away in his journal as if oblivious to the growing darkness in the car.

Livie squinted at her book as they passed shadows of trees, buildings, and the occasional ranch.

"Sure sounded that way. How could you say such a thing? After all he's done for us." Veronica stuffed her sketchbook into her bag. "He was going to spend a week with his family—and you—before leaving. He quit his job early and altered his travel arrangements. Did you ever thank him for doing that?"

"Of course. But he's getting free train fare." And she'd helped him with expenses.

"Rennie, you beat all. Can't you see he's trying to figure out whether to chase his dreams? See if he's good enough to make a living as an author?"

"We need a reliable income."

Veronica had grown up in the same household Rennie had, a home where money didn't always stretch as far as it needed to. Rennie had gone without necessities time and again so her siblings could have what they needed. She didn't want to put her children through that.

"Then keep working after the wedding."

"John will make more as a reporter."

"Didn't you listen to him today? He's taken care of everyone for years."

"I know." Rennie folded her arms and stared out the window.

"Right. And you were mad when he stayed near Cora to watch over her while she was away at school."

"I didn't know you knew that."

She rolled her eyes. "*Everyone* knew it. Especially your beau.

Mama finally had to tell you to stop nagging at him or you'd lose him."

That reminder stung. "I did stop."

"You're *still* nagging him. What if someone comes along who's interested in books and writing? John's writing?"

Rennie went still. Beth had talked with John about books and authors. More than once, she'd given him a look...

"John didn't pay any attention to Beth until she asked about his writing." Veronica's cheeks reddened.

"What are you saying?" Did her sister imply that John was *interested* in her friend?

"Only that you've wounded his pride. John doesn't want to court Beth. But what if a pretty, unattached woman shows interest in his stories, maybe more than you show?"

Rennie covered her mouth with shaking hands. Was it possible he'd find someone else who'd follow his dreams with him?

"Don't look like that. He loves you, for crying out loud. And cares about your opinion. Can't you give him a chance to figure out his life's work in his own way? Let him come to you when he's ready."

Rennie was accustomed to telling John everything. Did Veronica know she asked the near impossible?

Livie closed her book. "You hurt his feelings."

Even the little girl knew Rennie was too blunt. "I'll apologize."

"You should just say 'thank you' because he keeps planning surprises to make you happy." Livie gave her a look filled with reproach. "But you don't stay happy. You just start worrying about something else."

The truth smote her.

"Good advice, Rennie." Veronica's tone was quiet, almost a whisper.

Her throat tightened. Livie was right. How was she to fix the muddle she'd made of everything?

CHAPTER 21

*J*ohn lay on his new berth. Though it was the most comfortable one by far on this journey, he couldn't sleep. It wasn't the snores from the gentleman opposite that kept him awake either.

The bad feeling that began when they'd left Ogden intensified. He prayed it didn't have something to do with the wedge between himself and Rennie.

It had been an emotional day. Who was he kidding? The whole journey had been a whirlwind of emotions. He was usually the steady one in the crowd. Tonight, his heart was in turmoil.

Today's speech was better than he'd have imagined in his wildest dreams. Rennie's encouragement had fired his imagination, helped him put new twists on old stories. She'd inspired him to believe he could tell his stories—and someone would care.

And then she'd started poking holes in his confidence, which was paper thin already, instead of celebrating the victory with him. The unexpected boon of making money at something he felt passionately about should have been cause for celebration, for Rennie craved the security it brought.

He turned over on his side and watched the night sky. No rain but a bit of haze blocked half the stars. The long blast of the whistle preceded a stop at a station. He twisted on his berth to peer outside. A water stop. They'd be here a few minutes.

Dim light from a few lanterns hung about the small depot, providing scanty light inside his curtained cocoon. He reached for his writing pad and jotted a few changes to the stories he'd told today. He quite liked some of them better than his original versions.

More whistle blasts and then they left the light behind. Sighing, he stowed away his writing supplies in the darkness.

If he returned with the girls to Ohio, he feared he'd never step foot in the West again.

Back in Ohio, his greatest ambition would be to become a first-rate reporter. Unfortunately, he'd practiced that type of writing when Ben was working hard to make it as a reporter. It had seemed a logical next step for John. He'd liked the act of putting a news story on paper. But reporting required a different type of writing.

And it didn't satisfy the need to share *stories* that nestled deep in his soul.

The kind encouragement he'd received at supper from the couple old enough to be his grandparents went into his journal, word for word. He recalled every nuance, every expression as the man from Reno had spoken his praise.

Beth Carlson and her father had also bolstered his confidence. If only Rennie saw his passion for writing as a strength, as others did.

John loved her. Wanted to spend the rest of his life as her husband. But did that mean he must give up his writing dreams?

At nearly twenty-one, a man ought to know what he wanted

to do with his life. Could he ever be satisfied unless he at least tried to write a book and publish it? Did some part of him believe that he needed to be away from Rennie for a few months in order to write that book without her nagging him to get a steady job?

Yes, that had entered into his decision to travel, but the greatest part had been a desire to add adventure to his writings. Meet cowboys and prospectors and small-town sheriffs. Speak with miners and ranchers and sheep herders. Dip his feet into the Pacific Ocean. Explore Yellowstone National Park. Hike a trail on the Rockies. Spend a day in a gold rush town. Step inside a silver mine such as the one Mark Twain had owned. And he'd already seen a herd of buffalo on the prairie before they were all killed off.

All that and so much more he longed to see so he could put it in his writings in an authentic manner before marriage, children, and that stable job she'd insist upon tied him to Hamilton until he died.

Rennie didn't understand that part of him—his creative side—would die first if he wasn't able to express himself on paper.

He felt as if he'd been born to write. To say it was his destiny, even in the privacy of his thoughts, seemed presumptuous, but he didn't believe any other career would fulfill him.

He turned toward the darkness of the curtain veil and prayed once more that God would either help Rennie understand his desire to write or remove it from his soul.

He must give it all over to the Lord. John prayed for guidance and strength if he wasn't meant to marry Rennie, after all.

A cruel fate, indeed, to choose between his two greatest earthly loves.

∾

*R*ennie woke up from a bad dream where John needed help and she couldn't reach him. At first, she didn't know where she was. A blast from the train's whistle as it pulled into a station shook the last of her dream away and reminded her vividly that she was somewhere in western Nevada.

John slept down the aisle. What would tomorrow bring? Where did she fit into his plans? Did what she wanted matter?

Veronica's advice that evening had made sense. John *had* watched over his twin for years and only relinquished responsibility when he knew Cora was going to marry Ben. Maybe John would have preferred to take this trip on his own so he wouldn't have anyone else to watch over.

Didn't he deserve the freedom to pursue his writing dreams?

Of course, he did. Just because Rennie had no big career dreams didn't mean he shouldn't. Sharing stories was in his blood. Why, the first time they'd met, he'd spun a yarn about a robbery on his train ride from Bradford Junction to Hamilton. She'd accused him of telling a mighty tall tale. His reply that some of it was true and the way he left her to reason out which parts had intrigued her. Somehow she knew, though only a child, she'd met her future husband.

She was the only girl he'd ever courted. She never seriously considered another boy, though she had gone to a Valentine's dance with Horace Bosworth. She'd asked John to come home and escort her to it. His refusal had frustrated her so that she'd agreed to go with Horace. John couldn't have come home if he'd wanted to. It was the fact that he didn't want to escort her to the romantic dance that had put her dander up.

She'd had a miserable time. Things were strained between her and John for the next couple of months until she finally convinced him she didn't have feelings for Horace. That she loved John.

He'd never mentioned it again. Did he hold it against her?

With another long blast, the train left the station.

A sigh came from her very soul. It wasn't Horace who'd caused this current wedge between them. It was her nagging for John to put his writing dreams on the shelf. It wasn't fair for her to ask him to be less than who he was. Essentially, she'd been doing that for months. Was that the reason he hadn't proposed yet?

Her heart sank at the possibility. She'd treated his dreams as unimportant. She'd been selfish to ask that he stay with a job that didn't fulfill him.

At their next private moment, she must apologize for her selfishness and tell him she supported his dreams, his aspirations. Even if it meant saying goodbye for a time.

She'd not force him to choose between following his dreams and marrying her.

~

Tossing and turning, John was still agonizing over his decision when they pulled into a town. Based on the lights outside the train, this was a larger town than most they'd traveled through. He leaned the face of his pocketwatch to the dim lantern light outside the station. Five minutes past one o'clock. He yawned. No wonder he was tired.

Some passengers alighted, among them the older couple who had been so gracious to him at supper. This must be Reno. They were getting close to California, a state he'd longed to visit since learning about the first gold rush there. He'd see it with his own eyes. Write about it even if no one ever read his descriptions.

His attention returned to the scanty train crew and a

handful of passengers on the platform. One woman tugged her shawl farther up onto her shoulders in the night air. A gentleman frowned at his pocket watch. Were they a bit behind schedule? Maybe it just seemed as though they'd lingered over stops because he hadn't fallen asleep yet.

They finally got moving. John took one last look at the couple before darkness again enveloped the train. His arm was around his wife, who huddled against him as if chilled. They'd never realize the perfect timing of their praise and how much it had meant to him.

What would Cora, his parents, Peter, or Emma have said if they'd heard his speech? Mama Rosie would have noticed the way most of the audience leaned forward as if fearing they'd miss a word. Pa would have noticed the changes to his stories, even the subtle ones.

Cora had held reservations about him going on this trip simply because they'd never been so far apart. His oldest brother, Peter, had hated that school starting back up again in a few weeks prevented him from tagging along. Emma would simply miss her big brother. He could do no wrong in his youngest sibling's eyes.

A whistle blasted. They were slowing down again. So soon? John had barely been aware of minutes passing. This must be the next station. He fished his ticket from his knapsack and checked for the station's name—Verdi, only two hundred thirty-four miles from San Francisco.

As good as that mileage sounded, an uneasy feeling stirred in the pit of his stomach. Something was wrong. If the train needed water or coal, surely the crew would have filled up during the long stop in Reno.

Taking on new passengers? He craned his neck. The conductor strode across an empty platform toward the front of the locomotive. Good thing that Rennie and the girls slept on the side away from the depot's lights.

Ah, there were several crates for the baggage car. Simply a short freight stop, then. But the bad feeling lingered as the crew loaded the crates into the car behind the express car. Were there many gold bars and silver coins or lots of cash in the safes?

Haze covered the moon, giving the area surrounding the depot an eerie feel.

His imagination, always strong, galloped at a frenzied pace, and he kept his focus on the crew, vulnerable because their attention was on their task. Did someone lurk among the trees, ready to pounce?

John stared at the building. Wait. Was there movement in the depot's shadow?

The conductor waved his lantern to signal the engineer it was safe to depart. Then he mounted the steep steps to the local passenger coach beside the mail and baggage car.

Three masked men ran from the shadows. Lantern light glinted on the revolvers in their belts. Two mounted a baggage car. The other ran forward, perhaps to the box express car or the actual locomotive.

Heart racing, John tugged on his boots. If they were simply vagabonds, why were they masked? He must warn the conductor. All the trainmen were armed.

No time to waste. He reached for the curtain and then paused.

Were those footsteps? Were the vagabonds inside their palace car?

Rennie and the girls would probably be asleep, unaware of the potential danger. He jerked the curtain open.

Dim light from the aisle chandeliers showed movement. The rug muffled quick footsteps. How could the men have possibly made it to their car in a matter of seconds?

Wait. The shadowy figure wore a dress. Was she simply visiting the ladies' convenience?

No. She halted in front of a long privacy curtain.

Something was wrong. John's heart hammered in his chest as the strange woman pushed aside the curtain to Rennie's berth.

"What are you doing?"

Rennie's outraged question spurred his steps, for a woman bent over her berth and was rummaging through her valise.

CHAPTER 22

*R*ennie, alone in her berth wide enough for two, had just drifted off to sleep only to wake to someone trying to steal her bag. She gave the woman a hard shove that knocked her off balance.

"Why, you—"

"Mrs. Birchfield?" Rennie's stockinged feet struck the rug. The woman wore a black riding dress and hat that shadowed her face. Gone were the fancy white gloves. "You aren't supposed to be in here."

John, his curls tussled but fully alert, rushed to her aid and rounded on the woman. "What's happening? Why are you here?"

The train squeaked to a stop.

"You'll know soon enough." Mrs. Birchfield grinned. "Now give me my sketch."

Truly? The woman came to steal a drawing in the middle of the night? Rennie stepped into the aisle to confront her. "It's not yours. You never paid for it." The nerve of the woman.

Heads poked from behind curtains, Veronica's and Livie's among them.

"I never intended to pay for it." She put her hands on her hips. "Just offered enough so that blamed girl would do her best work."

Shouts from the front of the train where the engine was drew John's attention.

Rennie wasn't about to look away from the conniving woman. "You can't have the drawing if you don't pay for it, Mrs. Birchfield."

"That ain't my name." She took a pistol from her pocket and aimed it at Rennie. "Now give it to me."

Heart thudding, Rennie stared at the weapon. Someone liked Veronica's artwork enough to *shoot* her for it?

"She doesn't have it." Stepping in front of Rennie, John raised his hands.

The woman leveled the weapon at John's chest.

No!

It felt as if some big hand squeezed the air from Rennie's lungs, making her dizzy.

"I have it." John's voice was amazingly calm for a man with a loaded pistol barrel three feet from his heart.

"Then get it." Her expression turned steely.

A whistle blew. A warning? Regardless, that woman better aim the weapon away from Rennie's man, or she'd be sorry.

Hands still raised, John jerked his head as if listening to the shouts outside the car. The sound of wheels rolling on the track ahead of them vibrated the car but, strangely, their palace car didn't move.

The door burst open. "Belle, come on. We're going to have to run for it. They took off without us." Her husband came in carrying a valise that flopped against his leg. "I ain't losing my share."

What was happening? Rennie craned her neck to look outside. All she saw was swirling smoke from the engine.

"I want my sketch," Mrs. Birchfield—actually, Belle—said.

Her mulish expression detracted from her looks, making her appear ten years older than Rennie had first thought.

"Then get it and let's go."

Her mouth tightened in a thin line. "You." The pistol waved back and forth at John's chest. "Get what I want. Now."

"It's over there." John pointed and backed toward his berth. "I'll fetch it."

Belle swung her weapon back to Rennie, who no longer cared what happened to the sketch as long as the woman didn't hurt John.

"Hurry, Belle." The man calling himself Birchfield peered out the door he'd left open. Running footsteps approached. "Get out of there. Now!" There was a thud as he jumped to the ground.

Belle shot a glance at John, who was digging into his knapsack. "You ain't seen the last of us." She raced after her husband.

Livie burst into tears. Now that no weapons waved in anyone's direction, other guests rushed forward.

"Are you hurt?" a man asked.

"Why, you were so brave," a woman murmured in awed tones. "Are you all right?"

More shouts and running outside the car. "The engine's gone. Where'd they take it?"

"Don't know."

"Bandits stole it!"

Bandits? Belle and her husband had been involved. Rennie's heart nearly burst, it was beating so rapidly. She reached up for the weeping Livie and sat with her on the lower berth. "There, there. No one hurt us. No one took anything." She met John's reassuring gaze. Their hero.

Veronica climbed down and sat beside them as shouts and wails from other passengers erupted the palace car into pandemonium.

"They won't come back, will they?" Livie cowered against Rennie. "The lady said she would."

"She won't." John crouched beside the bed and tucked her hair behind her ear, then grazed Rennie's cheek with his lips. "I'll see what's happening." He stood and strode away.

"I want my mama." Livie buried her wet face against Rennie's shoulder.

Patting her back, Rennie drew in her feet as several men strode past as if on a mission to learn what happened.

"I saw three men mount the train at our freight stop." Standing at the door, John called out to those on the ground.

"Come down here, sonny, and tell us what you know."

Rennie began to shake from the inside out.

Veronica left and came back with a dipper of water she offered to Livie and then Rennie. "I didn't want anyone to die for that sketch."

"No." Her shaking worsened to think how long that gun had been pointed at John's chest.

~

*J*ohn stepped into the cold darkness where some of the crew and passengers stood peering at the place where the missing engine should be and told the conductor everything he'd witnessed at the depot, as well as the threats from Belle or whatever the pistol-toting woman's name was.

They'd left the desert behind and were now in the mountains. Thousands of stars in the partially cloudy sky lent sufficient light to see the other men's faces, some scared, some excited.

"The bandits likely had horses hidden nearby, maybe in the trees, mining tunnel, or the rock quarry," the conductor told them. "The Sierra Nevada Mountains give them varmints plenty of places to hide."

A crewmember in his twenties stepped forward. "I'm going on ahead and see if I can't find our locomotive, engineer, and fireman."

"Got your revolver on you?" The conductor raised his brows.

"Always."

"Good." He turned to another man. "Henry, you and Zeke go with him."

"Sure thing."

All three men followed the tracks at a brisk pace. Hopefully, they'd apprehend all the culprits, especially the woman who'd pointed a gun at Rennie. Now the danger had passed, a shudder went through him at the thought of what might have happened.

One of the trainmen spoke up. "Me and Rufus will run back to Verdi and sound the alarm."

"Good idea, Cal." The conductor looked at John. "I'd appreciate you going along to give a description of everything. 'Course, it doesn't help none that the men you saw at the depot were masked. But you recalled the color of their coats and boots and such. I saw them get on the train but thought they were vagabonds. I hurried to the baggage car to either sell them tickets or kick them off. Didn't get a chance to say nothing or even pull my gun because two of 'em already had guns pulled on me. Told me to get back in the coach and stay there."

"Reckon it was good you listened." Cal gave a low whistle. "We'll tell them at Verdi."

The men took off running down the tracks the way they'd come.

"Please, tell Miss Hill where I went." His going would worry her, but he'd little choice in the matter.

"Sure will, son." The wiry conductor his pa's age clapped

him on the shoulder. "The rest of you, get inside and try to calm the passengers."

John ran after Cal and Rufus, following the train tracks through the valley. He quickly caught up with the men, who were both maybe a decade his senior, and then fell into a rhythm behind them.

Boy, it felt good to run, to exercise his muscles after being cooped up over a week. Pretty here with scant moonlight on a mountain peak ahead, casting silver shadows on the pines and shrubs on the mountainside. If he recalled, this was Crystal Peak. He was sorry for the mission that took him here but not sorry for the chance to see it.

John was starting to feel winded when he saw buildings up ahead.

"There's the depot," Cal wheezed. "All dark now."

"We'll have to wake up the stationmaster." John halted in front of the building.

"Abe, there's been a robbery." Rufus pounded on the door.

John didn't know the shorter man could shout so loudly. That ought to bring Abe and whatever law was in town.

The door banged open. "A robbery? What are you fools talking about?" The barefoot man had taken time to pull trousers up over his underclothes, John was relieved to see.

Cal quickly explained what they knew. "This passenger saw three fellers get on the train from this station."

"No." The bearded station master gave an unbelieving scoff. "You sure? From Verdi?"

John nodded. "The conductor saw them too."

"Describe 'em."

John described the clothing, hats, and coats of one tall man and two of average height.

"Ain't seen 'em." He scratched his head. "Reckon we'd best wake up the marshal."

"We should," John agreed. The man still acted as if he were

half asleep. Either that, or he was so discombobulated by the event that he didn't know what to do. "And alert the stations on either side that there are cars stranded on the tracks with no engine attached." Approaching trains were the greatest danger, in his opinion.

Within twenty minutes, John was giving his descriptions to the marshal, who'd brought a crowd of men to help.

"Much obliged." Marshal Jones folded the paper and stuffed it along with a pencil into the pocket of his red wool shirt. He scanned the faces of the group of deputies and rail-road men. "Let's get to the train and see what else we can find out." He mounted a horse. Nine other men followed suit. "We'll meet those of you on foot back at the train."

Dirt clods flew as they trotted away.

"Shame we're not a telegraph station." Abe yawned. "My boy's riding out to Reno to send a telegram. Sheriff'll no doubt be doing the same. Wish I could join the posse."

"You done what you could. You gotta run the station. Them fellers will be caught quicker than a cat can lick its ear." Cal clapped him on the back. "Let's get back. I'm ready to run again."

John was too. How were Veronica, Livie, and Rennie handling all this?

⁓

"*M*arshal Jones is outside." The conductor tapped Rennie on the shoulder. "He wants your version of what happened. He already heard your beau's side."

That ought to be enough. John was the one who excelled at describing things. If only he were here, for he never failed to calm her agitation. After trying to soothe a frightened child for an hour, she was anything but ready to talk to a lawman.

"Will you stay with her?" Rennie asked her sister as she

touched Livie's damp cheeks. The poor girl had worn herself out weeping from fright and calling for her mother.

"I'll stay. Good that she's able to sleep with all the ruckus going on outside." Veronica looked up at her. "You were brave tonight. You and I could have fought her down if she hadn't started swinging that gun at you and John."

"No doubt." Rennie forced a smile and then followed the conductor outside.

The train crew scurried all around. Men wearing wool shirts and suspenders stood near horses tethered to low-hanging branches. Other passengers milled about, telling what they saw to anyone who'd listen and unashamedly listening to reports as they came in.

Rennie picked her way over to where the marshal was giving directions to his posse. Some sat on horseback while others gathered close to hear every word in the melee.

The whole crazy scene took place in the middle of the night when they all should have been sleeping. Everything took on a dreamlike quality for Rennie.

The conductor indicated her with a nod. "This is Miss Rennie Hill, marshal. The one that woman threatened with a pistol."

"Miss Hill, I sure am sorry about what you went through tonight." He introduced himself and seemed to make an effort to speak in a calm manner. "I've got about a minute for you to tell me what happened. Don't leave anything out."

Rennie told him everything that happened from the time she caught Belle riffling through her possessions, looking for the drawing, to when the woman threatened them and then bolted off the train.

Breathing hard, John wove his way through the crowd and clasped her hand.

"You say we've got a drawing of one of the bandits? Maybe

two of them?" He rubbed his jaw. "Fetch me the picture. Won't hurt none to have it."

"I'll get it." John gave her hand a reassuring squeeze and sprinted away.

Feeling in the way, Rennie took several steps back as a deputy hurried forward. "The engineer and fireman have returned. They saw three men dividing a pile of gold coins. The robbers put the money in sacks and dragged them toward the quarry. The express messenger stayed with the car to guard what was left and calculate what was missing."

"Someone get the sketch from this woman. Then follow us on horseback as quick as you can." At the marshal's direction, the posse followed him to their horses. The crowd moved back so they could ride away.

The bandits had stolen so many gold coins that they must drag them? Rennie's heart raced in a mixture of excitement and fear. She felt safe, especially now that John was here. So why was she shaking?

A stranger, hat pulled low over his eyes, stood a respectful distance from Rennie. He'd lingered near the posse, so he must be waiting for the drawing.

John ran up with the sketch. "Where's the marshal?"

"Gone. I'll take that." The man's voice was more of a growl. He snatched it from John's hands and then ran to his horse and rode after the posse.

A niggling of something not quite right disturbed Rennie. Was it because the man's abruptness had bordered on rudeness?

Suddenly, a kaleidoscope of emotions swept over her... terror at seeing John's life threatened as well as her own, shock that the couple who commissioned Veronica's drawing ended up being far more embroiled in crime than she'd ever dreamed, sorrow for her sister's sake that her sketch was gone, relief that the danger had passed, and remorse that Livie had been terrified by it all. Her legs shook as if they could no longer hold her upright.

"Rennie?" John touched her shoulder.

She turned at the beloved voice, saw the compassion and concern in his eyes, and melted in his arms.

"You're safe now." He held her good and tight. "The girls are safe."

"When Belle turned that gun on you..." She tightened her hold around his waist. If something had happened to him...

"I felt the same way when she pointed it at you." He rubbed her back.

"You stepped in front of me. To take the bullet if she fired it." Her voice was muffled against his chest. She was where she belonged. She never wanted to leave.

"I'd die for you. You must know that." His fingers splayed against her hair as she nestled closer.

Rennie reveled in the security of his arms. Protected. Loved.

"Ahem." A throat cleared. "Miss Hill. Mr. Welch. You have an audience."

Rennie peered around. Men stared at them. Women passengers spoke to one another behind gloved hands.

Cheeks flaming, she stepped away from John's slackening arms.

The conductor gave her a fatherly look. "Get her out of the night air, son. That young'un probably needs her, anyway." He tipped his hat at them and hurried away into the crowd.

"Let's get you back to Veronica and Livie." He pushed his hat low over his eyes.

"I think that's best." Embarrassed that she'd so forgotten herself in front of all these people, she kept her gaze on the pebbly ground mingled with tufts of grass in front of her.

Still, she couldn't regret the most comforting hug she'd received in her life.

CHAPTER 23

$\mathcal{T}$he terror in Veronica's and Livie's eyes convinced John that Rennie needed to stay close to them. Livie had watched her two protectors be threatened with a gun while far from the protection of her parents. It was the stuff nightmares were made of.

Plucky Veronica, though not crying like Livie, was little better off. The posse's noisy exit on a dozen horses had awakened the child. The strain of trying to soothe her, not knowing what caused the chaos outside, had surely sapped Veronica's energy.

A few folks gathered in the aisles here and there to talk, but most were still outside in the cold night air listening for the latest report. Where John longed to be, since the girls were safe. However, his presence seemed to soothe the girls, and he wasn't sorry for that.

"Are the bad men gone, Miss Rennie?" Livie asked.

"They ran away. The marshal took a posse to go find all of them." Rennie took the child from her sister and cradled her in her arms.

"Will you stay with us?" She clutched Rennie's arm in a tight grip, still holding Veronica with the other.

"I'm not leaving again." Rennie rocked her back and forth.

John had a sudden vision of Rennie rocking their children someday in the future. The rightness of that dream washed him with certainty. He was meant to marry her, but what about his dreams?

"Mrs. Birchfield didn't hurt you, did she?" Veronica, sitting on Livie's other side, studied her sister's face.

"Just made me mad."

That was not her only emotion. Rennie had been rattled by that gun. The feel of her shaking arms around his waist, her shuddering breath, was something he'd never forget. Those bandits had stolen a lot more than money.

"Where's my sketch?" Veronica asked.

John gulped. He had hoped to tell her in the morning, after everyone had a chance to calm themselves.

"The marshal wanted it," said Rennie with her customary bluntness. "Said it might help the posse to find them."

Veronica straightened. "So my drawing might help bring criminals to justice?"

"We can only hope." John stepped aside as several folks wound past him and stopped at their berths.

"Won't Mama and Papa be impressed?" She gave her head a little shake. "George won't know what to think, will he?"

"He'll be proud." Rennie patted her shoulder. "Just like me."

Tears filled Veronica's eyes but didn't spill over. "I never heard you say that before."

"Don't reckon I have." Rennie sighed. "Doesn't make it any less true."

Veronica's mouth tilted upward.

"It seems quieter outside. Most folks must be inside. How about some water?"

"I'm thirsty." Livie yawned.

John brought them each a dipper of water.

"Folks, your attention, please." The conductor stepped to the middle of the palace car.

Conversations in the aisles halted. Every head turned toward the conductor.

"Not much more we can do here to help the marshal. The engineer is bringing the locomotive back for us as I speak."

A few cheers greeted the news.

"The stations on either side sent warnings for other trains on the track. Closest one waits on a side track for us to pass. We're about ten miles from California. After another five miles beyond the state line, we'll stop at Boca. It's a telegraph station. We'll pause long enough for passengers to send word to loved ones about the delay."

They'd need to inform Livie's parents as well as their own. John glanced at his pocket watch, chagrined to discover it was half past four.

"In the meantime, I suggest you get whatever sleep you can. We'll try to make up some time, but we'll be in the heart of the Sierras before long."

John heard what he didn't say. It was dangerous to traverse the mountains at high speeds.

"Get some rest, folks." The conductor strode from the car.

No one dared grumble after all they'd endured.

John watched the other passengers return to their stations before turning to Rennie. "You all try to sleep. I'll send telegrams to the Shermans and my parents, who will get the message to your folks."

The sound of a locomotive approaching cheered him. They'd soon be on their way.

"Thank you."

Veronica climbed to the top berth.

"I want to sleep with you." Livie clung to Rennie.

"Of course." She gave her a reassuring smile and then

looked up at John. "Get as much sleep as you can after sending the telegrams."

"Say your prayers." John bent to give Livie a brotherly hug.

"I already did. Last night."

"Never hurts to say more prayers." He smoothed back her hair.

"Will you say them, Mr. John?"

The car lurched as the locomotive connected to it.

"Of course." He got down on his knees in the quiet car. The train started moving. Rennie tucked her hand inside his as he closed his eyes. His prayer for safe travels, the train crew, the marshal and his posse, and the loved ones who worried for them back home finally wound down. Then he thanked God for keeping everyone safe. No one had been harmed. He ended the prayer to find that Rennie's eyes shone with tears.

"My man of words." She squeezed his hand and then released him. "Sweet dreams."

"Sweet dreams."

He waited until she closed the curtain before turning toward his own station.

"Amen."

He met the gaze of an older gentleman who gave him a nod and then ducked back into his berth.

Shaking his head, John climbed into the privacy of his own berth and closed the curtain.

But adrenaline still flowed through his veins. He was a mass of jitters. At first light, he'd be scribbling every detail he remembered into his journal.

His premonition was gone, so the bad feeling that had nudged into his waking hours was the train robbery. Possibly something stirred his senses when the Birchfields got on the train. He had never understood where the premonitions came from, but he'd learned to tread cautiously when he experienced them.

As the conductor had warned, the train picked up speed. John had grown accustomed to the rattle and motion of the engine at its normal tempo.

The locomotive jarred over rough places in the track. It swayed from side to side more than usual. Folks suffering from train illness might soon be visiting the convenience. Thankfully, John didn't become nauseous like his ma did. Although Livie might have some trouble. The little girl should eat soon after rising.

Memories of that revolver pointed at Rennie played over and over in his head. Pressing his forehead, he thanked God fervently for protecting her and, indeed, all of them.

~

*M*ovement in the palace car woke Rennie. She'd been so exhausted, so emotionally drained that she'd fallen asleep as soon as John left them.

Full sunlight streamed in the window, causing her to wonder at the time. The porter must have allowed passengers to sleep late due to the tumultuous night.

"Miss Rennie, I don't feel good." Livie rubbed her stomach.

The train did seem to be rocking more than normal. "Let me find my food basket." Two crackers. Nothing else. "Want a cracker?"

"Do I have to eat?"

"It might help. You get sick on trains when your stomach is empty." She gave her a cracker.

"You all ready for the washroom?" Veronica leaned over her berth.

"In a minute." Rennie smoothed back Livie's hair, allowing her to rest against her while she ate. "Her stomach bothers her."

"She needs breakfast. The quicker we wash and change, the

faster we can get to the dining car." She opened the curtain a few inches and then joined them on the bottom. "I see the porter down the aisle. He'll be here any moment to take up the beds."

"Another minute." Rennie gave Livie the last cracker. "Does that help?"

"Maybe." The child's cheeks were flushed.

"Fresh air might help her." Her sister stood in her crumpled dress in her stockinged feet. "Ready to open the curtains?"

"All right."

Veronica stepped into the aisle.

"Good morning, sleepy heads." John grinned at them. "You're the last ones to rise. Even the line for ladies' washing room is gone."

"What time is it?" Rennie stood.

"After eight o'clock. We'll be in Sacramento soon. The conductor left the bills of fare." He held them up. "The eating station at Sacramento charges only seventy-five cents."

"We'll eat there." That saved John fifteen cents on the cheapest meal in the dining car. "Livie's not feeling well."

Did Livie's traumatic night factor into her illness? Or were they dealing with an illness that could create another serious threat?

CHAPTER 24

*I*f John weren't so concerned about Livie, he'd enjoy his first steps in California's capital city. About four miles back, he'd been sorry to see that the American River more resembled a swamp than a watercourse worthy of such a name. The train had crossed a long, high bridge. On the other side, there were beautiful vineyards. The Chinese gardens he'd read about showed vibrantly green and productive.

The impressive state capitol building had been modeled after the one in Washington. John had read about the three-story domed building so often in the guidebook that he nearly had its description memorized. The main section was three hundred twenty feet long and reached eighty feet high with a tall dome adding well over a hundred feet to its impressive height. The first story was constructed of granite like the steps leading to it, while the other two were made of brick.

He'd studied the view as they passed so he could write of it. How he wished there would be time to explore this city. He'd intended to stop here two days.

His glance fell on Rennie, who had her arm around Livie to guide her into the clean eating station. He whispered a prayer that food, along with a twenty-five-minute break, would restore her health. No one wanted the little girl to feel poorly when she first saw her ailing mother.

Nothing would do her more good than seeing her parents.

Nothing would do John more good than a long, uninterrupted talk with Rennie. After last night's scare, the doubts that'd crept into his heart during the trip had been swept away. He wanted her to become his wife.

What he didn't know was if his other dream would ever hold a place in his life. *God, I have to trust You with this one. Show me the way to pursue writing as my life's work if it's Your will. And if it is Your will, I'm asking You to show it to Rennie.*

~

"*E*at your poached egg." Fried potatoes and ham weren't the best choices for a queasy stomach. Rennie fretted over the little girl's appetite. A serving of applesauce wasn't enough to keep her nausea at bay.

"I don't want it." She leaned against John's shoulder. "I'm sleepy."

"All right." Rennie pushed back from the table. "Sip your water. I'll go see what's available at the lunch counter." She took her food basket and the three dollars John had given her. She intended to make the cash stretch as far as possible.

There were two men ahead of her. She tapped her foot.

Finally, the motherly-looking serving woman gave her a harassed look. "May I help you, miss?"

"What kind of sandwiches are already prepared?"

"Roasted beef, fried ham, and toasted cheese." The woman brushed wisps of curly brown hair off her forehead. "We also have biscuits and plum jelly, crackers with cheese, and tea or coffee."

What would appeal most to Livie's appetite? "I'll take a

toasted cheese sandwich, two biscuits, and four crackers. Oh, and slices of cheese."

"Surprised you can eat so much."

"It's for a child who's suffering stomach complaints."

"Oh, then you'll want ginger snaps."

"Two-minute warning, folks." The conductor stood at the door. His voice projected over the chatter.

"Yes." Rennie didn't see them on the counter but was grateful just the same. She wrapped the food in linens from her basket and paid the woman. Almost two dollars remained in her reticule, and they were nearly at their destination. Mr. Sherman would surely take care of their expenses until their return journey, wouldn't he?

John, carrying Livie, met her halfway to the table with Veronica at his side. "She's fast asleep. Let's hope she ate enough to keep her from getting sick."

"I've got more." Rennie patted the bulging napkins. "I'll feed her as soon as she awakens."

∾

*T*wo hours later, Livie was still asleep. They rode in the day coach section that didn't have sleeping berths on this new train, their last one of the journey. Excited chatter raised the volume of conversation above what they'd grown accustomed to in the quiet palace car.

"Do you think we should wake her up and feed her?" Rennie peered at the sleeping child.

"Sleep is good medicine." John looked up from his journal. "At least, that's what Mama Rosie says."

Veronica, sketchpad and pencil in hand, ignored them.

Rennie sighed. "I don't want her to be sick when her father sees her. How much longer?"

John checked his pocket watch. "We'll be in Oakland in ninety minutes. Then we'll take a ferry ride."

Rennie wrung her hands. "You did mention in the telegram that we'd been delayed?"

"I did." John closed his journal.

"You already told me that, didn't you?" She gave him a sheepish smile.

"Four times." He sandwiched her hand between his. "What's worrying you?"

"I don't know Mr. Sherman. First, the train is robbed and then Livie arrives sick. What will he think of me?"

"Miss Rennie..." Livie's eyes opened, and her face paled.

John straightened. "Get her to the washroom."

Rennie half walked, half carried the child down the aisle. A passing man practically sat on someone's lap—a woman who screamed—to get out of their way.

It was no use. Livie cast up her accounts at the threshold of the washing room.

Veronica brought their bags and washed the stains from Livie's dress.

The porter cleaned the aisle floor while Rennie gave Livie a sponge bath and then changed her into the crumpled dress she'd worn the day before. The rest of her clean clothes were packed in trunks in the baggage car.

"I wanted to look pretty for Mama and Papa." Tears welled in the little girl's eyes.

"You will never be anything but beautiful in their eyes." Rennie rinsed her washcloth at the basin and wiped the tears away.

"This dress is dirty. Can't I have a pink one from my trunk?"

"I'm sorry." If only that wasn't against the rules. "I shook out as many of the wrinkles as I could."

"I washed the stains from her dress. Let's stand with it on

the landing." Veronica touched the largest wet spot not much larger than her hand. "I'll bet it will dry in the wind and sun."

It might work. Rennie met Livie's hopeful gaze. "Want to try it?"

She nodded. "I like standing outside. My stomach is happier out there."

That decided Rennie. "Let's go see if Mr. John wants to come with us."

Back at the seats, John gave the little girl a pleased smile. "You look like you feel better."

"My dress is wrinkled and dirty." She tugged on his hand. "Want to come outside with us?"

Rennie explained their plan.

"I'll come with you." John stood. "We'll be in Oakland in an hour."

~

A half hour later, John followed the girls inside and found the conductor waiting for him. "A word with you, Mr. Welch. We can talk out here."

"Of course." Probably more questions about the robbery. John told Rennie he'd stay outside a few minutes and then closed the door behind him. He joined the red-haired man leaning with one elbow on the rail. "What's on your mind?"

"Tell me about the sketch the marshal wanted." His eyes were watchful.

John explained everything again.

"The marshal wired that he never got the sketch of the bandits."

An uneasiness started in the pit of his gut. "I gave it to a member of the posse last night. He was waiting for it. Took it from me and rode off after them."

"It's missing." The conductor looped a thumb in his belt. "What did the man look like?"

"Average height. Wore an overcoat with his hat pulled down low." John had been more worried about Rennie at that point. He'd never seen her so shaken.

He grunted. "Describes half the men in that clearing, no doubt. Anything else?"

"The man had an abrupt manner. Something familiar about him, now that you mention it." A terrible possibility occurred to him. "Wait...you say Marshal Jones never received it?"

"That's right." He rubbed a finger over his rust-colored mustache. "What are you thinking? Out with it."

"It's just that Mrs. Birchfield—or Belle, as her husband called her—was mighty insistent about getting that sketch. I wonder if her husband doubled back after meeting up with his fellow bandits to get another shot at taking it from us since it identified them." The way the man snatched it from his hand before he offered it had troubled him even then.

"Marshal Jones's wire said none of the posse had it. I think it's lost to you, sonny, and to the law, too, which is more important. I'll pass on what you said. Don't know as I'd tell the little lady. Thinking she gave up her sketch to help a lawman might just comfort her enough she won't mind losing it."

There was wisdom in that advice. "Thank you, sir."

"Where you staying, in case we have questions? Ain't likely, but I've learned it's best to know rather than regret not knowing."

"The ladies will be at Mr. Paul Sherman's home in San Francisco. I don't have his address at the moment."

"Fair enough." The trainman gave him a nod and left.

John looked out over a cattle ranch while pondering what he'd learned. The more he considered the matter, the more certain he became that Mr. Birchfield had doubled back for the drawing. The couple had realized it could identify them too late. Not so smart.

Yet, in the end, they'd been wise enough to outfox all of them.

It was actually a relief to be rid of it, now that John knew the lengths the couple went to steal it.

Both sisters felt good that they'd been able to help the marshal. No need to tell them otherwise unless something in the newspapers demanded they know. With how much money the bandits had stolen, this part of the story seemed a minute detail that might never surface. Good riddance if it didn't. The girls needed to put this behind them as soon as possible.

~

*J*ohn believed he felt the ocean breeze from the Sixteenth Street Station when he alighted the train in Oakland. They were some six miles from San Francisco. Somehow, despite all the obstacles thrown in their way, they'd made it.

"Is Papa here?" Livie searched the crowd.

"We have to take a boat, and then he'll meet us at the wharf." Rennie reached for her hand and spoke to John. "How do we get to the ferry?"

"Either a streetcar or a carriage. With all we must carry, I want a carriage. I'll claim our trunks first." He peered over the crowd pushing toward the baggage cars. "Find a bench. This could take a while."

The next few minutes were as frustrating as any of the other waits to claim their possessions. Seemed the fellows who shouted the loudest got their trunks first.

He craned his neck to see how the girls were faring. They sat on a bench munching on bits of a sandwich.

His stomach growled at the sight. It was half past one, and

they hadn't eaten lunch. He must buy ferry tickets. After that, there wasn't much money remaining from his speech earnings. He certainly hoped Mr. Sherman planned to feed them.

Still a dozen passengers ahead of him. He widened his stance. The lone man emptying the car had sweat pouring down his face even in the mildest weather of the entire trip.

At least they didn't have to worry about missing the ferry. It ran every half hour.

More baggagemen climbed onto the car and began clearing it. Within five minutes, he had claimed their possessions. He hired a nearby driver to take them to the ferry in his carriage. By now, the depot was nearly empty.

Leaving the driver to load the trunks, he left to fetch the girls. Saw a tall stranger in a dark blue jacket, trousers, and waistcoat striding purposefully toward them.

This wasn't a crew member or passenger from the train that John recognized. The smartly dressed man's eyes fastened on Livie.

It couldn't be someone connected to the Birchfields, could it? John quickened his pace.

"Papa!" Livie ran and threw herself into his arms.

CHAPTER 25

*T*ears burned the back of Rennie's eyes.

"Livie." Mr. Sherman's top hat fell off as he knelt to hold her close, revealing thick brown hair. "Are you all right? I was so worried when I got Mr. Welch's telegram."

She pulled away to look up at him. "How is Mama?"

"She's better just knowing she'll see her pretty little girl today."

"I'm glad. I miss her." Livie's eyes lit up. "I got sick, but I feel better now."

"On top of the robbery, you were ill? Why was I not informed?" Mr. Sherman gave Rennie a piercing stare.

Rennie hastened to explain. "Livie suffers from train sickness if she doesn't eat enough. She was sick for two days in Wyoming Territory and then again when our train sped up to make up lost time. As you know, we were delayed about three hours due to the robbery."

He hugged his daughter closer.

"That meant breakfast was delayed." Rennie rambled on. "I gave her crackers to stave off the hunger until we stopped in Sacramento. She still felt poorly." Could she have done more?

"How unfortunate." The man stood. "My apologies for not introducing myself. Paul Sherman, which you've already surmised, I'm certain."

"A pleasure to make your acquaintance." Rennie relaxed slightly at this return to good manners. She introduced herself, her sister, and John as their escort.

They each returned his greeting.

"News of the bandits so distressed me that I had to learn the details for myself as soon as possible. I took the liberty of talking to the conductor before I found you."

"Papa." Livie tugged on his light-wool jacket. "I want to see Mama."

"You're right, Liv. We can talk on the way." He looked at John. "I've rented a carriage to take us to the ferry."

"I didn't know." John shoved his hands into the pockets of his favorite brown jacket. "You see, I just rented a carriage and had our bags loaded onto it."

"No problem. You can ask the driver to load them onto the one I rented." He pointed out the large red vehicle a few yards away. "Save your money."

"I'll see to it." John's glance cut toward Rennie before he strode away.

Did Mr. Sherman's displeasure bother him too?

"Let's wait in the carriage, shall we?"

They were soon seated in the spacious, comfortable interior. Livie sat by her father, and the sisters sat opposite them on soft leather seats. Rennie doubted John had rented something this nice. She'd have to tell Mama about this luxury.

"Miss Hill, it seems you were in the worst incident involving passengers. Will you tell me what happened?"

Rennie told him everything, even the details the marshal hadn't cared to know. "Unfortunately, Livie saw most of it. She was frightened and wanted her mother." He had a right to know how upset his daughter had been.

The carriage swayed as bags were loaded on top.

"Are you feeling better?" He touched his daughter's shoulder.

"Uh-huh. I was scared but Miss Rennie was brave. I only want to see Mama."

John climbed in and sat beside Rennie. The carriage set off immediately, its swaying motion reminding her of the sleeping berths.

"May I ask how Mrs. Sherman is faring?" Rennie glanced at Livie, whose apprehension seemed to be growing. "We prayed for her every night."

"And when asking a blessing on our meals, Papa." Wide-eyed, Livie stared up at him.

"I'm certain that's what made all the difference." He gave her a tender smile. "Your mama's fever broke three days ago."

"Praise God," John whispered.

"Oh, boy." Livie clapped her hands. "Did you hear, Miss Rennie? Mama's better."

"She's still weak and lying abed most of the day." He gave Livie a one-armed hug.

"That's fine." Her blue eyes glowed. "She's getting better. God answered our prayers."

"He did, indeed." Mr. Sherman's eyes misted. "And seeing you will be the best medicine in the world."

~

John stepped out on the ferry boat landing in San Francisco at the foot of Market Street. He'd arrived at long last. Carriages and horse-cars waited to take passengers and their luggage to one of several hotels within a mile's radius. Heavy trunks would be harder to maneuver on the omnibuses that led into the city.

Their host hadn't thanked any of them for their services.

Either he wasn't grateful, or he figured the salary Rennie had earned was thanks enough. Or all his thoughts were focused on his sick wife and the daughter he hadn't seen in months.

Mr. Sherman hadn't asked if they'd eaten lunch or extended an invitation to his home, and it was now mid-afternoon. He directed their trunks be taken from the ferry to a waiting carriage, greeted the driver, and introduced Livie. The man's employee expressed his pleasure at meeting Miss Sherman, which caused her to smile.

Rennie frowned. They'd received no introduction. She didn't seem to know how to proceed either. Best John discover the man's intentions.

He stepped forward. "Mr. Sherman, may these ladies stay at your house for a few days while they rest up for the trip home?" They deserved the courtesy after escorting his daughter.

"Yes, that's what my wife wants. In fact, I meant to ask you, Miss Hill, if you will act as Livie's governess until my wife is up and about."

"Eleanora gave me to believe that we'd stay with you about a week and then return home." Rennie gave him a direct look. "If you'd like my sister and me to stay an extra week, I will send my employer a telegram."

Good for you, Rennie. Ever practical. Always got to the heart of the matter as she saw it. If her sister wasn't included, Rennie wasn't interested.

"One week truly may be enough. We have a cook, a driver, a housekeeper, and a maid, so Cynthia will not be overtaxed." He named a modest weekly salary. "Of course, I'll include your travel expenses back to Hamilton. Your sister is also welcome to stay. Is that acceptable?"

"Yes, sir." Rennie nodded, no doubt relieved not to have to travel home tomorrow. "Thank you. Spending time with Livie has been a pleasure. I'm glad it hasn't ended." She smiled at the little girl. "We also need to send a telegram to inform our family that we arrived safely."

"Write your message, and George here will take it to the telegraph office."

"That will be lovely. Thank you."

The tension in John's shoulders relaxed. The ladies had a safe place to stay.

"Mr. Welch, where shall I direct your luggage to be sent?" He turned a pleasant face toward John—though was careful not to meet his eyes. Likely ashamed to leave him standing in the street, so to speak.

"I'll find a hotel. Where do you live?"

"On Fifth Street." He gave his address and then motioned for a carriage for him.

John would have preferred to pay for the less expensive horse car, but pride kept him silent. The man might be well-to-do, but he wasn't very gracious.

"How long will you be in the city?" Mr. Sherman asked while John's trunk was loaded onto the carriage.

Rennie's gaze captured his.

"My plans are uncertain. I need to speak with Rennie." There'd been no opportunity for them to have that private conversation he craved.

"Yes, that's an excellent idea." Though the tension in her face lessened, she didn't take her eyes from his. "Let me know where you're staying."

"I will." Once he figured it out.

"Eleanora wrote that the two of you are courting. Miss Rennie will be busy until eight o'clock every evening." He lifted Livie into the carriage. "That's when my daughter goes to bed. You may call then."

He was treating Rennie as an employee, not a guest. Eight o'clock was late to call, but he'd be there.

"Bye, Mr. John. Come see me, please." She waved from the window.

"It appears my daughter wants you to visit." Mr. Sherman helped Veronica into the vehicle. "I'll speak with my wife. She will want to meet you when she's more recovered."

"I look forward to that, sir." He gave Rennie his hand to help her up. It was difficult to say such a quick goodbye in front of her employer—for one more week.

She didn't make a move to mount the high step. Her clasp tightened. "This isn't the way I wanted to say goodbye," she whispered. "Come tomorrow at eight."

"I'll see you then." He gave her a slow smile, hoping she understood he wasn't leaving her alone.

"Ahem." Livie's father cleared his throat behind them.

Rennie's look held a tinge of desperation John longed to soothe as she entered the waiting carriage.

"Until tomorrow evening." Mr. Sherman touched the brim of his hat as he sat beside his daughter.

Rennie waved until an omnibus hid her from view.

This wasn't the way he'd envisioned his first day in San Francisco.

CHAPTER 26

*R*ennie fumed at the way Mr. Sherman had treated her beau. The least he could have done was drop John and his baggage off at a hotel. Their host had been rude to all of them. John had missed a meal entirely while she and the girls snacked. The man had never inquired about their comfort, not even his daughter's.

To be fair, he'd said he watched them while speaking with the conductor. They'd been eating at the time to distract Livie's nervous excitement.

Mr. Sherman passed the short ride asking his daughter about her trip. She told him about her new slate, the drawings she'd made to cheer her mama, and seeing the canyon.

"You've had a good trip despite being sick." His expression softened.

"Oh, I did, Papa. I like Miss Rennie, Veronica, and Mr. John. They're my new friends." Livie beamed at them. "They brought me to see you and Mama. Praying for her every night helped me sleep."

"It seems that you've taken excellent care of my daughter."

His ears underneath his top hat turned red. "My apologies that I didn't see it at first. All I could think about was that woman waving a gun."

Rennie blinked at his apology but hastened to reassure him. "It was pointed at me and John." It made sense that all he could see was the danger to his daughter. "All of us were afraid. Thankfully, Livie and Veronica were never in direct danger. And my sister was right there with her the whole time Mrs. Birchfield threatened John and me."

"I'm relieved to hear that."

"Mr. Sherman, I understand why you might be angry your daughter was in the middle of a frightening, dangerous experience, but know this—John would have taken a bullet to save any of us. And I would too."

"Ahem." His mustache did nothing to hide the mottled red of his face. "I wasn't precisely angry..."

Lifting her eyebrows, Rennie gave him a direct look.

"That is to say, I'm angry with the bandits. And it seems you felt the brunt of that anger." He ran a finger under his collar. "My apologies."

"That's all right." She'd pass that apology on to John tomorrow. "I feel mighty protective of my family, so I understand."

The carriage stopped in front of a modest two-story wood frame home that didn't live up to their host's lofty attitude.

Mr. Sherman jumped out.

"Are we here, Papa?" Livie's feet wiggled as he lifted her to the ground.

"Mama's waiting." He took her hand and shot a look over his shoulder at Rennie. "Mrs. Burke, my housekeeper, will see to your needs." He allowed the child to pull him along the short walk to the front door. They disappeared inside.

"That child's waited so long to see her mother." Rennie stepped from the carriage carefully. "I'm glad we're finally here."

"Me too." Veronica accepted Rennie's supportive hand to alight. "Though it was a mighty uncomfortable ride, you said what needed saying."

"Thanks, sister." Rennie smiled at her.

A squeal of pure joy came from a second-floor window. Rennie's eyes misted to imagine the joyful reunion. It had been anything but a peaceful journey to get the child here. But Livie's shout made it worth every sacrifice.

~

"*W*here do you want to go?" The driver, a bearded man in his mid-twenties, had stowed John's trunk atop a carriage on the overcrowded street.

"I'm not certain." Though it had never been stated, John had expected he'd be invited to spend at least one night with the Shermans while he figured out his next steps. At least the ladies had room and board included with Rennie's temporary job. Given how sweet and kind Livie was, one could only assume that Mrs. Sherman was far different from her husband. If so, they'd have a good week.

"I'm Collier Brandt. I run my own carriage company. Most folks call me Coll." The driver held out his hand.

John shook it. "Glad to meet you, Coll." At last, a genuine welcome. "John Welch. Just arrived."

"Come to seek your fortune?" Coll's direct brown gaze was levelled at him. They were of the same height.

"Not my fortune." John considered. "Not the way you mean it, anyway."

He quirked an eyebrow.

"I'm more in search of my future. I want to be a writer, but my girl's not too happy about it."

"You're not the first to face that dilemma."

"I need to find a place to stay."

Coll peered behind John. "The Grand's up here at Market and New Montgomery Market." He considered John's coat. "I'm guessing you don't want that or the Baldwin either. The Lick, the Occidental, and the Russ are on Montgomery Street. You'll run out of money quickly if you choose those."

Which hotels had his guidebook recommended? "My girl and her sister are staying with a family on Fifth Street for the next week or so." He gave him the direction. The man had an honest face. He'd trust him. "Know of any modestly priced hotels in that area?"

"Our city has lots of hotels and furnished lodgings with restaurants nearby. Most folks live in furnished lodgings and dine at the restaurants for every meal."

"Sounds expensive." John gulped. His savings wouldn't survive long in that environment. "Do you know of a family who rents out a room to bachelors?" That was likely the cheapest option.

Coll studied him. "Mrs. Goldie's Boardinghouse is maybe a fifteen-minute walk from where your girl is staying. She rents by the week. It's cheaper than staying at any of the hotels near here."

John surveyed the street astir with carriages, horse cars, omnibuses, and wagons while he considered the option. There was a cable car leading from the ferry. Women in landaus holding parasols and wearing colorful frocks in the latest fashions. Men in work clothes, mothers with children scampering behind them, and gentlemen sporting expensive canes all claimed their place on the crowded Market Street.

"Last I heard," Coll said, "she charges four dollars a week for room and board. The food's good but don't be late. She doesn't wait the meal for anyone."

Sounded perfect for his wallet. If he missed a meal, he'd dine at one of the restaurants. "Let's try her place first."

"You won't be sorry. My charge is a dollar." Coll held out his hand.

Steep fare, but it was what his guidebook cautioned travelers to expect. John paid him and climbed aboard. Coll took off as soon as the door snapped shut. He had done him a service by suggesting the boardinghouse instead of a hotel. John hadn't considered that possibility since he wasn't making San Francisco his home.

Seemed he had a lot to learn.

About women too. He'd be here at least a week. Everything depended on his talk with Rennie. After the robbery, he felt even less comfortable about the sisters traveling back with an escort provided by the Shermans. True, train robberies were rare. It was doubtful another one would occur for many months—years, even—but that didn't change his desire to protect the woman he loved.

He was still shaken by seeing her life threatened. It strengthened his conviction that this was his task. His privilege. No matter the outcome of their talk, he'd accompany them home. Both Rennie and Veronica were strong women—it ran in the family—but that didn't change his decision. Undoubtedly, Mr. Hill would agree.

Before long, the carriage moved closer to the cable car running along Market Street. An iron arm from the car gripped the three-inch wire rope. John had never seen one of the horseless vehicles that ran by means of a cable. It had two cars. The one enclosed with windows and a roof was empty on this pleasant but breezy day. The other was completely open with no walls. The benches facing outward on all four sides were occupied by two women, and men filled the rest. Three who stood at the ends didn't look at all uncomfortable.

John wanted to ride on the cable-roads, as they were commonly called. If Rennie could break free from her duties, he'd escort her, for he was certain she'd love the novel experience. It was reported that this was the preferred way to travel through the city because the cars easily climbed the steep hills, and the descents were equally safe.

If only Mr. Sherman wasn't set on his own importance, John might have been invited to join the family, Rennie, and Veronica for luncheon or maybe supper. On their final day in the city, he vowed to treat them to a meal and to see what they could of San Francisco in those few hours.

To think that Mark Twain had strolled these very streets. After spending a couple of years in the silver mines in Nevada, he'd gone to San Francisco while the War Between the States still raged. Anticipating income from the mining stocks he owned, he lived the lifestyle of the wealthy. Then his stock became worthless, and he found himself penniless.

John sympathized with the suddenness destruction had struck Twain because he and his sister had lived through something similar. Their destruction might have been complete if not for meeting Mama Rosie. Those terrible days spurred the deep-seated desire in him to write stories.

Twain had written of those harsh experiences when he was at his lowest. How could even the hardest of hearts fail to be touched by them?

Rennie had suggested that he tell stories of being orphaned. He had skimmed over the topic in his talk. Should he write of that dark place in his soul? Might it bring comfort and hope to some orphan boy, convince him that he could grow up to become something more than he dreamed?

The carriage stopped, and John alighted and looked around. A grocer, a watchmaker, a milliner shop, a life insurance company, and a ready-made clothing store were mixed in between homes. Across the street was a three-story gray frame building with five steps leading to a porch that ran along the front of the building.

"There it is." The driver joined him. "Mrs. Goldie's Boardinghouse. She and my mother became friends at church. I'll introduce you because she's mistrustful of strangers."

"I appreciate you bringing me here." She was a Christian. Even better.

"Let's leave your trunk in case she doesn't have a room available."

"Good thinking. Is Goldie her last name?"

Coll shook his head. "Never heard it. Rumor is that her husband died in the war and nobody was sorry."

A terrible testament for a man's life. What must he have been like that no one mourned him? "She didn't want to keep his name?" John climbed the steps.

"Right." His driver rapped on the door. "Mrs. Goldie? It's Collier Brandt."

The door opened, and a bright-eyed woman in her mid-forties stepped out. "Coll, what a surprise." The breeze blew brown curls across her face, and her green gingham dress whipped around her legs.

They exchanged brief pleasantries on her good health. Then Coll turned to John. "I hope you have a vacancy." He made the introductions.

"A pleasure to meet you, Mrs. Goldie." John met her direct gaze, as she seemed one who'd see through deceit. "If you have a vacancy, I'd like to rent week-to-week. I may be here one or two weeks."

"He's a writer, Mrs. Goldie."

Her gaze returned to him. "Then I'll give you a room on the third floor where you can see the San Francisco Bay—when the fog cooperates, that is."

"Perfect." Was she serious? He didn't even have to see the room. "That view will inspire me." Riding a ferry across the bay had given him a taste of what he imagined the ocean to look like. He planned to see the Pacific Ocean while here.

That and having a candid discussion with Rennie topped his list.

"It's the only room with a desk. Will you be writing?"

"That's my dream."

"Well, then, young fella." Her eyes twinkled at him. "Fetch your baggage and make it a reality."

CHAPTER 27

"We're pleased you all made it safely after the robbery." The Sherman's housekeeper, Mrs. Burke, placed a plump hand to the high collar of her green floral muslin dress, which was partially covered by a frilly white apron.

"Thank you. We're happy to be here." Rennie looked around at her home for at least the next week.

They stood in a small foyer in front of a wooden staircase. A hall to the side of the stairs likely led to the study and kitchen. An open door on the right side of the main entrance showed a dining room with a table for eight. A vase of red-and-yellow dahlias added vibrancy from the middle of the white linen tablecloth. The wallpaper was yellow with blue vertical stripes. Curtains the color of a summer sky touched the floor over one window on two adjacent walls.

On the left of the hall was a parlor with a harpsichord in the back. Two sofas with four cushioned chairs were arranged in two groups, all in soft green, allowing for multiple conversations in the spacious area. The rug's green swirl pattern complemented the lime color on the wallpaper.

Pretty. This would be the nicest place Rennie had ever stayed.

"Why, your beau's telegram about those bandits ..." The short woman in her forties shook her head. "Mr. Sherman's been pacing about all morning. It wouldn't do Mrs. Sherman any good to know about it before Miss Olivia arrived, so no one told her."

That made sense, but... "I hope he tells her now because Livie will. She was upset last night. Other than suffering train illness, she's been fine today."

"Just wanted to see her mother," Veronica added.

"Poor child." The motherly woman patted Veronica's arm. "You've all had a fright."

"Yes, ma'am." The housekeeper's concern soothed Rennie. "I'm glad to put that behind me."

The driver carried in their trunk and valises.

"Thank you, Thomas. He's my husband." Mrs. Burke beamed at him. "Have you met these sisters?"

"Not been introduced." Removing his bowler hat revealed a gray streak in his brown hair. "How'd do?" He nodded at them.

"I'm Rennie Hill." She smiled, for the introduction made her feel more welcome. "This is Veronica, my sister."

"Pleased to meet you both. I'll carry these upstairs. Are they in Clara's room?" At his wife's nod, he climbed the stairs with the trunk on his shoulder.

"Miss Olivia's room is next to the master bedroom. I've moved our maid, Clara, in with the cook while you're here. Mr. Sherman has inquired for a governess, but no one fit his requirements." She peered up the stairs and then leaned closer. "He's a mite...selective about who will care for his little girl," she whispered. "Four young women applied for the position. I'd have hired any of them, but it's not my decision, as he reminded me."

So even the friendly housekeeper had felt the brutal honesty from Mr. Sherman. "Is Mrs. Sherman like him?"

"Night and day, my dear. It's a joy to work in Mrs. Sherman's household. You'll find out soon enough. I expect she'll talk with Miss Olivia until she's ready to lie down. Insisted on sitting in a chair this afternoon. Didn't want the child to see her abed and sick to boot." She looked up as the stairs creaked. Her husband descended, scorning the gleaming wood rail. "Thank you, Thomas."

"I'll stable the horses."

Rennie understood why he didn't talk much. His wife made up for it.

"Best thing for her, in my opinion. Sitting up, that is. And seeing her daughter, of course. Mr. Sherman wanted her to rest in bed. He coddles her." She rolled her eyes. "Longer than what's needed. Of course, my opinion's not wanted."

Good information. Perhaps Mrs. Sherman was far more improved than her husband had suggested. "Should we get settled while Livie is with her mother? Or can we help you with something else?" Might as well earn their keep.

"Best take what free time you can find." Mrs. Burke led the way up the creaky stairs. "You'll do your own laundry—that'll keep you on friendly terms with Clara. The washtub and everything else you'll need is stored in the pantry. I may as well show you Miss Livie's room." She opened a door right off the stairs. Another door was down a small hallway beside it.

"This is beautiful." Rennie stepped inside a room that was a little girl's dream. A pink coverlet on the bed where a doll nestled against the pillows. A small rocking chair facing the pink-curtained window. A table under a mirror on the wall contained brush, comb, and hair ribbons. A wardrobe as tall as John stood against the wall opposite the bed. A kerosene lamp with a pink bowl and pitcher sat on top of a two-drawer chest.

"It was a pleasure to prepare this room. Yours is to the

right." Mrs. Burke closed the door behind them and led them to the last room in the hall.

This one was a quarter of the size of Livie's spacious room. Their trunk took up most of the space between two narrow beds on opposite sides. There were plenty of hooks on the gray walls for their dresses and a four-drawer high boy for the rest of their clothes. A three-foot square table nestled underneath a window. A welcome cool breeze fluttered the short white curtains. A lantern, bowl, and pitcher sat atop the chest. Sparse. Clean. Quite different from the one they'd just seen, but nicer than what they were accustomed to. "Thank you very much."

"You're welcome, I'm sure." Mrs. Burke released a breath. "The staff shares a convenience off the kitchen. The bathroom is there too. We can use it any time the family doesn't need it. Plan on bathing in the evening. Simply clean it when you're done."

That sounded heavenly. "I'll use that tonight after Livie goes to bed."

"Me too." Veronica spoke in fervent tones.

"The family dines at six. The staff eats after they're finished." Mrs. Burke frowned. "I think that's everything. Any questions?"

"Does the family entertain much?" That big dining room suggested it.

She shook her head. "Not since Mrs. Sherman took sick. They often entertained railroad men when they first moved here. Mr. Sherman traveled to the San Joaquin Valley several times and stayed away for days at a time, but I don't think it did any good. His mood sure turned sour after that last trip." Mrs. Burke peered down the hall and then stepped back inside. "If you ask me, the family will move back to Ohio as soon as Mrs. Sherman is well enough to travel."

~

*J*ohn's room in the boardinghouse had a narrow bed, a high boy, plenty of hooks for his shirts and jackets—and a roll-top desk under a window with a view of San Francisco Bay. Was he dreaming?

"Mrs. Goldie gave you the best room in the house." Coll dropped John's valise on the bed. "Not the biggest or most expensive, but her favorite."

"It's my favorite. I don't have to see the rest."

"You plan to write a book while you're here?" Looking at the bay, Coll put his hands on his hips.

"I'll start this evening." John was itching to start it now, but he felt grimy from the trip. Once Coll left, he'd seek out Mrs. Goldie and ask about the cost of a bath. It had been included with his room in Cincinnati.

Coll turned to him. "Do you ride?"

"Yes, I'm hoping to rent a horse for the day and see the Pacific Ocean."

"I rent horses on Saturday and Sunday. How about tomorrow? It's my day off, so I can be a guide for you. If you want one."

Excitement surged in John's veins. "The sooner the better." It was worth the extra cost. "How many people work for you?" He liked Coll. As much as he enjoyed being with Rennie, it felt good to talk to someone not wearing a skirt.

"Just one. I'm using my mother's stable for my teams and to store my vehicles. I've built my business up to two carriages and eight horses. Saving for a third one. Summer visitors help." He sighed.

"That's great. Mind if I take my journal and write a bit at the ocean?"

"Not at all. Kind of like a few minutes by myself when I'm there too." His averted gaze indicated a bit of embarrassment at the admission. "Let's leave about nine to give a chance for the sun to burn the fog away."

"I've heard about the fog here. Is it bad?"

"It can last all day." He shrugged. "Most days are sunny in July. You'll see the fog roll in this evening. It'll get colder. You'll need a light coat then."

"Good advice." John had heard how fog could blanket the whole city in late spring and early summer. "What's your fee?"

"Three dollars ought to cover it." Coll headed out the open door. "I've got to get back to the wharf. See you at nine." He turned back. "Ask Mrs. Goldie to pack a lunch for you. We'll return mid-afternoon."

John closed the door. He'd be back in plenty of time to see Rennie tomorrow evening. If only he could take her with him.

He peered out over the distant bay. Bright sunshine cast sparkles over the dark-blue waters. What appeared to be tiny birds dotted the sky over the water. They must be large for him to see them from so far inland. Could be the pelicans, cormorants, and gulls known to inhabit the area.

Grabbing his knapsack, he fished out his journal and a pen. First impressions were important. He'd describe them while they were fresh in mind.

Laundry and that desperately needed bath could wait a few minutes.

CHAPTER 28

*R*ennie managed to unpack before Livie ran through their open door.

"Mama's so much better, Miss Rennie." Livie threw her arms around Rennie's waist. "She wasn't in bed the whole time and said she was so happy to see me that she wasn't even tired."

"That's wonderful." Her heart lightened at the answered prayer. Livie's joy was infectious. "Where is she now?"

"Papa told her to lie down." She sat on Rennie's bed.

"I thought she wasn't tired?" Veronica placed a stack of underclothes in a drawer and then gave her a one-armed hug.

"Papa said she was." She brightened. "But she'll eat supper with me and Papa. She's not been downstairs since the fever hit, and she said she's not missing her first meal with me."

Rennie checked the clock on the high boy. "That's in an hour, enough time for a bath." Her thick hair would still be damp. Perhaps there'd be a fire built in the parlor at least to help dry it. "Let's pick out a pretty dress from your trunk for you to wear afterward." Too late, she realized she should have unpacked Livie's clothes before her own. She was unaccustomed to this governess job.

"I'll finish up in here," Veronica offered.

The next hour flew. With Livie's hair still damp from her bath, Rennie gathered up only the top and secured it with a ribbon.

"Do I look pretty?" Livie held out the folds of yet another pink dress, this one patterned with white daisies.

"Pretty as can be." Rennie grinned at her. This little girl commanded a piece of her heart. It would be difficult to leave her. And even harder to leave John. But she was determined to be brave about her loneliness. He deserved an opportunity to pursue his writing dreams.

A door opened down the hall.

Livie's mouth opened wide. "That's Mama. Come with me." She grabbed Rennie's hand and dragged her into the hall.

"Mama, you look beautiful." Livie halted a couple of feet from her parents.

"Why, thank you, Livie." The blonde dropped her husband's arm and stooped to gather her close. She was of medium height and appeared somewhat fragile. "You look lovely too."

"I'm the luckiest man in California to dine with the two most beautiful ladies in the state." Mr. Sherman spoke gallantly with a smile for both.

"And you must be Miss Hill." Mrs. Sherman stepped forward with a radiant smile to clasp Rennie's hand. Her hair was brushed into a smooth coil. "Livie can't stop talking about Miss Rennie, Mr. John, and Veronica. Why, I feel as if I already know you."

"It's a pleasure to meet you, Mrs. Sherman. And may I say how happy we all are to see you up and about?"

"Thank you." Tears brightened her eyes, to be quickly blinked away. "I'll call you Rennie, shall I?"

"Yes, ma'am."

"You have my sincerest thanks for your excellent care of my daughter. And for protecting her, you understand."

"My pleasure." Rennie nodded. The woman didn't want to speak of frightening events in front of Livie. "It was my privilege to bring your wonderful daughter to you."

"I hope you understand that tonight is a family supper." There was an apology in her brown eyes, as if she guessed how her husband had acted. "And perhaps tomorrow night too. On Sunday, we'd like for you and your sister and Mr. Welch to join us for supper. Do you have his address?"

"Not yet." Had he even found a place to stay? She now understood how there was no room for him here. "He plans to call on me tomorrow evening at eight."

"That's wonderful. I'll meet your sister tomorrow as well. Thank you for giving us another week or two of your time to care for our precious girl." She put her arm around Livie. "She'll be with us until half past seven. You may come for her then to ready her for bed."

"Of course." She stepped back to give them ample space to reach the stairs.

With her husband's arm securely around her waist, Mrs. Sherman held onto the banister as she descended.

Rennie held her breath, recognizing how the illness had weakened her. Little wonder that her husband tended to be overly protective.

Mrs. Burke greeted her when she reached the bottom. "Mrs. Sherman, how good it is to have you below stairs again. Your meal is ready."

"Thank you."

Their voices trailed away.

Mrs. Sherman truly was night-and-day different from her husband. It made the arduous, eventful trip worth the effort. What a pleasure to do something that mattered for her.

Hunger pains struck at the same moment exhaustion seeped into Rennie's very bones. There'd been little sleep the night before. She vowed to go to bed as soon as Livie fell asleep.

Then she remembered that evening was the only time for staff to use the bathroom. Sleep would be a little delayed tonight.

~

*J*ohn plowed into his meal as soon as Mrs. Goldie finished saying grace. Breakfast seemed eons ago, and the baked ham and boiled potatoes hit the spot.

There were nine other boarders at the table, all men aged from early twenties to older than his pa. There was one vacant chair in a rectangular table for twelve. He'd exchanged names with everyone before seating himself. Some wore the wool shirts and suspenders of working men. Others wore the jackets, vests, and trousers of businessmen.

"Where are you from?" Ray, a man in his late twenties, passed a basket of corn muffins to him.

"Hamilton, Ohio." John helped himself to a muffin and then passed it on. "I lived in Cincinnati for two years while my sister attended college there."

"I like a man who takes family responsibilities seriously." Mrs. Goldie gave an approving nod.

"What did you do there?"

He set down his fork and explained about quitting his job at the newspaper. "What about you, Ray?"

"I'm a banker." Ray expounded on his job at a bank on Market Street, giving John a chance to eat. "Emory here"—he nodded to the man little older than John on his right—"is a teacher."

"Let the man talk for himself." Jack, a wiry man with the weathered skin of someone constantly outdoors, spoke up from across the table. "By the way, I work at the wharf."

"That seems a fascinating job." John worked to associate jobs with the men's names as he listened.

"How so?" Jack quirked an eyebrow.

"I'll bet you meet some interesting folks getting off the ferry."

He grunted.

"No more than I do." Red-headed Grant spoke up at his side. "I work on the ferry."

"I rode it this afternoon." John grinned at him.

"How'd you find your way here?" Grant ate a large slice of potato while eyeing John curiously.

"Collier Brandt, the driver of my carriage, suggested it."

"I operate a cable car on the Clay Street Hill Railroad." Kent's broad-shouldered frame suggested few would want to pick a fight with him. "It's the car on Kearny, Leavenworth, and Larkin Streets."

"I'll look for it. I want to ride a cable car this week."

"That mean you won't be here long?" Kent pushed his empty plate away.

He sighed. "Doesn't look like it. My girl and her sister need to return to Ohio in a week or two."

"Say, you weren't on the train that got robbed last night, were you?" Jack leaned forward.

"Actually, I was." Scanning their faces, he knew he had captured everyone's interest.

"What happened? News has been sparse." Ray stared at him. "Don't leave us in suspense."

John didn't. He even went back so far as meeting the Birch-fields to tell his story. He included details he might have skimmed over. Every now and then, someone broke in with "you don't say," or "don't that beat all," but for the most part, they let him describe the event as he experienced it.

"We'll never read all that in a newspaper." Kent eyed him. "You should write it down while it's fresh in your mind."

"Excellent idea." There were so many ideas in his head, he hardly knew what to pursue. "I jotted some notes this morning."

"None of you asked him what he quit his job to do." Mrs. Goldie gave him a triumphant look. "And may I say that story was an excellent example of why."

"What's your job?" Ray frowned.

"I'm a writer." Boy, that felt good to say.

~

John didn't remember to jot down his boardinghouse address for Rennie until after supper. He verified the directions to Fifth Street with Kent. Then he scribbled a note for her in case he wasn't allowed to talk with her directly and set out to the Sherman home at dusk. Fog had already settled over the area at half past seven, making it difficult to see. He buttoned his coat against the chilly breeze.

After expressing his desire to write to his fellow boarders, Kent had said he could see that become a reality after hearing him talk about the bandits. Ray called him "a born storyteller" and asked if he'd considered speaking to audiences.

Serving as a speaker? Such as he had done on the train? That had been fun, pure and simple. Seemed like robbery to take someone's hard-earned money for doing something he loved.

It was one more thing he'd mention to Rennie tomorrow evening. He whispered a prayer that she'd support his hopes for his life's work. He'd return to newspaper work for Rennie if she thought it best. Maybe she'd been right all along. Maybe his dreams had blinded him into giving too much credence to the encouragement he'd received.

But if the woman he loved could support his dreams through those first lean years...

John came upon an unpretentious, two-story home. Could this be the place? He had expected something much bigger. He applied the knocker.

A motherly woman answered the door. "Yes?"

"My name is John Welch, ma'am. I escorted Miss Olivia Sherman west along with Miss Rennie Hill and Miss Veronica Hill. I'm sorry to make an unexpected call so late, but I promised to let Rennie know where I'm staying."

"I'm Mrs. Burke, the housekeeper. I've heard a lot about you this day." She smiled. "I'd invite you in, but Rennie's putting Livie to bed and then she'll be...indisposed."

"I understand." He was ready for bed himself after a sleepless night. "Will you give her this message? It tells her where I'm staying and that I'll be here tomorrow evening at eight."

"I've learned she expects you then." She accepted the folded paper. "I will give her this and see you about this time tomorrow. Good night."

He strode back quicker than he'd come as exhaustion descended.

CHAPTER 29

*R*ennie had finally managed to calm Livie's excitement. The child had missed hours of sleep the night before, witnessed her governess being threatened with a gun, suffered from stomach complaints, and been reunited with her parents all in less than twenty-four hours. It was little wonder that Rennie needed to read a bedtime story to her before she relaxed enough to allow sleep to claim her.

After a luxurious soak in the tub, Rennie cleaned the bathroom.

When she headed to her room, a robe tied securely over her nightgown, Mrs. Burke stopped her at the foot of the stairs. "Your young man came around earlier and left you a note."

She hated that she'd missed him. She read it while Mrs. Burke waited. "He's staying at Mrs. Goldie's Boardinghouse."

"He's fortunate to have found such economical accommodations. Goldie attends my church. Good woman."

"I'm relieved to hear that you know where he's staying." Indeed, it was as if a great burden lifted from Rennie's back. "There's a chill in the air this evening. The end of July is a strange time of year to need a fire."

"We build fires every evening and every morning. You've a heat stove in your room. Veronica already lit the coals in it, so you should feel toasty warm in no time."

Sounded deliciously cozy after all the travel discomforts. "Livie's room was already warm when she had such difficulty falling asleep—"

"My husband lit it while the Shermans ate supper."

"Please thank him for me." Rennie loosened her grip on the banister. Next time she'd remember.

"You look all done in." Mrs. Burke patted her arm. "Breakfast for the staff is at seven. Sleep well, Rennie."

As she suspected, Veronica was asleep with the lantern light turned low. With a sigh, Rennie sat on the edge of the bed near the stove to dry her hair.

Exhaustion descended in waves, but her mind couldn't rest. She must discover John's plans. There was a lot to see in San Francisco. Many adventures awaited him in this state.

Her stomach clenched at all the money he'd spend seeing the sights. But was that the reason she'd balked, really?

No, not if she was honest. She had many concerns, not the least of which was him traveling alone in the Wild West. Why, entire train crews carried loaded revolvers. John had told her that many passengers did also. This land was even rougher, more dangerous than she'd first realized, and she'd worry about him until he arrived safely back in Ohio.

She splayed her fingers through her damp waves as she probed the root of her fears—losing him altogether. She had no doubt her beau would thrive with the adventure and excitement here. He'd meet interesting people, ruggedly different from those back home. What if he met another woman like Beth who enjoyed talking with him about books? What if she was beautiful and talented? What if he decided he liked it here?

What if he never came home?

Her heart squeezed at the mere possibility. She wanted to

marry this dreamer. Had loved him since she was a schoolgirl. She couldn't bear the thought of not becoming his wife.

Yet, as Mama had warned, when she'd held onto him too tightly—nagging him to come home when he'd felt responsible for his sister—it had damaged their relationship.

He loved her, but she'd given him nothing but grief about his writing.

Tomorrow evening was her opportunity to show the support he craved. Could she do it?

She must. She bowed her head and prayed for the strength to encourage his dreams.

Several people had praised his work, folks who knew more than she did about such things. What if he did possess the talent of his hero, Mark Twain? Dare she rob the world of his books?

No, she must not be so selfish. And if his books didn't sell to match his dreams, so be it. If the table was bare, she'd return to her job at the telegraph office.

Peace seeped into her heart. Supporting his dream was the right thing to do.

And if he didn't return from his adventures to marry her, she'd die an old maid, because there'd never be another man for her.

~

The salty breeze stung John's fresh-shaven face, though he couldn't see the ocean from his current position. His overcoat provided welcome warmth on these hills. Following Coll Brandt on horseback through low-lying fog required concentration, for it was easy to become disoriented.

It was about seven miles from his boardinghouse to the beach, and his backside reminded him it had been three months since he'd ridden a horse.

"Not much farther." Coll spoke over his shoulder as his horse picked its way over the hilly terrain. "Hope the fog's better at the beach."

"Me too." This might be his only opportunity to see the ocean.

"The sun should burn off most of it. Might see a mist instead, then. It's kind of pretty."

They descended another hill.

"There it is." John halted halfway down the hillside at his first glimpse of the Pacific Ocean. The white rolling waves crashed into the blue water in a foamy arc. Faint sounds of the surf prompted him to urge his horse on. They descended through the fog, which hung above them, allowing a view of the ocean.

"Thank you, God," he whispered. "It's even mightier than I imagined."

"What's that?" Coll stopped at the bottom and looked back.

"Just praising God for this wondrous sight."

"I feel like that every time I come. I bring my girl sometimes. She's always reminding me about God's creation." He pointed to some bushes. "Let's tether the horses. Meadowlark here doesn't like the sand."

John, journal in hand, was soon sitting out of the reach of the tide in front of the vast expanse. He was glad he'd worn his work clothes, else he'd be standing in his suit to scribble his thoughts.

But words failed him. How did one describe the feeling of insignificance against the power displayed in front of him? He began writing phrases, impressions, praises to the One who created this beauty. The swell of the waves three times his height. A pelican's low soar over the water that ended in a sudden dive. The bird disappeared only to emerge a moment later. Had it been successful in seizing a fish?

He tried to capture the sounds on his page. The call of a sea gull. The crash of the waves that drowned out all but the closest of noises.

Wait. Did a fish leap above the waters in the distance? He stood and walked closer.

"Best take off your shoes and stockings." Coll already carried his shoes. "You're mighty close to getting wet."

The tide stopped a mere yard away. Here was his chance to experience the ocean, the sand. He looked around. There were a few groups of people to the right and left. They might not even notice his bare feet.

He stowed his journal out of reach and then removed his shoes and stockings. "Does the water feel good?"

"Bracing. Best fold up your trousers to your knees."

John did so and then ran toward the foamy tide. It covered his ankles. *Brr.* "Bracing is the right description, Coll. Mind if I use it?"

"Not at all." He grinned.

John spent the next half hour running back and forth, playing with the tide. He donned his sandy stockings and shoes when the chill of the water caused him to shiver.

Then he wrote in his journal, wishing Rennie were there to experience the ocean with him.

It was a revelation. He'd enjoyed this day. The ride. The ocean. Playing with the tide.

But everything would have been infinitely more special with her at his side.

Would his adventure in the West leave him always wishing Rennie were with him?

It was only natural for a man to want the woman he loved beside him, yet he'd been pulling away from her for months because she'd dug in her heels about everything that mattered most to him.

He didn't want to pull away anymore. He'd propose while they were in San Francisco—but not in the Sherman's parlor.

Someplace special. Someplace that San Francisco was known for.

Ah, he knew the perfect place. But Mr. Sherman wasn't the friendliest person. He'd already stipulated that Rennie would only be free from her duties after eight.

Must he wait until the day they left this amazing city to propose?

Perhaps there was another way.

~

It was Saturday evening. Rennie could scarcely contain her excitement. She'd asked Veronica, who also wanted to visit with John, to busy herself with her sketches in another part of the room because she feared Mrs. Burke would not allow her to speak with John alone.

While Mr. Sherman was out, Livie had spent two hours with her mother in the parlor that morning and another two in the afternoon. Mrs. Sherman's cheeks were still pale, yet she seemed stronger, her steps less hesitant. It did everyone in the household good just to see the two of them reading a book together or watching Livie practice her writing while her mother looked on.

Everyone in the small household knew John would arrive at eight, including Livie.

"But I want to see Mr. John." Livie bounced on her bed. "Papa didn't let me hug him goodbye."

Another reason to dislike the man. "I don't believe your father knows how much you like Mr. John." Rennie had been trying to get the child settled for twenty minutes. "I'll ask your mother if he can come over and see you."

"My answer is yes." Mrs. Sherman stepped through the open doorway. "I can see that taking a trip across the country together has built a bond between you."

"He's my friend, Mama, just like Miss Rennie and Veronica." She gave her mother a pleading look.

"Pardon me, ma'am, but I have a suggestion." Rennie waited until Mrs. Sherman waved at her to continue. "I had hoped to take Livie and Veronica to church tomorrow. I'll invite John to come."

"What a lovely idea." Mrs. Sherman sat next to Livie on the bed. "I don't feel well enough to attend, and I'm certain my husband will stay home with me. When you return, we'll all have lunch together."

"I'd like that." Though Mrs. Sherman had hinted an invitation was coming, this would be the first time Rennie and Veronica dined with the family. "Perhaps we could take Livie for a stroll sometimes when you're resting."

"As long as you don't go too far, I have no objection. If your beau is with you, I'll have Mr. Burke drive you around the city, if you like." She smiled at her daughter. "I'm feeling stronger already. I just needed my girl here with me."

"Can we go back to Ohio?"

"Papa and I have been discussing that very thing. His business ventures haven't gone as planned, and there's nothing to keep us here." She gathered Livie close. "We'll travel as soon as I'm strong enough. A month at the soonest, likely two."

Good news. This was confirmation of what Mrs. Burke had suspected. She could see the little girl more often when they returned. In fact, she and Veronica could travel back with them. John could rest easy about their safety and continue his tour.

"With Miss Rennie and Veronica?"

"I hope so." She gently guided Livie onto the pillow and arranged the pink coverlet over her. "Rennie, I want you to travel with us, if possible."

Rennie's spirits deflated. She couldn't stay until the end of August, and the end of September certainly was not an option. "I have my job waiting for me, and Veronica has to go to school.

If you leave in two weeks, we'll happily make the journey with you."

"I will try." Mrs. Sherman sat on the edge of the bed. "If not, will your young man go with you?"

"No." She wouldn't ask it of him. "He's an author. There are stories waiting for him in the West. He'll return in a few months." That was her prayer.

"Then my husband will find an escort if you must leave before I'm ready." Mrs. Sherman patted her hand. "I'll ask him to hire a couple because it would be nice to have another woman along. And, of course, we'll bear all expenses."

"Thank you." It was the best Rennie could hope for. She glanced at the clock. Four minutes after eight.

Mrs. Sherman followed her gaze. "Let me say evening prayers with Livie tonight. Go get ready for your beau."

"Thank you." She bent to kiss Livie's cheek. "Sweet dreams."

"Tell Mr. John we're going to church with him."

"I will. See you in the morning."

The knocker sounded as she stepped into the hall. Her heartbeat quickened as Mrs. Burke greeted him. *Lord, give me the right words.*

She patted her braided coil. All seemed in place.

Taking a deep breath, she hurried down the stairs.

CHAPTER 30

he parlor was cozy with the three of them sitting before the crackling fire. John heard about Rennie's job, their room, and Mrs. Sherman's improving health. He admired Veronica's latest sketch of the view of the city outside her bedroom window before sharing about his lodgings, his new buddy, Coll, and his ride to the beach.

Both girls tripped over one another to ask for descriptions that he happily provided.

"Mrs. Sherman said the four of us—you, me, Veronica, and Livie—can attend morning services together." A wide grin wreathed Rennie's face. And indeed, this was good news, for they'd missed church altogether on the train. "She's invited us to lunch here afterward."

"I didn't know that," Veronica said.

"It just happened." She turned to John. "She doesn't feel like going out yet, but it will happen soon. She was up several hours today. You can accompany us, right?"

He grinned. "It was one of the topics I wanted to discuss tonight."

"What's the other one?" Rennie gave Veronica a look.

"I'll sit at this table over here and finish my sketch. You two can talk." She moved to the opposite side of the room and began working on her drawing of the city.

This didn't feel right. "Do you want to take a stroll? Although, it's chilly out. You'll need warm wraps."

She hesitated. "Let me ask Mrs. Burke." She disappeared into the hall.

Low voices were followed by a light tread on creaky stairs. Soon Rennie was back wearing a hat and coat.

"She said not to venture far and to return by half past nine."

He glanced at the mantel clock. Hopefully, it would be enough time.

The housekeeper brought his hat and overcoat. "Just an hour, mind you."

"That's fine. Thank you, Mrs. Burke."

Once outside in the thickening fog, John offered his arm as they began to stroll. She encircled it with both hands.

"I've missed you." He smiled down at her.

"I've missed you too." She tilted her face up at him, looking into his eyes.

He stopped walking to kiss those upturned lips. It was a promising start to their time together.

When they continued on their way, even with her head turned, the curve of her cheek told him she was smiling.

They passed a streetlamp shrouded in mist. It gave the sense that they were all alone. Echoing hooves on the cobblestone street proved otherwise. Carriage wheels rolling behind them and footsteps on the plank sidewalk ahead reminded him to speak softly. "There are things I must say."

"Yes?" The darkness of the building they passed shadowed her face.

"I'll escort you and Veronica back to Ohio. I won't return to California. I'll get that job at a Hamilton newspaper like you've always wanted." There. That ought to satisfy her.

She stopped and looked up at him, her mouth pursed. "No, you must stay here."

He froze. "What?"

"Mrs. Sherman told me tonight that they're going back to Ohio as soon as she's well enough to travel. She suspects it will be at least a month. We'll travel with them if it's two weeks since Veronica has to get back to school and Zach can't do my job after school starts. Otherwise, they'll hire a married couple to go with us." Her hands tightened around his arm. "We'll be fine."

He rubbed his jaw, surprised at her resolve. "You've got this all figured out." What had caused her change of heart?

"I do." She gazed at him steadily.

"I'd rather come with you myself."

Her fingers slid off his arm. "You've got things to do here. Finish your adventure." She sat on a bench beside a misty streetlamp. "And write that first novel."

She supported his dream? It felt as if a thousand-pound load slid off his back. He hadn't realized how heavy a burden it had been.

But was he wrong, or did a certain sadness emanate from her? He sat next to her, not daring to give rein to his joy. If she was truly unhappy, he'd become a reporter. "I've decided what it will be about...the novel."

"What?"

"Becoming an orphan. Living as an orphan." He caressed her tense shoulder. "That was your suggestion."

"Reckon it was." She didn't look at him. "I was wrong to give you such a hard time about becoming a writer. It's what you were born to do."

He sucked in his breath. Could it be...? Supporting his dream and believing he had talent were two very different things. "Rennie, look at me."

She raised miserable eyes to his.

"Rennie, please tell me." His chest nearly burst. He'd never felt more vulnerable. "Do you believe I have talent?"

"So much it oozes out with every word you say."

It was as if a lightning bolt jolted through him. He pulled her close and kissed her lips, her face, her eyes, and then her mouth again, reveling in the way her lips clung to his. "Oh, Rennie, I was ready to quit. To push the dream aside."

"Don't do that." Her arms were around his neck, her shaking fingers entwined in his curls. "The world can't lose your books."

He gave a soft chuckle. "The world won't miss what it doesn't have."

"Then give it to them." Raising her cheek from his chest, she looked at him squarely. "Write that first book and then send it to a publisher."

"What if they don't give me a contract?" He finally voiced his insecurity. She must understand the risks. "Or what if they do and readers don't buy it?"

"Can't we leave that part up to God?" She caressed his cheek. "Your part is to write the best book you can...tell the story as only you can tell it and then trust God with the rest."

Could be as simple, as complex, as unbelievably difficult as that? The back of his eyes burned. "How did you become so wise?"

"I've been praying for the courage to let you pursue your dream." Her cheeks flushed. "It won't come as a surprise that I'd originally planned to use our time together on this trip to change your mind."

"You want security. Weekly pay." Becoming an author meant he couldn't guarantee those. How he hated that aspect of his dream.

"I heard that man on the train say that your gift for story-telling is one he's rarely seen." Tears glistened. Spilled over.

"Please forgive me for saying that people only listened to you because of boredom."

"You spoke your mind." He wiped a tear from her cheek with his thumb. That still stung. No need to make her feel worse.

"I was wrong. It was what I wanted to believe. But it wasn't true." She stared at him in wonder. "John, they listened because you tell everyday stories in a fascinating way. You put little twists on them so that folks see the heart of the matter in a way they might not have understood otherwise."

"Oh, Rennie." He covered her mouth with his and then cradled the most precious woman in the world to his chest. "Have I told you how much I love you?"

She smiled shyly up at him. "You might have mentioned it. But I don't mind hearing it again."

"I love you." He brushed a wisp of her hair off her forehead and kissed her again. Then he helped her to her feet. "When I was at the ocean today, I realized experiencing it wasn't nearly as special without you. Rennie, I will go back with you to Ohio. It's not the sacrifice it once was."

"I love you, John." She gave him a soft kiss, which he returned. Then, realizing they'd been gone a while, he put his arm around her and walked her home.

Maybe it was the fog or maybe it was sheer happiness, but either way, it seemed they walked through a cloud of joy.

～

*A*t church services the following morning, Rennie gave special thanks to God that her sacrifice had convinced John she believed he was meant to write. For she did. The journey to become willing to relinquish her own desires seemed farther than the miles she'd traveled across the country.

On the carriage ride back, John showed her a telegram he'd received in reply to the one he'd sent his parents. News of the train robbery had reached them. Both sets of parents knew they were safe but wanted letters immediately. Rennie vowed to get one from her and Veronica to the post office early Monday morning.

By scouring the papers, John learned that a Wells Fargo detective and his agents were working to track down the bandits. Veronica seemed disappointed that the article didn't mention her sketch.

Lunch was a pleasant meal. Mr. Sherman sat at the head of the table and Mrs. Sherman, sitting opposite, seemed genuinely interested in getting to know them.

Livie bounced around in her seat, happy to have her friends and her parents with her. She told them about church and finally getting to hug Mr. John.

Mrs. Sherman gave them a meaningful nod toward Livie as she asked them about the train journey. John soon had them all laughing. His stories led them to the discovery of Veronica's artistic talent.

"My dear, I'd love to see your sketches." Mrs. Sherman picked at her apple pie.

"Oh, Mama, I forgot something." Livie's eyes widened. "May I be excused to go fetch my present for you?"

"Has everyone finished their dessert?" Their hostess looked around as they all nodded. "Then let's move to the parlor while you fetch my gift, Livie."

She ran from the room.

"A bit more decorum," Mr. Sherman called after her.

Rennie had barely settled onto the sofa beside John when Livie burst through the door.

The girl glanced at her father and slowed her steps. "Here it is, Mama." She gave a page to her. "My gift for you."

Mrs. Sherman gasped and covered her mouth. "Where...

who? Why, this is lovely. My sweet angel." Tears flowed down her cheeks. "Who drew this?"

Livie pointed to Veronica. "She gave it to me as her gift, but I never wanted to keep it. I always wanted to give it to you, Mama, so you'll remember what I look like when you and Papa go away without me."

"Oh, Livie." She gave the sketch to her husband and reached for her daughter. "I'll never forget what you look like. And I'm not going away anymore unless you come with me, all right? At least until you're much older."

Livie scooted into the small space on the sofa between her parents. She leaned her head on her mother's arm. "All right."

The little girl's happiness touched Rennie's heart.

"Veronica, thank you for this gift." She stared at her. "You're very talented." She focused on her husband. "Don't you think so, dear?"

"Indeed." He studied the sketch. "It's most lifelike. Thank you for drawing it."

"My pleasure." She flushed.

"An artist and a writer accompanied our Livie on her journey." Mr. Sherman returned the sketch to his wife. "If I neglected to give you my thanks for your good care of my daughter, I'm saying it now."

Rennie gave him a half-hearted smile. An artist, a writer, and a plain ordinary woman was what he'd implied.

"Speaking for all of us"—John glanced at the sisters—"it was our pleasure."

Mrs. Sherman gave him a gracious smile.

"And speaking of pleasures, have you ever been to Golden Gate Park?" John leaned forward.

"My wife and I have been there on a few occasions." He patted her shoulder. "Did you realize it was once a desert, a wasteland?"

"I've read a bit about it," John said. "It was known as the Great Sand Bank."

"More commonly called the Outside Lands. A barren desert until William Hall took on the task to plant grass and trees there. He had a bit of luck with making grass grow amidst the sand dunes." He chuckled. "Barley that fell from his horse's feedbag quickly grew into hearty grass."

"A lucky accident." John grinned.

"He got some grass seeds from France. Bent seeds." He shook his head in wonder. "Amazing that they took root in the sand and began to stabilize it."

"The trees are my favorite thing about the place." Mrs. Sherman looked out the window toward the nearly treeless cobblestone street. "There are thousands of Monterey pine, Monterey cypress, and eucalyptus trees growing inside the park."

Rennie's interest was piqued. It would be fascinating to see a forest built on sand dunes.

"Golden Gate Park is larger than New York City's Central Park. San Francisco residents are quite proud of it." Mr. Sherman spoke with a measure of pride himself.

"It's one of the places I want to see." John clasped his hands together. "May I escort all of you to Golden Gate Park on Tuesday? Perhaps enjoy a picnic lunch there?"

The married couple exchanged a glance.

"I've no objection to you taking the three girls with you. It will be a treat for Livie." Mrs. Sherman sighed. "Though I'm feeling stronger every day, I'm not ready to ride a carriage on those hills."

Her husband nodded. "I'll actually be in the San Joaquin Valley for a few days, but you've my permission to take the girls. My driver will take you in our carriage."

"Cook will pack a lunch basket for you." Mrs. Sherman beamed at them.

Rennie blinked. Did they just agree to the three of them spending a day with John?

At her side, John released a pent-up breath. "Thank you both. I can't wait to see the park."

Rennie couldn't wait to spend a leisurely day with the man she loved.

CHAPTER 31

*G*olden Gate Park was as picturesque with its pine-
covered hills and various lanes as its reputation
claimed. The sun hadn't yet burned off the morning
fog on the last Tuesday in July. John prayed they'd see sunshine
before they left. Still, the mist was pretty against the green hills.

John had asked Mr. Burke, whose wife sat beside him on
the driver's seat, to take them directly to Golden Gate Strait that
connected the Pacific Ocean to San Francisco Bay.

"Will we see the ocean?" Veronica stuck her head outside
the carriage, one of dozens already in the park at half past nine.

"Nearest I've heard, the strait is up to three miles long."
John breathed in the pine-scented air. "Golden Gate leads to
the bay and the harbor. We'll see it from the beach—"

"We'll all see the ocean and the bay today." Rennie's foot
jittered against the floor. "I can't believe it."

"George never saw the ocean, that's for sure." Veronica gave
a happy sigh. "I brought my sketchbook so I can show him."

"I brought my journal"—he tapped on the knapsack
between his and Rennie's feet—"but don't expect to capture it. I
saw the ocean on Saturday. There was no land in sight."

"I never saw it either, Veronica." Livie poked her head out the window on the opposite side. "I want to see it first."

"All right." He winked at her. "There's an esplanade by the ocean."

Rennie's brow furrowed.

"It's a promenade, a pedestrian walk that allows us to stay off the sand if we want to."

"Do we want to?"

He grinned. "Considering the amount of sand in my clothing and shoes when I got back to the boardinghouse, you might."

When Rennie laughed and wrapped her hand around his arm, John fought down an attack of butterflies. If there wasn't an opportunity to propose beside the harbor, there was always one of the lakes in the park that Mr. Burke had mentioned as a wonderful place to picnic. Either would be romantic. Would she be as happy as he hoped?

~

*R*ennie stood near John on the promenade, scarcely able to take in the beauty of the dark-blue water and jutting hill across from it. White bubbles of foam crested near the shore and spilled out onto the beach. Sunlight had burned small patches into the fog over the harbor to shine on the water in sparkling brilliance.

Scores of folks crowded the walkway and picked their way over the sand. Several families and other groups had quilts spread out and sat on them to gaze out over the bay. The Burkes seemed content to occupy a bench facing the water.

"I can't believe it. Toward my left is the ocean." She stared at the distant expanse in awe. "To my right is the San Francisco Bay."

"Another impressive body of water." John reached for her hand. "This is what I wanted to experience with you."

"Rennie, come join us." Veronica, barefoot and holding her dress up to her ankles, called to her from the thick sand.

She needed to warn her sister not to lift her skirt any higher for modesty's sake.

Livie bent to pick up something and held it up.

"I'm going out there. Ready?" She looked up at John and caught her breath. Why, he looked at her as if she was the most precious woman in the world.

"You bet."

They left their shoes on the promenade. Soft, thick sand slowed Rennie's progress. She held her skirt up with one hand. "This is difficult to walk on."

"Not for long." He intertwined his fingers with hers.

He was right. They soon reached harder-packed sand as they joined the girls.

"Look at my pretty shell." Livie lifted a brown-and-cream shell that resembled an open fan.

"It's beautiful." Rennie scanned the area. "Let's all see if we can find one to remember this day."

They spent the next hour combing the area. Livie went back and forth to the Burkes to show them her treasures. The stack on the bench beside Mrs. Burke grew, but the little girl didn't stop her search.

Veronica sat on the edge of the promenade, sketchbook in hand, and studied the vicinity.

"Reckon you want to write in your journal." Rennie sighed.

"I don't want to do anything that takes me from your side."

"You don't?" The intensity of his gaze took her breath away. Did his words have a deeper meaning?

"Let's sit on the promenade." He gestured to a spot several yards from Veronica.

"Let me put on my shoes first."

"How about we wait on that?"

Mystified, she perched on the walkway.

He sat beside her, so close that his broad shoulder brushed against hers. "Remember how we traipsed all over the farm barefooted?"

She laughed. "That was a long time ago."

"Not so long. And today I'm in my best brown suit. You're wearing your favorite peach dress. We look so grown up except for our bare feet." He sandwiched her hand between his. "Seems an appropriate time to ask you a question."

Her heart skipped a beat. "Yes?" She shifted to face him. He had her complete attention. Could this be the moment?

"We've both been on a journey. Riding a train to California was the least important one." His fingers trailed the curve of her face. "We'd drifted apart. Been at cross purposes. That changed on our journey together."

"We're not the same," Rennie said. "I've grown, John. I really have." It wasn't what she expected him to say, but they needed to discuss it. "I meant what I said on Saturday. Work hard on your writing. It's what I want."

"I'm not the same man, either, Rennie. Feeling forced to choose between you and my dream of becoming an author—it seemed like my heart was ripping apart."

"I'm sorry." Learning of his inner struggles tore at her soul. She looked away.

"I prayed for God to take away my love for the written word. I prayed for guidance. What did God want me to do with my life?"

Shame burned a brand on her heart. She'd put her strong, loyal beau through so much turmoil with her demands.

"Then Mrs. Birchfield—Belle, that is—aimed a loaded pistol at you. From three feet away. She couldn't miss." He kissed her fingers clenched around his. "I knew if she pulled the trigger, I couldn't take it."

"I was ready to hit her over the head with my valise when she turned it on you." The very memory stirred her ire.

He laughed. "Oh, Rennie, I don't want to live my life without you."

Rennie's heartbeat quickened. "That's certainly my preference."

He laughed again. Then he bent down on one knee. He looked up without a trace of mirth. "Miss Renita Hill, will you do me the very great honor of becoming my wife?"

She stared into those wonderful brown eyes and found a love to last a lifetime. "Yes, Mr. John Welch. I believe I will."

He rose to his feet, pulling her along with him, and gave her a tender kiss that curled her toes into the sand. She'd never forget this proposal kiss, full of promise for the future, as she wrapped her arms around his neck and leaned into his embrace.

Whoops and shouts and claps reminded her they weren't alone. Dazed, she stepped back and discovered everyone on the whole beach looking at them.

"I reckon she said yes." One man grinned.

Veronica ran up, clutching her sketches. "Is it true, Rennie? Are you getting married?"

Joy such as she'd never known bubbled up and spilled down her cheeks. All she could do was nod.

"I'm so happy for you." Veronica clung to her as Livie slammed into them both.

"You're marrying Mr. John? I saw you kiss him."

She had indeed. Her cheeks blazed at the sight of the watching crowd. Out of the corner of her eyes, she saw the Burkes struggling to walk over in the thick sand. "Yes, I'm marrying the man of my dreams."

She reached for his hand, reveling in the warm clasp.

~

*T*heir picnic on quilts spread over the grass beside Mallard Lake was as hazy to John as the fog had been. She had agreed to marry him. Not that he'd doubted it, but now it was official.

"Mama will be so mad at you." Veronica smeared blackberry jelly on a biscuit.

"That I didn't get engaged in Ohio?" Rennie sighed. "I miss her. She'll be thrilled to know we'll be married. I want to tell her. Today."

"We'll send a telegram to both our families this afternoon." Now that the proposal was behind him, John had a hearty appetite. He munched on his second ham sandwich and stared out at the placid water. "I've a hankering to write my family a long letter tonight."

"I'll stop at the telegraph office on the way back." Holding his own sandwich, Mr. Burke frowned skeptically at birds cawing while in flight above them.

"Excellent idea, my dear." Mrs. Burke beamed at the couple. "This is just the kind of good news Mrs. Sherman needs to revive her health the rest of the way."

John hoped so. He'd like to do the gracious woman a good turn. "Rennie, there's one more thing."

"What is it?" She tilted her head.

"I have a ring waiting for you back in Hamilton. It was my mother's, so it has sentimental value, though it's not worth a lot. If it had been, Cora and I could have sold it to save the house after Mama died. Will that suit you to wear for our engagement?" Hopefully, it would be enough. "I'll buy a nice wedding ring, of course."

"It suits me very well, indeed." She dimpled at him. "When have you ever known me to want to spend money needlessly?"

"Never." He laughed. Rennie would always be the practical one in the marriage.

God knew what he was doing when He finagled to get John to Hamilton and living next door to this feisty girl. He needed her to keep his feet planted on the ground.

~

*M*rs. Sherman's delighted reaction was everything Rennie had hoped. In fact, she didn't lie down the rest of the day. She insisted that John stay for an early supper. She lamented her husband's absence for the celebratory meal, but Rennie didn't believe anyone else did. Though Mr. Sherman had been friendlier toward them after discovering how they'd protected Livie, his manner was too abrupt for her taste.

There were many questions about when they would marry and where they would live, a reminder that they had much to decide.

John asked if they all wanted to take a stroll after supper. Veronica declined, saying she had a sketch to finish. Mrs. Sherman said she wanted to read books with her daughter but asked them to return in time to say goodnight to Livie.

Rennie fetched her coat, and soon they were strolling with other pedestrians on the crowded sidewalk. There was still a lot of wheeled traffic at six o'clock. A chilly fog was descending, and she adjusted her coat securely about her shoulders.

"Mrs. Sherman asked when we planned to marry. What are you thinking?" John tucked her hand onto his arm.

She'd marry him as soon as her wedding dress was made if she could, but being practical... "Perhaps it's best we wait on that first book to be written to set a date."

"Agreed. I think your father will be happy with that plan. I'll live at home, help with the chores, and write my book. Maybe start the second one while I'm waiting to hear from a publisher. I have a feeling that first book will be done before

Thanksgiving. Maybe sooner. Ideas are swirling around my brain."

"Write about becoming an orphan first."

"Thanks. It was a wise suggestion. I've nearly finished the second chapter of that book."

She'd helped him. That felt good. "John, can I ask you something?"

His pace slowed. "What's troubling you?"

She stopped walking to look into his eyes. "I can't write or paint worth a lick." She had to know the truth. "Am I too ordinary for someone as talented as you?"

He burst out laughing. "Rennie, you are anything but ordinary."

"I'm serious."

"Let's sit." He indicated a bench. The sun hadn't set yet, but the streetlights already glowed.

Her insides twisted. She didn't want to talk him out of marrying her, but neither did she desire to hold him back.

"If I've never told you in so many words"—he clasped her hands between his callused ones—"you are perfect for me."

Her heartbeat sped.

"You are honest, blunt, compassionate, funny, practical, sensible, and a fine Christian woman who will make the perfect wife and mother."

"Some of that sounds good." *Blunt* wasn't much of a compliment.

He chuckled. "*All* of it sounds good to me. You know why?"

"Why?"

"Because that's who Rennie Hill is."

Her heart melted. "I love you."

"I love you." He lowered his head and finished the kiss that had been interrupted by the crowd earlier that day. He made a thorough job of it too.

To think that they had years of such kisses ahead.

CHAPTER 32

*O*n Friday afternoon, August fifteenth, Rennie accepted John's hand departing the train in Hamilton. She scanned the few people at the depot as he turned to help her sister on the steep steps. Rennie squealed when she spotted a beloved face. She took off at a run, her valise bumping against her leg.

"My girl." Her father closed the distance between them and held her close. "Don't like nobody threatening my daughter with a gun."

"I'm fine, Pa." She stepped aside so he could hug Veronica.

John threw his arms around his pa.

"Good to see you, son. You all gave us a scare."

"I'm sorry. Good news, though. They caught everyone except Mrs. Birchfield."

"We got your letter about them being in jail." He shook his head, then hugged the girls while Pa shook hands with John.

"I've made peace with it," John said. "God was with us on our journey in so many ways."

"I want to hear all about it."

"You will." John looked toward the empty wagon. "Is everyone else at home?"

"Yep." His father winked at him. "And the women warned us within an inch of our lives about dawdling."

"We don't dare be late." Pa laughed. "Let's claim your baggage."

It took far less time to claim their trunks when they were the only ones in line. Pa kept looking back at his daughters in the wagon bed and smiling in that contented way he had. John and his father talked as if they were determined to catch up on weeks of news before supper. That was fair. Enough had happened that it felt as though they'd been gone for months.

They went directly to the Walker farm, where both families waited for them in the yard. Even Ben had come from Cincinnati to greet them.

Rennie ran to hug her mother first.

"Look at you, coming home an engaged woman." Tears shone in her ma's bright blue eyes. "What happened to mend the breach between you?"

"I stopped nagging, just like you said, and opened my eyes. Ma, he's such a good storyteller. I know he'll do well."

"He will." Pride shone from her mother's face as she stepped away to greet Veronica.

Hugs were exchanged all around. Rennie's sisters wanted to see her nonexistent ring and asked the wedding date. Each of her brothers offered to punch the bandits in the nose for her and Veronica.

Mrs. Walker hugged Rennie. "My prayers have been answered. I'll have another sweet daughter."

"Not many folks call me sweet." Rennie sighed. "I'm too blunt."

"No one ever has to wonder what you're thinking." She laughed. "You take after your mama, my dearest friend. Honesty is a good quality. Remember that."

Cora stood to the side, waiting her turn to greet Rennie. "I'm so happy you'll be my sister." Her hug was good and strong. "God had the best woman in mind for my twin."

"Me?" Rennie gaped at Cora. She thought that, even having witnessed some of their arguments?

The rest of John's siblings nudged them apart to hug her, but Cora didn't step away. She laughed. "Absolutely. I prayed you'd resolve your differences on this journey. You were thrown together a lot."

Conversations stopped and everyone moved closer to listen.

"That's true enough. But we usually had other people around us. We hardly got to talk privately until we got to San Francisco." She met John's gaze.

He left Ben's side and crossed the yard to hold her hand. Ben moved to stand beside Cora.

"But I don't think we were ready for that conversation before that." Her hand tightened around his. "Not one minute sooner than that foggy San Francisco evening. I think we had to experience what the whole journey taught us first."

"Agreed," John said. "We both had some growing to do."

A sudden thought struck her. "John"—Rennie turned to him—"if we can afford a wedding trip out West, I will be happy to go with you."

His eyes softened. "See what I mean? You're perfect for me." He placed an arm around her waist and held her snug against his side. "It's a resounding yes from me—if we can afford it. How about we make that decision together when the time comes?"

"Fine by me." She'd always want to have a say in things. But that appreciative look in her fiancé's eyes made her offer less a sacrifice and more of a gift.

"And soon the next part of your journey will begin." Pa looked at Rennie with so much love and pride that tears pricked her eyes.

"Just wish we could have been there when you proposed." Ma heaved a sigh.

"Want to see what it looked like?" Veronica asked.

"What do you mean?" Ma covered her mouth. "Never say that you..."

"I did." She ran to the wagon and selected a page from her sketchbook. She put it in her mother's hands.

Everyone gathered around her except the newly engaged couple.

Stunned silence.

Rennie exchanged a look with John. "You going to let us see it?"

"It's amazing." Ma gave it to her. "I didn't know you could draw like this, Veronica."

Rennie gasped when she saw the sketch of John on one knee looking up at her as she stared at him in wonder. Veronica had sketched the promenade, Livie gathering shells on the beach, and even a handful of spectators. "It's beautiful."

"Do you like it?" Her eyes were huge.

"I love it." She held her close. "Who knew?"

"George. Just George." Veronica stepped back to smile at Rennie. "I'm glad you like it...because it's your first wedding present."

Both Rennie and John wrapped their arms around her at the same time. It seemed fitting to end the journey as they had started it.

Together.

Did you enjoy this book? We hope so!
Would you take a quick minute to leave a review where you purchased the book?
It doesn't have to be long. Just a sentence or two telling what you liked about the story!

Receive a FREE ebook and get updates when new Wild Heart books release: https://wildheartbooks.org/newsletter

ABOUT THE AUTHOR

Sandra Merville Hart, award-winning and bestselling author of inspirational historical romances, loves to discover little-known yet fascinating facts from American history to include in her stories. Her desire is to transport her readers back in time. She is also a blogger, speaker, and conference teacher. Connect with Sandra on her blog, https://sandramervillehart. wordpress.com/.

ACKNOWLEDGMENTS

I want to thank my agent, Joyce Hart, for her perseverance, guidance, and friendship for the past several years. Because she retired last year, *A Not So Peaceful Journey* will be the final book I publish with Joyce as my agent. She's encouraged me through the mountains and valleys of this lonely writing journey. I'm more grateful than I can express for her wisdom, business savvy, and Christian values that govern her life. I cherish her friendship and support. Thank you, Joyce, for your persistence in submitting my proposals, for suffering with me through the rejections, and for rejoicing with me in the successes. You made a difference. God bless you.

It's a joy to work with Misty Beller at Wild Heart Books. I was privileged to meet with her at a writers' conference last fall, and she is as kind as she is professional. It's also been wonderful to work with gifted editor Robin Patchen, who continues to push me to become my best.

Part of my research led me to Kentucky Railway Museum, Inc., in New Haven, Kentucky. My husband and I took a tour of the older cars with Executive Director Greg Mathews as our knowledgeable guide. Back inside the gift shop, Brooke Routt answered several of my questions. I was at the beginning of my research for my book and was just soaking up all possible details about old passenger trains I could find, not yet knowing what would be significant for my story. I appreciated the tour, Greg!

Thanks to my wonderful husband, who took me on a

writing retreat for this book. It ended up being a week of reading and taking notes because this story required lots of research. Thanks for joining me on this writing adventure. It's been a rollercoaster ride, for sure!

Thanks to family and friends for their continued support. Love you all!

Most of all, thank you, Lord, for giving me the story that grows inside of me until I must put the words on the page. Just like with the hero in this book, it's my job to write the best story I can at the time of the writing. It's up to You, Lord, to take it where You want it to go. It's as simple, as complex, as unbelievably difficult as that. More than anything, I'm glad You're with me on this journey, Lord. Without You, I don't want to go. Without You, I can't go.

AUTHOR'S NOTE

This story took our characters on a journey, both physically and emotionally. Both our hero and heroine have opposing goals when beginning the train journey west. Things change along the way.

Our heroine is a telegraph operator. Women worked in that profession as early as the 1840s. As I researched how messages were sent and received, I found a novel written by a female telegraph operator in 1879. *Wired Love* by Ella Cheever Thayer gave me many specific insights about the job's daily tasks. By the way, the public became so interested in the role of women in telegraphy that it became the topic of romance novels and short stories, creating a new genre called "telegraphic romance" in the latter 1800s. There's a little-known fun fact for you!

In 1884, train travel across the country presented many challenges. Those who could afford to pay for luxuries enjoyed a more comfortable journey. Because there were so many palace cars on the Central Pacific Railroad between Ogden, Utah, and Sacramento, California, I was able to show the more luxurious train travel for the last leg of their journey.

This novel was a joy to write because it allowed me to take

the journey west with them through my imagination. I found an amazing guidebook, *The Pacific Tourist* by Henry Williams, published in 1882-83. Our hero refers to it within our story. The author gives amazing details about each station stop along the Union Pacific and the Central Pacific Railroads, providing wonderful tidbits for me to enhance the readers' experience. It's my dream to find these historical books written just before my story begins. What a blessing! Williams breaks from his itinerary often to tell stories about the areas the train passes through, well worth the read for train and history buffs. Of course, I read many other books and articles while preparing to write this book, but this one was a treasure I wanted to share with my readers.

I hope you enjoyed spending a few hours in Chicago, Omaha, Sacramento, and Oakland. It was such fun to include an excursion to Weber Canyon at an overnight stay in Ogden, Utah. I was delighted to discover the Thousand Mile Tree and included it in my story where another significant event takes place.

Eating stations must have been a nightmare for early travelers. While the passengers would have been grateful for a meal, it was sometimes inedible and those stops too rushed to enjoy. Meal stops were often twenty minutes, forcing passengers to almost shovel food into their mouths to finish. Lunch counters offering sandwiches and fruit were a quicker, lighter option. I love how this aspect of the story tied in with our hero working at a train eating station in *A Not So Convenient Marriage,* Book 1 in this series. It was a happy surprise for me as a writer.

What a joy it was to show readers the early sights of San Francisco. The busy wharf, the cable cars, an uncrowded beach, and Golden Gate Park must have been quite a treat for travelers from eastern states. In 1884, folks mostly lived in furnished lodgings and ate every meal in one of the many restaurants. That was beginning to change as the city became more settled.

I didn't find a train robbery that happened at the time of my story. I patterned the robbery off one that occurred in Nevada around Verdi on the night of November 4-5, 1870. Depending on the source, details vary from having one train passenger who got on in San Francisco (possibly Oakland) heading east to six of them being on the train. The accounts agree that $41,600 in gold coins were stolen from the express car and that three men sneaked aboard the train in Verdi. My story had a fictitious married couple who realized too late they could be identified by a sketch in the possession of our hero. Train bandits usually robbed only the express car because it held lots of bills, gold coins, and gold bars. All the bandits were arrested in the 1870 robbery as they were in my story—except the woman. It seemed fitting for her to go free because, historically, only men took part in the 1870 robbery.

If you haven't already done so, I invite you to read the entire Second Chances series with *A Not So Convenient Marriage,* Book 1, and *A Not So Persistent Suitor,* Book 2, to spend more time with the characters.

Thanks for taking a journey west along with me and our characters.

Sandra Merville Hart

If you love historical romance, check out the other Wild Heart books!

The Pirate's Purchase by Elva Cobb Martin

Escaping to the New World is her only option...Rescuing her will wrap the chains of the Inquisition around his neck.

Marisol Valentin flees Spain after murdering the nobleman who molested her. She ends up for sale on the indentured servants' block at Charles Town harbor—dirty, angry, and with child. Her hopes are shattered, but she must find a refuge for herself and the child she carries. Can this new land offer her the grace, love, and security she craves? Or must she escape again to her only living relative in Cartagena?

Captain Ethan Becket, once a Charles Town minister, now sails the seas as a privateer, grieving his deceased wife. But when he takes captive a ship full of indentured servants, he's intrigued by the woman whose manners seem much more refined than the average Spanish serving girl. Perfect to become governess for his young son. But when he sets out on a quest to find his captured sister, said to be in Cartagena, little does he expect his new Spanish governess to stow away on his ship with her six-month-old son. Yet her offer of help to free his sister is too tempting to pass up. And her beauty, both inside and out, is too attractive for his heart to protect itself against—until he learns she is a wanted murderess.

As their paths intertwine on a journey filled with danger, intrigue, and romance, only love and the grace of God can overcome the past and ignite a new beginning for Marisol and Ethan.

∽

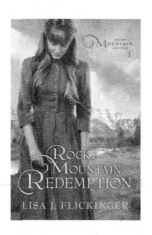

Rocky Mountain Redemption by Lisa J. Flickinger

A Rocky Mountain logging camp may be just the place to find herself.

To escape the devastation caused by the breaking of her wedding engagement, Isabelle Franklin joins her aunt in the

Rocky Mountains to feed a camp of lumberjacks cutting on the slopes of Cougar Ridge. If only she could out run the lingering nightmares.

Charles Bailey, camp foreman and Stony Creek's itinerant pastor, develops a reputation to match his new nickname — Preach. However, an inner battle ensues when the details of his rough history threaten to overcome the beliefs of his young faith.

Amid the hazards of camp life, the unlikely friendship growing between the two surprises Isabelle. She's drawn to Preach's brute strength and gentle nature as he leads the ragtag crew toiling for Pollitt's Lumber. But when the ghosts from her past return to haunt her, the choices she will make change the course of her life forever—and that of the man she's come to love.

∼

Lone Star Ranger by Renae Brumbaugh Green

Elizabeth Covington will get her man.

And she has just a week to prove her brother isn't the murderer Texas Ranger Rett Smith accuses him of being. She'll show the good-looking lawman he's wrong, even if it means setting out on a risky race across Texas to catch the real killer.

Rett doesn't want to convict an innocent man. But he can't let the Boston beauty sway his senses to set a guilty man free. When Elizabeth follows him on a dangerous trek, the Ranger vows to keep her safe. But who will protect him from the woman whose conviction and courage leave him doubting everything—even his heart?